Also by Sarah Elle Emm

PRISMATIC
Harmony Run Series, Book 1

OPALESCENT
Harmony Run Series, Book 2

CHATOYANT
Harmony Run Series, Book 3

NACREOUS
Harmony Run Series, Book 4

MARRYING MISSY

Last Vacation

Sarah Elle Emm

Next Chapter Media

Last Vacation
Copyright © 2016 by Sarah Elle Emm

Next Chapter Media, LLC.

www.SarahElleEmm.com

Cover design by Natasha Brown
Editing by Sherry Foley
Typesetting by Odyssey Books
Author photo by Brand Photo Design

ISBN: 978-0-692-62771-6

Published in the United States of America

For my daughters, Audrey and Sabrina

I pray you always are there for each other, that you will treasure your friendship, and trust in God to guide your steps. I love you.

Prologue

Maddy awoke to a throb in her head that traveled from her beaten, swollen eye and shot throughout her broken body. Panic swept over her as she recalled how the rope slashed against the flesh of her wrists and ankles, binding her to the chair, and the moment the red light on the camera had illuminated. As unwelcome memories flooded her thoughts so did the realization she had survived.

They didn't kill me...yet.

She shuddered from the reminder of the inevitable. Though his face had been covered with a ski mask, the pleasure in Trevor's eyes before he had raised his fist to punch her confirmed her biggest fear: He would have no problem killing her. She willed herself to think of something other than the bloodlust in his eyes and focused on her immediate situation.

From the hard dirt floor of her prison, she took a slow steady breath and was struck by the overwhelming stagnant, musty air. It made her think of the livestock barn at the farm her grandparents had worked in Florida, minus the strong scent of animals. She and Meg had been brought up helping out on that property, and the scents, among other things about farm life, would never leave her memories. Yet, the unrelenting heat of the small space was unlike any she had felt before. And Meg had been with her at the farm. Coping with the aftermath of their parents' accident had been tolerable with her sister. But the walls of her prison would never see Meg. Maddy was all by herself, and she was entirely to blame.

The throbbing at her temple seemed to grow, and she wished for Excedrin. Or a bottle of the Cruzan Rum Miguel enjoyed so much. It had been sixteen months since her last drink, but offered the potent island rum right now, she could imagine herself guzzling it. Maybe it would numb the pain and soothe her increasing fear.

What were they going to do with her? Why had they filmed her beating? And who was the video intended for? Was it a ransom? Maddy was as broke as it got. Why would anyone kidnap her for a ransom? The only person she knew with money was Meg, but how could these people, whoever they were, know about Meg? As her thoughts came back, she remembered how the older man had mentioned her sister. They knew something about Meg, but even so, Meg was well off, but she wasn't super rich. There had to be another reason.

Time and again, Meg had warned her about serial killers and psychopaths she read about in novels or saw on episodes of Dateline. Women were kidnapped, sold as sex slaves, killed on camera for psychopaths, she had heard it all. If she knew which scenario was hers, perhaps she could try to accept her fate. And if Miguel wasn't behind this, as Trevor had informed her with a smug expression, then who were these people?

She hadn't understood the Spanish Trevor, and his sadistic sidekick, Luis, had spoken throughout the filming, but she had stopped caring when the potent taste of blood had filled her mouth. Crying had seemed futile after that. No matter how she screamed or begged Trevor to stop, he'd kept going. His calloused hands on her neck had squeezed until she was sure she would die. Maddy was the star of their show, but clueless to their intentions and had turned to prayer, begging for an out of body experience. At last the small red light on the end of the video camera had faded away, and so had she.

Maddy's ribs ached, and she felt the sting of cuts across her face and body. But she wasn't dead. She vaguely recalled Trevor's hot breath on her ear at one point whispering to her before she fell unconscious, that if she survived, they might feed her and clean her up. Had that happened, or was she imagining the memory? She wasn't sure how much time had passed since she had eaten, but more than anything, she craved water.

She fought through the pain and pushed herself up to a seated position, shocked to discover her hands and feet were no longer bound, though the rope-burn lingered. With her palms pressed to the ground she edged closer to the front of her prison and peered through the bars with her uninjured eye. No sign of Trevor. Luis was at the table drinking beer, focused on a small TV screen. Maddy figured it was just her luck she would get guarded by the man whom she couldn't communicate with. Her mouth felt like it was made of cotton balls. What she would give for a drink of water.

"Hey, Luis," she croaked.

If he heard her, he made no indication of it. She tried again. "Excuse me, I'm thirsty. Can I get some water, please?"

He cast an annoyed glance over his shoulder and turned back to the TV screen. Maddy's voice dipped with desperation. "Por favor, can I get some water?"

He still ignored her.

"Luis, agua. Por favor!" she pleaded.

He twisted around in his seat. "Cállate!"

Maddy's voice hardened. "Agua. Agua, por favor!"

Her tone must have struck a chord. Luis got up from the table and retrieved a bottle of water from the cooler. He stalked over to her cell and stopped, clearing his throat as he looked down at her. "Quieres agua, bonita?"

Maddy's heart sped up as their eyes met. "Sí, por favor."

He shrugged his shoulders and unscrewed the bottle cap. Maddy's hopes soared as she waited for him to give her the water. It would make the hell she was living somehow bearable, if just for a moment. Luis knelt down on the other side of the bars and reached the bottle through, but inches before Maddy could grab the bottle, he stood up. With the flip of his wrist, he poured the water out on the ground near his feet.

"No, no, no," Maddy protested, trying to get closer to the water. But it was too late. The water soaked into the ground, mixing with the dirt, just a foot out of her grasp.

Luis's snicker squashed out all hope left. "Cállate, mujer."

He tossed the empty bottle through the bars and trekked to his chair in front of the TV. As it rolled towards Maddy, she clutched onto it. Her lip quivered as the plastic touched her mouth. A single drop fell onto her chafed and bruised lips.

A tear slid down her cheek and stung as it hit one of her cuts. "Please, God, please send..." A sob escaped her lips, and she wiped another tear. "Send someone to find me." She moaned as her head clouded with reality and overall despair. "I'm so sorry, Meg. I'm sorry."

Maddy curled into a ball and closed her eyes tight. She had never been so scared in her life.

If only she had listened to Meg.

One Week Earlier

1

The lanky fourteen-year-old sat up in his bed, narrowly missing the basketball hoop on the headboard. He had shot up four inches over the summer so the goal was kind of in the way, but he was too relieved about the growth spurt to mind. His day was coming. His tall family genes were starting to kick in, and tomorrow at tryouts the other boys, who tended to tower over him, wouldn't start off the season calling him Lil' Gabe. Though smaller than the starting five, he had still impressed the coach with his speed and agility last season. As consciousness returned, thoughts about proving himself to the other guys faded away, and he noted the moonlight pouring through the window and voices drifting from the living room.

"Abigail, we love you."

He rubbed his eyes and looked towards the open door.

"Look at me, sweetie."

So Abigail was there.

"We can help you. Please come home." His mother's voice cracked, and he pictured her worry lines around her eyes and tears pouring down her face. It had been months since his parents had seen Abigail.

As total alertness returned, his body tensed. Abigail showing up in the middle of the night meant she was desperate for drug money, and he dreaded the days ahead. His dad or mom would give her money, but his mom would be a wreck for at least a few days. Then her tears would dry up, and while the vacant, haunted expression would remain on her face, she'd pretend that everything was going to be fine. And that her sixteen-year-old daughter wasn't a heroin addict runaway living with criminals.

Until Abigail showed up again, and the cycle continued.

His heart raced as he threw the covers off and planted his bare feet on the tile floor. Most often Abigail came when their parents were at work. She'd take cash from the shoebox in their closet, their emergency money, and be in and out within five minutes. She'd ignore her younger brother's pleas to go back to rehab. Even when he'd promise to go with her. He'd promise to convince the rehab center that he was addicted to heroin too, so she wouldn't have to go alone. But it never worked.

Sometimes she would hug him and say she was sorry. She'd say the pain was too much. And that it was agony to go through rehab. He felt sorry for her, but he'd always tell their parents when she'd been there. Abuelita told him to call the police when Abigail showed up, but his parents wouldn't let him. They were determined they could convince her to come home.

But Gabe knew they couldn't. His grandmother was right.

He'd followed Abigail before. And he'd seen the way her eyes changed the moment she shot up. His sister was still in there somewhere, but she'd become a slave to the heroin. It controlled her.

He walked to the top of the steps, hating the sound of his mom's sobs. He paused, wishing it could just be a bad dream. *Why tonight Abigail?* Basketball tryouts were in the morning, and his dad had been helping him with his jump shot for weeks. Basketball was the only thing that made sense anymore. It freed his mind from the numbing pain in the house. Getting his parents' permission to keep up normal activities hadn't been easy. Everyone at school whispered about his high school dropout sister, the daughter of respectable professionals, a teacher and a doctor, and her multiple trips to rehab. People stared at Gabe's parents when they showed up for a sporting event or parent teacher night.

But just because Abigail wasn't Abigail anymore didn't mean he had to stop living. His mom had said she would try to make the games this season, but he wouldn't pressure her. It was difficult for her to watch the dance team at the games. Abigail had been on the squad before she met Matthew.

He hated Matthew.

Matthew had been the one to introduce Abigail to heroin, and at once she was hooked. While their dad attempted to have him arrested, he'd always been too slick for the police. The charges never stuck.

"I promise I'll help you get through it, Abi-girl. I'll take a leave from work. I'll quit my job. I'll do whatever I have to."

He swallowed a lump in his throat, hearing his dad call her by the nickname. His dad had always been better than his mom at hiding his emotions, but he could hear the longing in his voice now, and it frightened him.

"They don't love you, Abigail. They're just saying that to manipulate you," interjected another male voice.

Gabe's stomach dropped. *Matthew is here, too?* He tried to shake off his anxieties. Hate aside, the eighteen-year-old scared him. But he had to go to his mom. He could hold her hand or hug her. It couldn't hurt.

He heard his mom again as his foot found the first step. "I love you more than anything, Abigail. I can't stand to see you go through this. Sneaking in and stealing money out of my purse in the middle of the night? You don't have to live like this. Please, Abigail, let us help you. Just stay. Don't leave with him. He's lying to you. We really do love you. Stay, please."

"She's lying, Abigail. She wants to send you back to that hospital where they hurt you."

"No, Abi-girl. Don't listen to him," his dad pleaded.

"I just need some money." Abigail spoke for the first time, her voice stressed with nerves. Gabe figured the need for heroin made her sound so irritated and distant. "I'm really sick, Mom. You want to help me? Then give me more money. I know you have more than this."

"Tell us where the money is, Mama," instructed a new voice.

Gabe heard a collective gasp, and his chest constricted. He couldn't imagine who the new person was or what they were doing in the house. A chill ran down his spine, but he had to know more. He descended two more steps so he could peer into the living room.

Fear froze him as he spotted the gun pointed at his mother's head. His dad inched closer to the gunman. "Put that thing away. We'll give you everything we have. Just lower the gun. It's not necessary."

"Relax, T. They'll give you what I owe and then some." Abigail sounded indifferent, and Gabe wondered how it was possible his sister could be so relaxed while a gun was aimed at their mother's temple. Was his sister still in there somewhere?

Gabe began to tremble so much he wondered if the concrete stairs were moving beneath him. Still, no one had seemed to notice him yet. His mind raced, imagining what he should do, but he didn't think he could pry his feet up or down, forward or backward if he tried.

The guy, "T", standing beside Matthew was a stranger to Gabe, but he was without a doubt not a stranger to guns. The weapon rested in his hand as his steely gaze fixed on their mom.

"Please, put the gun down," she cried.

His dad stepped towards his mom, and T hit him across the face, knocking him down. His mom fell to the floor and reached for his dad as she sobbed. "Just take what you want and leave."

Gabe took another step down and his dad made eye contact with him. With one hand hovering over his fresh wound, he shook his head, just a fraction, motioning behind Gabe, back up the stairs to his bed-room. Gabe knew he was telling him to get out of there or maybe he wanted him to call the police. Adrenaline rushed through his body. He tip-toed in reverse determined to call the police.

T waved the gun at his mom as he proceeded up the stairs. "Open your safe, empty your valuables, give me everything. Your Abi-girl owes us a lot."

"Just do it, Mom, and hurry," she snapped.

Once Gabe had made it a few feet up, he turned on his heel and finished the climb. He tiptoed to his room, afraid to alert them to his presence. He'd call the police—just like Abuelita would tell him to do—and maybe Abigail would get arrested and forced into rehab. And he'd get his sister back. Their mom and dad could be happy again. Hope surged as he picked up the phone.

But the next second it was squelched by a loud popping noise. *Pop, pop, pop, pop*. He couldn't believe his ears. Ringing blared through his head as he crawled into the closet a few feet away. *Pop, pop*, it was so loud, he wanted to block it out. He covered his ears and curled into a ball. Darkness enveloped him, and he faded away.

A loud wrap sounded on the door, jolting Gabe from the darkness. He sat up in bed, realizing at once he'd been having a nightmare. The same nightmare he always had.

The reoccurring one that'd been haunting him for twenty long years.

He wiped the sweat from his brow and listened for the sounds beyond his door, sagging as he realized it wasn't his door, but one of the neighbors in the sardine packed apartments in the rundown complex. He walked to the refrigerator and retrieved a bottle of water, downing half before taking a breath. The nightmare always took its toll on him. Setting the bottle on the counter top, he jumped and grabbed the chin-up bar hanging in the doorframe to the kitchen. He pulled himself up, over and over, until he counted forty repetitions.

As he lay down on his side, he heard the Reggae music turn up next door. Of course, they'd think it was okay to have a party at two a.m. The laughter poured through the windows and thin walls as he closed his eyes. But he wasn't thinking about the music in the dive next to his. He thought about the countless lives lost to drugs from Victor Torrez over the past few decades and how at last he had a chance to stop him. He remembered how close his team had been last year and the runner who'd agreed to testify against the boss. Torrez had somehow found the man and spooked him once they'd gotten him into witness protection. After their informant had escaped, Torrez had found him, and varying body parts had been mailed to the witness protection unit.

He considered the dozen or so cases of teenagers overdosing on drugs they knew came from Torrez's supply, which was growing, from the Caribbean to cities across the U.S.A. He recalled the expressions of the last set of mourning parents he and Smith had met in their investigation in Miami before he'd gone undercover. Unlike most agents on cases like this, Gabe had a firsthand understanding of losing a loved one because of the drug trade, specifically, Torrez's drug empire.

And he recalled Abigail, their mom, and dad. The pain he'd carried around since that night so long ago had hardened him and pushed him to become the man he was today. In less than thirty seconds, a stranger called T had killed his parents, Abigail, and even Matthew.

The police had never solved the murders. Gabe knew he might never find the guy who fired the gun, but he knew the drugs that had hooked his sister and destroyed his family had come from Victor Torrez. Everyone knew Torrez controlled the drugs on the island. He always had and always would. Until someone could stop him.

Gabe exhaled a slow breath as he shifted onto his back. His fingers found their way to a scar above his ribs, tracing over it as his mind raced.

He was going to take down Victor Torrez if it killed him.

2

"Wait in the car, Madeline. This won't take long."

"But where are you going? You left the main road awhile ago. It's like we're in the middle of nowhere. Where are we anyway? I thought we were going on a sunset cruise," Maddy eyed Miguel suspiciously.

A solid wrap on the truck's hood interrupted Maddy's questioning. Standing beside Dalbert was Trevor, and his hostile expression was fixed on her. Maddy shifted in the passenger seat. "Have I mentioned that I don't like him?"

Miguel laughed, but it had a nervousness to it Maddy hadn't heard before. "Ah, he's just wound up too tight. He needs a little love in his life. Like me."

"You still didn't answer my question, Miguel," Maddy complained, arching her brow at him.

Miguel leaned across the central console of the SUV and tilted her chin up. His grin was self-assured. "Don't worry. The cruise won't leave without us. I own the boat."

Before she could protest or ask about the trouble she still sensed in his body language, he gave her a quick kiss. "I'll only be a minute, Amor."

As he opened the door Maddy called after him. "You don't own the sun, do you? Think it will wait for you too, Mister?"

Miguel winked at her as he stood up. "There is that spirit I love so much, Madeline. Be right back."

She spared him a small grin as the door to the black, luxury SUV closed with a thump, but once he had turned away, her shoulders slumped. The unpleasant tone Miguel's voice had taken when the phone call interrupted their drive to the harbor moments ago had left her spooked. Maybe if she had paid attention in her high school Spanish class, she would have understood something Miguel had said during the conversation.

She lifted her eyes just as Miguel disappeared through the thick mass of trees surrounding the vehicle, followed by Trevor and Dalbert. Maddy wondered about the quick errand Miguel had explained was the reason for the stopover. She had been having a lot of weird feelings the past couple of weeks, and wasn't sure if it was the occasional oddity in Miguel's behavior, like his random mood changes, or her own personal turmoil. Perhaps, it was the fact she had something important to tell Miguel today, and she knew he wasn't going to be happy. But she was sure her decision to move on was the right one for her, and telling Miguel, despite the unpleasantness, was something she intended to do that very night on their date. It was more than a sunset cruise. It was a farewell cruise, and she was more than ready to continue the next leg of her journey.

So if it wasn't nerves about telling Miguel she was leaving, maybe the uneasy feeling she was having had nothing to do with her own personal issues. Maybe it was the uneasy feeling Trevor gave her. If he could just be more like Dalbert. She liked him.

Despite Dalbert's physical appearance, standing at 6'3" and weighing about two hundred twenty-five pounds, the extremely large, dark-skinned man, with muscles ripping through the short-sleeved button downs he preferred to wear, was a gentle giant as far as Maddy was concerned. His huge smile, hip-length dreads, and deep, infectious laugh toned down his imposing build and were complemented by a great sense of humor and a charming Crucian accent. But then there was Trevor.

Trevor was native to St. Croix as well, about six feet tall and on the skinny side, a pallid complexion, with brown hair and dark brown eyes. He had told Maddy how his ancestors had arrived in St. Croix in the mid 1700s, during the time of slavery, as representatives of the Danish crown. She hadn't had a good feeling about Trevor since meeting him, and had a very difficult time believing he had descended from any sort of royalty, but had accepted the fact that wherever Miguel went, his two assistants were sure to follow. Whether sitting across from them in a crowded restaurant or walking twenty feet behind them as they strolled along the waterfront, the pair was always nearby. Had she not known about Miguel's multiple local businesses, she might have thought he was a politician or movie star and that the men were his bodyguards. Still, the tourist industry was more competitive than ever because of the bad economy, and Miguel said having two assistants was integral to his continued success. From the way Maddy had seen Miguel throw cash around, she knew he wasn't struggling for money.

The economic crisis hadn't dampened Maddy's spirits. Staying in one place for too long, on the other hand, certainly did. Not that she hadn't enjoyed St. Croix. She was quite content on the tropical island, but that feeling she hadn't been able to shake since her teenage years was still with her. There was something out there for her. She just knew it, and one of these days, she was bound to find whatever she was looking for. Her search for inner peace had taken her on a nine year global adventure. She had only been back in Florida for a matter of weeks, fresh from Denver, via California, via New Zealand, via Italy, via Switzerland, via Guatemala, via Aruba, and on the list went, when she had gotten stir crazy.

As promised to Meg, she had tried to make it work in Naples, but she couldn't help it. It wasn't home. The old farm they'd been raised on after their parents' accident had felt like home after some time, but when her grandpa had died, Grandma Lynn had moved into a retirement home in Naples, and now there really wasn't a physical place she could call home. Not yet, anyway. She had returned to Naples just long enough and had worked just enough doubles to buy a one-way plane ticket for the next leg of her on-going journey, and the low-fare airline tickets to Caribbean destinations had popped up right in time. Meg hadn't been happy, of course, but Maddy had given up trying to explain her need to travel to her sister long ago. Maddy went by the retirement home to say goodbye to Grandma Lynn. Then, she re-packed her backpack, even emptied her hollowed-out book full of saved-up waitress tips, her emergency money, she kept hidden at Meg's house, and kissed her waitressing job goodbye.

She had intended to spend a couple of weeks in St. Croix before moving on, but within hours of arriving to the serene tropical paradise the thought of leaving, even to go to another island, became less appealing. The slow-paced, relaxed feel about the island made her want to stay. The endearing local accents of the Crucians, the local islanders, the food, the simple beauty of the landscapes, the feel of the white sand between her toes, and the crystal clear tropical waters were intoxicating. And then one week after her arrival, in a waterfront restaurant in downtown Christiansted, she had met Miguel and gotten sidetracked from her travel plans. Against her better judgment, something she would never admit to Meg, she had spent a lot more time with him than she should have. He fit the type she would have fallen for in the past, but sixteen months ago, she had decided to clean up her act. Her lifestyle change wouldn't work in the long run with someone like Miguel.

Just yesterday, she had accepted the fact it was time to move on, even if Miguel didn't understand. She knew in her heart her quest for peace needed to continue, and Miguel wasn't part of the plan. Though she would treasure the memories of the time they had shared, she would tell Miguel the news.

She sighed, closing her eyes as she recalled how fast she had fallen for his charm that first meeting. She was used to dining alone, with the amount of traveling she did, and the night she met Miguel should have been no different than any other night out for her. Especially considering the sixteen months of sobriety she had made it through, without a man by her side. The more time that passed since her last drink, the stronger she became and to her surprise things like eating alone were quite enjoyable. But for some reason the night she met Miguel had been different.

The moment she walked in to the ocean front restaurant, she saw him sitting at the bar. Unlike the other bar and restaurant customers enjoying their vacation, he sat motionless, staring out at the ocean with sad eyes, she was all too familiar with. An instant later, his eyes darted to hers, and the lifelessness vanished as they lit up. Even as she broke eye contact she tensed. The new look in his eyes was also one she was familiar with. The old Maddy would have taken it as a compliment, maybe even expected the attention her striking looks got her. Her hair made her stand out more than anything, but she knew there was more to it than that. At 5'5", she had red hair, pale porcelain-like skin and bright hazel eyes. Her face was sculpted with delicate features, high cheekbones, and naturally rosy lips. People couldn't help but stare at the classic beauty, and the old Maddy would not have denied that she tended to let it go to her head. These days, however, she wasn't interested in repeating past mistakes, and letting a man back in to the picture wasn't on her new plan. At least not until she had found the inner peace she craved. Maddy refused to glance in his direction, but from the corner of her eye she could see him as he leapt up from the barstool.

Seconds later, he was beside her. Maddy felt her pulse quicken as he grabbed her hand and pulled it to his mouth to kiss. Speechless, she arched a brow, studying him as she searched for the words to get rid of him.

"I've been on this rock for over ten years. It's about time you got here, Hermosa."

She told herself he was playing on one of her obvious weaknesses, her vanity, but somehow, she still couldn't help the blush that flushed her cheeks. She fought the urge to return his smile. Calm and in control, her eyes met his. Her voice was steady. "I'm sorry, but—"

He cut her off, "No apology necessary. It was worth the wait, Hermosa." His eyes, only moments ago dead, danced with life as he smiled at her. Something was exciting, maybe dangerous, but intriguing still, about this newcomer with the Spanish-sounding accent.

The hostess interrupted their exchange. "Table for two?"

3

Maddy recalled the look on the hostess's face as she waited for a response. "Table for two?" she had repeated.

Maddy broke eye contact with the raven haired man beside her. In her thirty second assessment, she hadn't missed his attractiveness. He was olive-toned with chin-length hair parted down the middle, framing a dimpled smile and brown eyes, which moments ago had been so grief-stricken, but were suddenly so alive.

"Table for two?" the hostess repeated, jolting Maddy out of her thoughts.

She couldn't keep making the same mistakes. She would focus on her recent re-commitment to herself to keep searching for her peace. Even if this man was intriguing with his unique approach. "Actually, I…"

The man interrupted with a polite but commanding response. He gently draped her arm around his and smiled at the hostess. "Yes, Señorita, table for two. And we want the best view of the harbor. The sun will be setting soon." He had nodded at Maddy, and winked at her reassuringly. "I think a sunset on the harbor of Christiansted should be on a top ten bucket list somewhere. Right below dinner with you, Hermosa. Even if it did take you ten years to get here."

A sunset view did sound intriguing. One dinner with the newcomer would be harmless, she was sure. She recognized his determination, and inclined to enjoy one meal with this stranger, and one alone, if only for a bucket list experience, she ignored the faint voice of doubt and made her decision, angling her head upwards to look into his eyes. "I'm assuming *Hermosa* means something spectacular."

The dimples in Miguel's cheeks appeared as his smile spread. "You are truly a spectacular beauty, Señorita. But beyond that, my heart just awoke from a long slumber when you walked in. Allow me the pleasure of your company. My name is Miguel Torrez."

She thought about the words she had last spoken to her sister. *You have to start living, Sis. Before it's too late.* She gave him a friendly smile. "Madeline MacKenna. Everyone calls me Maddy."

Miguel beamed. "Then I'll call you Madeline."

Two weeks later, and multiple meals together, along with scuba diving, boating, and exploring the island, Maddy knew she would treasure her time with him. Beyond his charm and good looks, there was something more. She could relax around him. He didn't seem to mind her free-spirit nature or that she wasn't interested in sleeping with him. Typically, that had been the easiest way to get rid of an admirer. Most of the men who had tried to date her since she had quit partying after a bad experience in Amsterdam could handle the fact she didn't drink, but the no-sleeping-together rule was one that had them finding the nearest exit.

But not Miguel. He hadn't asked questions about her past. He told her he respected her decision. Still, she had been determined to stick to her plan. She'd travel to St. Thomas and pick up a waitress job when her funds ran low. She'd heard it was easy to find server jobs in the many cruise ship stops on the busy island. So one week after meeting him, she had checked out of her hotel and told him she was heading to St. Thomas, but Miguel refused to accept it. "Stay a few more days, Madeline. You can have the guest apartment at my house all to yourself. Save some money for now. You can extend your travels if your hotel budget is put to rest for awhile."

Again, Maddy had let her guard down and taken him up on his offer. Though she had fallen for his charms and finally kissed him, something she wouldn't pretend to not enjoy, she knew that Miguel was just stalling her. She knew he wanted a different kind of relationship with her and by staying at his property she was simply leading him on. But if her plans worked out, she would be off island within twenty-four hours. She didn't know how long she would work in St. Thomas. She had heard Tortola and some of the other British Virgin Islands were captivating and wanted to explore them as well.

Though Miguel would never understand, she was ready to keep moving. She tried to ignore the small tug of guilt. The real kicker had been when he had opened up about the pain of losing his mother. As an orphan, her heart had gone out to him. The longer she stayed on St. Croix, the harder it would be for Miguel to accept her leaving. Below his teasing exterior and charm she could sense layers of pain and anguish. He was deeply scarred, and she feared she wasn't the one to heal him anymore than he was the one to heal her.

Maddy glanced through the window at the dark clouds gathering above, and shivered at the sudden rush of goose bumps she felt all over. Thunder growled nearby as the storm edged closer. Three weeks into her trip, now October, she was well aware that hurricane season ended in November, and the storms and rain showers associated with the season often came with little warning.

She cringed as lightening crashed nearby. *So much for a sunset cruise.* She sighed, feeling more on edge than ever. She hated to be trapped in a car when it was lightening. And of course, the sky was darkening as the sun would be setting soon. The fact that they had driven way off of the beaten path, or at least one Maddy had recognized, didn't offer her much comfort either.

After a decision to find Miguel, she grabbed her purse and abandoned the air-conditioned vehicle. At once, she felt the unwelcome caress of the humid air. With a fleeting glance towards the climate controlled vehicle, she walked over to the thin dirt trail, enclosed by thick, over-grown Tan-Tan plants covered in clusters of green oval and flat leaves and long brown pods. She took a deep breath and began down the path she had seen Miguel and his assistants follow moments ago and hiked deeper into the forest.

A sudden grumble of thunder made Maddy flinch, and her gaze shot up as lightening flashed across the spec of sky barely visible through the crest of treetops. She looked down at the dirt trail, and caught a scream in her throat as a dark green iguana, with a white face, about four and a half feet long, crept into her path. With a laugh, she poked fun at herself for being so jumpy. She was still getting spooked by iguanas? Her first day at the beach side resort, she had discovered that while iguanas may be hideous, in her opinion at least, they were totally harmless. She snapped a picture of the ugly reptile with her cell phone and watched as it scurried across the path and disappeared into the mesh of trees. Meg would get a kick out of it or at least jump when she downloaded the picture on her smart phone, which was practically another limb of her body.

She brushed the nerves aside, pressed send on the photo, and tossed her phone into her purse. Seriously, she needed to get a grip. Wildlife and thunderstorms were all part of her upbringing in Florida. Miguel would likely have a clever line for her about why she should have stayed in the truck since he couldn't be by her side to protect her from the scary iguana. He called it 'taking care' of her, but Maddy was starting to feel more like his possession. Lost in her thoughts, she exhaled a heavy breath as she tromped through the forest. Even if the sunset cruise was cancelled, she would tell Miguel that she was leaving St. Croix. Afterwards, she would call Meg to tell her she was moving on again. She had already perused ferry rates and flights and discovered she could just hop on a ferry in the morning to go to St. Thomas.

The crunch of debris at her feet alerted her to the thinning of the path. She glanced down to find that the dirt was no longer visible. As she ventured further through the leaves, twigs, and overgrown bushes, she ignored the sudden voice in her head telling her to walk to the SUV.

It had to be nerves about ending things with Miguel and nothing more. Meg would have returned to the vehicle. Of course, Meg wouldn't have even been there in the first place. She was safe behind her meticulously organized desk right now, thousands of miles away, probably preparing to meet the last client of the day.

Miguel's distinctive voice caught her attention. She would never admit it to Meg, but his sexy Puerto Rican accent had been one of the reasons she had let her guard down. His family had moved from San Juan to St. Thomas when he was a boy, but he had settled in St. Croix, enjoying its peacefulness in contrast to bustling St. Thomas he had told her. She loved to listen to him speak. She was certainly going to miss that accent.

He was talking to someone nearby. Relieved she had made it through the patch of woods successfully, she turned now, heading towards the voices. She peered through the trees, and her gaze landed on him. If her plan worked out, she would have the dreaded conversation over with soon enough. In anticipation of the next leg of her journey, the lightning and thunder were quickly disappearing from her thoughts.

About to step through the camouflage of the trees, she stopped dead in her tracks. Eyes wide in disbelief, she watched as Miguel leaned down and punched a bound man in the nose, chin, and chest over and over again. Dalbert and Trevor stood over the man, who was on his knees begging Miguel to spare him. Frozen, she tried not to breathe. Her mind told her that Miguel wasn't capable of harming a fly, but as he continued to punch the bound man at his feet, her heart sank to a new depth. All of those weird feelings she was having begun to make sense. Disappointment and sadness were quickly replaced with tremendous fear. Now thankful for the droning of thunder, she took a careful step, praying to flee undetected. Meg was going to kill her when she told her about this.

Just as she turned away, lightning crashed again, illuminating the sleek, black gun Miguel retrieved from his back. Paralyzed with fear, she stared as Miguel pointed the weapon directly at the helpless man at his feet. "No one betrays my family," he said, in a cold, steel-sounding voice she didn't recognize.

Before another thought could cross her mind, she had already released the first scream of protest. "Noooo!" echoed through the trees and above the sounds of the storm. Miguel and his crew turned in unison towards the source of the scream and all eyes fell on her, trembling terrified before them.

With a slight nod of his head, Miguel communicated something to his men, and they started after her. Positive she was going to end up like the man on the ground, she forced her feet to move and took off running as fast as she could. The strappy sandals were a handicap along with the twigs, rocks, and leaves as she ran away from the men. Disoriented all of a sudden from the shock of the scene she had just witnessed, she only knew to run, unaware of which direction would lead her to the road.

A quick glance over her shoulder confirmed that Dalbert and Trevor were right behind her in pursuit. The cruelty she saw in Trevor's eyes made her stomach flip. She wished she had trusted her initial gut instinct about him. Maybe she would've left St. Croix.

A gunshot exploded, causing her to shriek, and she ran harder. The realization that she might not ever see Meg again overwhelmed her. Tears stung her cheeks. She reached into her purse as she ran. Her fingers retrieved her cell phone and yanked it out of her purse, but the device slipped from her grasp, falling into the greenery at her feet. Not even a last call to Meg. Her feet, cut from the chase, burned as the elements of the path rubbed them. Dalbert and Trevor yelled behind her, but she didn't recognize the words. She had a difficult enough time understanding them because of their accents and slang as it were, but the sound of her heart beating erratically filled her ears and head, blocking everything else out. Death was closing in on her.

A sudden incline surprised her and her heavy feet, and she tumbled recklessly down the hill. Over rocks and branches her body twisted. She opened her eyes suddenly as she felt the weightlessness of a free fall. The rocky edge of a tidal pool waited to greet her below. Death closed in. As she fell the short drop and prepared for the end, her thoughts returned to Meg. *I'm sorry Meg.*

4

Thirty-eight hours and thirty-two minutes. Exactly the length of time she had spent on the so-called island paradise. Megan glanced at her iphone again. Thirty-eight hours, thirty-three minutes. Not one of those minutes had been in any way, shape, or form, productive or helpful.

Her first full day on the Crucian island had been spent in the police station being told to wait, wait some more, and for the last part of it... wait. When the police officer assigned to assist her had finally summoned Megan to his desk, he had simply told her the same thing she had been told via telephone before arriving in St. Croix. They had no reason to believe anything had happened to her sister and with no evidence of wrongdoing, other than the fact Megan hadn't heard from her in over a week, there was no missing persons case to solve. They would make sure to keep a lookout for Madeline and circulate the photo of her throughout the police unit and of course, let Megan know if anything changed, but they were certain Madeline had already left the island. Furthermore, they were treating Megan as if she were wasting *their* time.

How could she convince the police this was a real case? Completely frustrated, Megan had returned to her hotel and walked around the place interviewing the staff. She had chosen the same beachside resort Maddy had been staying at before her disappearance.

Though very sympathetic to her situation, the staff wasn't very helpful either. No one seemed to remember any significant details about her sister's stay other than her vivid, red hair and good looks. Apparently, she had spent very little time at the island resort other than the first few days. After that, no one saw much of her other than her leaving early in the morning and returning late at night. The hotel records indicated Maddy had checked out after one week, but no one knew where she had been staying after that. She had been on the island for almost three weeks the last time Megan had heard from her sister.

Truth be told, she hadn't actually heard from Maddy, but she had received a photo of an iguana. But as unpredictable as Maddy was, no matter where in the world her travels led her, she always checked in with Megan before she went to her next destination. In a strange way, it was how Maddy said goodbye to Meg. Just in case something happened to her during the journey, like it had to their Mom and Dad. But the police didn't seem to believe Megan.

To add insult to injury, the police were convinced that Maddy left the island after she checked out of the hotel, even though Megan insisted the photo of the iguana Maddy had sent her would prove she had still been on St. Croix one week ago. "That photo coulda ben on any island. Yoh sista island hoppin, Miss," one officer had remarked. Sure, there were no airline or ferry boat records of Maddy leaving St. Croix, but the officer had pointed out that someone who was such a free spirit, like Megan was describing, might have taken off on a yacht or sailboat with someone.

They took her for a flighty tourist, having a good time. Even when Megan had told them how Maddy quit drinking sixteen months ago and never even indulged a little, they hadn't seem convinced she was in real danger. One officer had pointed out that she could have relapsed. Megan had wondered the same thing herself, but she hadn't voiced her agreement with them. Maddy had been a heavy drinker for so many years. What if she had started again? Yet even if that were true, Megan knew without a doubt that something had happened to her sister. She could have taken up her old habits, and she was still the type to jump on a yacht or even a sailboat with strangers she met at the beach and sail the open seas, but she wouldn't leave without making that phone call to Megan.

Besides, the two had an emotional connection that was practically unbelievable. It was so unbelievable in fact, that Megan had refrained from informing the local police about a terrifying feeling which had overcome her just moments after the last communication she had received from her sister.

"Mo' coffee, Miss?" The server interrupted her thoughts, smiling brightly at her.

The coffee canister staring her in the face aided Megan more than she would have admitted, as the thick Crucian accent, which many of the locals had in common, was quite difficult for her to understand. The server's black hair was pulled back tightly in a barrette, showing off her golden hoop earrings nicely. She wore several gold bracelets, each clasped together with a u-shaped latch. The white jean shorts and sun-flower yellow tank top were the perfect compliments with her dark skin.

Megan wished she could get away with a yellow tank top, but the color had never gone over well with her own pale, freckled complexion. A few of her teenage years had been spent trying to get a tan but had only resulted in multiplying the freckles, not exactly flattering in her opinion. She thought the olive, tailored shirtdress that she wore, clasped together at the waist with a thin dark brown belt was one of her color matches.

Megan smiled. More coffee was never a bad idea. "Yes, please…Oh my gosh!" Megan gasped suddenly and jumped, moving the plastic chair away from the table.

The server chuckled now, nudging the small lime-green reptile from Megan's tabletop gently. "'Tis only a gecko, Miss. Notin' ta worry bout," she said. "Are yoh enjoyin' yoh visit ta St. Croix?"

"Is it that obvious I'm a visitor?" She was genuinely curious, especially considering the number of stateside residents she had heard of who lived year-round on the island.

"Well, de gecko tip me off," she said, good-humoredly, stretching her arm to refill the coffee cup.

Megan glanced around the outdoor restaurant. From a small hut-style kitchen, the strong smell of bacon frying drifted towards her, reminding her of any other breakfast place. But geckos didn't lurk on tabletops in most breakfast diners. Her eyes scanned her surroundings for more of the tiny lizards. She knew it was a silly phobia, especially considering her upbringing on a farm in Florida, but anything that crawled, slithered, or crept left her unsettled and dealing with that sort of thing was a thing of the past. She had a reoccurring pest control service back home for a reason.

A tent covered the small space, which was equipped with wobbly, white plastic tables and matching chairs. One of her hotel's security entrance guards mentioned it was a neighborhood hangout, and Maddy had a knack for finding places to mingle with locals. Maybe her sister had been here. While the humble diner was certainly in a scenic area, situated on the waterfront in the heart of Christiansted, one of two towns on the island as she had learned on the flight down, it wasn't what Megan was accustomed to. Fortunately, there didn't appear to be more geckos slinking around.

"I can't say I care much for lizards," she confessed. Or insects, or heat, she thought to herself. The air-conditioned space of her office was where she generally preferred to be. Of course, jetting around to appointments in her Maserati wasn't so bad either. Nice, luxury, indoor environments were what Megan preferred. If it weren't for the money she'd made in real estate living in Naples, she'd probably live someplace with seasons and escape the excessive heat altogether. But being a commercial and residential real estate agent in Naples had paid off for her, and she could work from her air-conditioned office anyhow.

She wasn't thrilled about being outdoors, period. It stirred up memories of the life she had run away from. She had worked strenuously to earn that full ride to college and invested every ounce of her energy from the first day of college on into her financial success. Bugs, reptiles, and being outside were all aspects of the poor farm life she had worked so hard to escape, and she had vowed to never spend a day out in the Florida heat feeding livestock or harvesting crops again.

In the ten years since leaving for college, the only time she concerned herself with a plant of any kind was to ask her landscaper to clip roses from the climbing rose bush he had planted and tended to on the side of her house. It yielded a nice bouquet for her dining room table. And having him take care of the roses and the yard meant she never had to encounter reptiles of any kind or bugs for that matter. In the new life she had built for herself, she could control everything, and she avoided reminders of her past at all costs. A fly buzzed across her face suddenly, as if reading her thoughts. She hated bugs.

"Don' worry, bout dem geckos hurtin' yoh…It's de centipedes yoh need watch out foh." The waitress smiled now, picking up Megan's empty breakfast plate before walking away from the table. She turned back towards Megan, winking at her over her shoulder.

Megan examined the ground uneasily. Her palms were clammy all of a sudden. Centipedes? Unpleasant images of creepy insects crawling over Harrison Ford, from Indiana Jones' movies, flashed through her mind. What had she gotten herself into? Shaking her head, she thought of her carefree and reckless sister. Even after years of sound advice from Megan, Maddy had not once paid a bit of attention. If she had listened to Megan, she would have been working in Naples, paying her taxes, and participating in society like a normal person. Unfortunately, Maddy had never warmed up to the idea of normal. Ever since she turned eighteen, her sister had been jumping around the globe on a quest for some unknown thing that would supposedly give her peace. Instead of peace, all she ever found was more trouble.

Megan peered out at the vast expanse of ocean gleaming in the bright morning sunshine before her. The turquoise waters seemed to go on forever. From the Caribbean Airways in flight map, she had noted the islands of Puerto Rico, St. Thomas, and St. John were in the far off distance. She had been told a faint view of the densely populated St. Thomas could sometimes be seen on a perfectly clear day, but no matter how she strained her eyes, she couldn't quite see it today.

Had Maddy hopped on a sailboat and continued her travels to another island as the police officer had suggested? It wasn't like Maddy not to check in. Her cell phone had been going straight to voice mail since the last photo Maddy had sent, and according to the cell company, the cell phone was out of service range. Something had happened to her sibling. The last communication with Maddy had been an unexplained picture of an iguana. No message, no text, nothing. Just an enormous, slimy, dragon-resembling lizard. Megan sunk her head to her chest. Where in the world was her sister?

"Everything okay, Miss?"

Startled from her hopeless thoughts, Megan sat upright at the sound of the low voice. Her eyes scanned the length of the man standing before her, and she pursed her lips together. She guessed he was probably about six-foot-two.

As she sat silently, observing him, the man repeated his question, "Are you okay?" His tone bordered on cautious, but concerned.

"Everything's fine," she finally managed with a tight voice.

With a smile, his concern faded away, and he reached behind his back to untie a grease-spotted apron. He folded the apron up, pulled out a chair at the table right next to Megan's, about a foot and a half from her, and sat down.

An internal alarm went off, making Megan feel extremely uncomfortable with his proximity, and she fidgeted with her hands as he stared at her, finally forcing them into her lap. How could a voice so soothing go with a gruff-looking character like him? And what in the world was he doing sitting down so close to her?

5

His black hair was smoothed under a navy bandana into a short pony-tail, and she saw a hint of a nicely chiseled face and jaw line, but it was hidden below a disarray of facial hair with a full beard and mustache. If he were to clip the beard a little closer or shave it off completely, it would further reveal his dark bronze skin tone, and Megan might consider him handsome, but as it was, the beard gave him an edge, making Megan imagine he was dangerous. Thin lines wandered from the skin around his dark brown eyes, which were fixed on her, causing her pulse to quicken, uncharacteristically. She imagined he was in his mid to late thirties, but couldn't be sure. While his eyes seemed older than the rest of him somehow, his arms, wide chest, and athletic frame were so fit, she figured he could be in a triathlon if he wanted to. She had no doubt he exercised regularly. He was dressed in worn shorts and an old white t-shirt, which had at least two holes in it that Megan could see.

She wondered if he had any idea how scruffy he looked or if he even cared. More than anything, she just wanted him to widen the space between them. Even with the list of reasons he was definitely not her type that she came up with in her ten second assessment of the man, there was something alluring about him, which just made her want to kick herself. She needed to think about finding Maddy.

"I have a quick break, so I thought I'd escape the heat of the kitchen and enjoy this breathtaking view for a moment," he said, breaking the silence with another easy smile. His accent didn't sound even the slight-est bit local and was likely American, though she wouldn't have been able to pin it down to a region.

Megan raised an eyebrow, surmising that the breathtaking view he was referring to was her and not the pristine Caribbean waters surrounding them. She was not flattered. In fact, she was irritated at herself for letting him distract her at all. Even if she weren't on an indefinite relationship break, she wouldn't even consider falling for the charms of a man with holes in his clothes. Maddy had repeatedly accused her of being snobby, but Megan just accepted that she knew the type of man she was interested in dating, if she ever ventured down that reckless path again, and it was her prerogative to be picky if she wanted.

Suddenly, it struck her that maybe he was being so familiar because he had met Maddy or seen her before. Maddy wouldn't have put off the cool, uninterested vibe like she would. But if he had met her or knew her, was he one of the good guys? As anxiety crept through her, she took a deep breath. Either way, she wasn't telling him anything. He had probably just decided to try his bad boy looks out on her thinking she was a tourist. And she wasn't interested. She decided her nerves were simply shot, and since she was accustomed to being hit on, even by the occasional hoodlum-looking type, she would simply get rid of him before he proceeded any further.

"I'm waiting on the check," she informed him in her best business-like manner.

"You might be waiting for a moment, Miss. Looks like Celia stepped around back for a quick break," he finished with a small grin.

Megan shifted towards the kitchen, searching the restaurant to verify this piece of information. With her waitress nowhere in sight, she let out an aggravated sigh. Apparently, she was trapped with the intruder.

"So are you enjoying your stay in St. Croix?" he asked politely.

Megan narrowed her eyes at the unwelcome stranger. "How do you know I'm a visitor? Maybe I live here."

He chuckled, shaking his head in disbelief. "I may have overheard some conversation in the kitchen about a gecko taking you out of your comfort zone."

Megan angled her head slightly before responding in an icy tone. "Perhaps my discomfort is a result of the unexpected company I find myself in."

This time, he let out a deep laugh. "Where have my manners gone? I should have introduced myself." He held out his hand to Megan, waiting patiently for her to accept it. "Gabriel Sanchez. Or just Gabe."

Megan glanced skeptically at his outstretched hand. Why wasn't he getting the message? Normally, men understood and fled with one cool response from her. Debating another cold remark, the manners Grandma Lynn had instilled in her won out. She placed her hand in his, "Megan MacKenna."

He held onto her hand firmly, forcing her to look into his eyes. She pulled her hand back after some effort, reprimanding herself for also noticing the rough, but strong feel of his hand.

"Megan MacKenna, huh?" he sounded out her name slowly.

Megan was tempted to roll her eyes. Her trust issues aside, for a man on break from a breakfast kitchen, he sure was being nosy. Maybe he had met Maddy before and was just confused about the different first name. She debated asking him but couldn't shake the unsettling feeling he was giving her. "Last time I checked," she said haughtily.

"Is that where you get your vibrant red hair? Irish ancestry? Or Scottish?"

"My great-great grandparents were from Dublin," she said automatically, wondering why she was answering him as if she owed him any explanation.

"What brings you to Captain Sully's?" he asked, never taking his eyes from Megan's.

"I heard the veggie omelet was delicious," she replied vaguely, feeling her irritation escalate from the intrusion.

If he noted her irritation, it didn't phase him. His smile widened. "Was it everything you hoped for?"

It was the first meal she had actually finished since Maddy had vanished, but she decided she would have slept out in the wild with the centipedes for a night before admitting that to her new companion. Megan glanced away from his intense gaze, wishing he would just leave her alone. She was planning to find a print shop to make flyers to hand out with information about Maddy. Megan skimmed the area for Celia. She needed to take advantage of daylight hours. The local diner had been a waste of her time. Maddy had obviously not been there.

"Excuse me… Mr. Sanchez. Not to be rude, but I really need to get going. I have a million things to do."

She grabbed her medium sized, tan, sateen Coach bag from where it was tucked into the plastic chair beside her hip, and unzipped it, taking out what she figured was more than enough cash to cover her meal. She placed it under the saltshaker. Celia was nowhere in sight.

"What sort of urgent matters do tourists find themselves rushing off to do these days? Beach volleyball?" he asked.

"I'm not a tourist."

"Well, I admit you seem a little intense for a vacationer."

Guilt tugged at her. At the very least, she should ask the man if he had seen her sister. She reached into her purse. "Maybe you can help me then, Mr. Sanchez."

She placed a picture of Maddy before him. She had chosen this spot to talk to locals she reminded herself. This man may have been unexplainably causing her to feel uncomfortable, but what if he had met Maddy? Good guy or bad guy, she just had to find a clue for the police. Hopefully, she could read his reaction to the photo. "Have you seen this woman? Has she been in here before, maybe?"

Gabe wrinkled his brow, appearing genuinely confused. "You're sitting right in front of me."

Megan took a deep breath before continuing. "Well, I guess if you had recognized her, you would have mentioned it sooner. It's my *sister*, Madeline."

"You have a twin?" Most people expressed fascination at the news, but Gabe seemed like he might fall over from shock.

"Identical in looks…but not exactly in lifestyle choices."

As he held her gaze, a somber look filled his eyes. His voice lost its teasing tone. "You're carrying a picture of her around like something happened." He paused. "Have you lost contact with her?"

"My sister disappeared a week ago without a trace. No one has spoken with her since. When I realized she hadn't checked in with me, I reported her missing, but the police think she left the island. They don't believe me, but I am sure she's in trouble. She wouldn't just drop off of the face of the earth like this. I know her."

A range of emotions crossed his face from alarm to concern, but never doubt. Megan felt her hopes rising for a moment. Why did it feel like he accepted what she had said without any questions? Why couldn't the police have looked at her like they believed her? Maybe he had seen her and that was the reason he approached her in the first place. Hope consumed her. "Have you noticed her around? She flew to St. Croix three weeks ago."

His expression turned apologetic. "I'm sorry about your sister. I thought you were just overreacting. She hasn't been around here." He studied Megan for a few seconds, then added, "Trust me. I wish I could help you."

Megan grabbed the photo from the tabletop, shoved it into her purse, and retrieved her car keys before she zipped it shut. She stood up, placed her purse strap on her shoulder, and clutched the keys to her rented Ford Focus. "Enjoy the rest of your break." She turned away, exited the tent, and walked the short distance across the gravel lot to her car.

Footsteps dug through the rocks behind her. "This is my phone number. Maybe I can help you find your sister." Gabe stood next to her car now. He held out a napkin.

Accepting help from a complete stranger, and one who wasn't even in law enforcement was the last thing she would do. "Thanks, but I think I'll go about this my own way. I'm going to post flyers up today. Somebody has to know something."

"I've only lived in St. Croix for three months, but I know my way around pretty well. You never know, maybe I could be of some help. I get off work by two o' clock every day, and I always have Sunday off."

Megan couldn't imagine getting off of work at two o' clock. She studied the imposing man from behind her Dolce and Gabbana sunglasses. She wondered what he did every afternoon but figured it wasn't much. He looked like the type who would park himself at a beach bar, order bucket after bucket of cold beer, and drink the afternoon away in the hot sun, flirting with bikini-clad tourists. That was not the sort of help she was looking for.

"I'll call you if I need some help," she lied, taking the napkin from him.

Gabe shrugged his shoulders. "I've got to get back to work. Seriously, I would love to help out in any way."

Megan studied him again, wondering about his interest. Was he just being friendly or did he know more than he was letting on to? She settled on the facts. She needed to spread the word, and question people, but Gabe obviously didn't know Maddy.

"I will bring a flyer here sometime today in case anyone knows anything or recognizes Maddy. I didn't even show my server the picture. Maybe you can hang the flyer up here."

"It's the least we can do. Think about my offer, Miss MacKenna."

Megan nodded her head slightly and turned away from him.

She wasn't quite sure why, but she couldn't resist glancing in Gabe's direction as he walked to the kitchen. She felt sad all of a sudden thinking of Maddy. If Maddy were there, she would probably be making plans to meet the cook after he got off work. Then, at least Megan would be scolding her sister and dealing with the normal type of Maddy behavior.

She started her Focus and began her search for a print shop. She had to force herself to drive on the left side of the road. It was among the quirks of the strange island she so unexpectedly found herself on…driving on the left hand side, street names in Danish, 17th century buildings, and bumpy stone roads.

Her sister dropping off the face of the earth for a week wasn't something Megan was used to dealing with. She glanced longingly at her cell phone and prayed that it would ring. Maybe Maddy was okay and this was just a major prank.

"The jokes over Maddy. It was a good one. You got me to leave my job on a whim and fly to the Caribbean. I'm finally using those vacation days. Ha ha. Now, call me, Sis. We'll laugh about this over a quick shoe shopping spree before we catch a flight home."

Megan sighed. She wished Maddy had pulled a joke on her but knew, with all of her heart, that it wasn't so. The heartsick feeling and chills which had overcome her that early evening a week ago had yet to go away. The shivers and goose bumps had inexplicably linked the twins when something was wrong their entire lives. Maddy was in trouble, and Megan was the only one who believed it or seemed to care.

She wiped fresh tears away and concentrated on the road. She needed a printer so she could hand out flyers about her missing sister. She spoke loudly, attempting to sound convincing. "Hold on Maddy. I'm going to find you, I promise."

6

Gabe climbed into the faded, blue clunker and carefully closed the door. He grabbed a new prepaid cell and dialed a number he hadn't called in a few weeks, but one he knew by heart. He was always careful to dispose of the phones every so often, just in case. Especially after the one man willing to testify against Torrez had been murdered two years ago. Gabe didn't want to think someone was on the take, but he had to be careful. After all, they'd never confirmed how their informant had been discovered.

Paul Smith was one of two people who knew the exact details of his cover. Gabe noted a couple walking near the waterfront but no one else was around. October was a slow month on island, but people didn't pay much attention to Gabe either way. As far as any of the locals knew, Gabe was just a poor fella trying to make it, who showed up from down island a few months back, willing to work wherever there was cash to be made. To anyone who asked questions or dug a little, they'd learn he'd served a little time on gun charges and grand theft charges. They might also learn he sent money to family—a mother in Puerto Rico and an ex for child support in Miami, nothing but an alias. Being raised bilingual in Fort Lauderdale after the rest of his family was murdered in their St. Croix home, and earning his bachelor's degree and later his master's degree in Chicago, Gabe had learned a few accents, which were quite impressive, and could blend in easily without raising questions.

"Hello," answered a gruff voice.

"Don't sound so excited. I might start to think you actually miss me."

"Have you perfected your omelets yet?" Smith's tone lightened up at once.

"Don't make me fly a thousand miles to kick your ass."

Smith laughed. "You're welcome to try. Been lifting?"

Gabe sighed. "Some people don't have time to train for King of the Beach."

As Smith laughed, Gabe allowed a small smile. Ever since they'd met on Gabe's first official case, a decade ago, he had teased Smith that he should've been a body builder instead of a DEA agent since he spent every spare moment away from the job lifting weights. Though the perfect fit for a King of the Beach contest with his stocky build many females swooned over, he was actually an ex-marine with a passion for lifting and endurance training. He was a couple of inches shorter than Gabe, bald, with light brown eyes and a pale complexion, and built wide and strong like a linebacker. The truth was, he probably could kick Gabe's ass. But he would not admit that to Smith.

"So, made it into the family circle yet?"

"No, but something interesting turned up. Or someone that is."

"Someone? A female, I'm assuming. Do I need to come down there to keep an eye on you?"

"No, she's not involved with the family. It's not like before."

"I trust your judgment. It's just that I'm not there to drag you to the ER if you get mixed up with the wrong informant again."

"That was ten years ago."

"Just cautioning you to watch your back. You're flyin' solo down there."

Ungrateful for the reminder of his near-death experience, Gabe got to the point. "I'm being careful, but listen…Looks like Miguel's girl-friend has a sister."

"Which girlfriend? The new one you were telling me about?"

"The red head I asked you to get me info on…which you never gave me by the way."

"Look, man, boss decided since things have been pretty idle with your operation, he'd put us on another case. We're swamped here. And my new partner is a real tool," Smith's voice was suddenly agitated.

Gabe paused, allowing the small tug of guilt to linger before sighing into the phone. When the DEA decided to send a new undercover in three months ago to once again gather intelligence on Victor Torrez, and possibly establish a relationship with him or one of his men, a thus far untouchable on the list of suspected and notorious drug traffickers, Gabe had begged for the assignment. It had meant leaving a ten-year partner behind in Miami, but it was the chance of a lifetime to go after the man responsible for the deaths of his sister, mother, and father. Even if it was an impossible mission. No one had ever come close to taking down Torrez, and those sent in on past undercover assignments hadn't lived to tell about it. "Look, I know you don't really get why I had to take this assignment."

"Forget it. Tell me about the girl."

Gabe recognized the stubbornness in his partner's voice and moved on. "She walked into Captain Sully's just this morning. They are identical twins, too. I thought it was Miguel's girlfriend at first. I was so surprised to see her that I stepped out of the kitchen to talk to her. That's when I found out she has a twin."

"What were you planning to do? Ask her if she wanted to rat on her boyfriend's dad?"

"Funny, man. No. I just thought I would feel her out. See what she knew about her new boyfriend. Maybe she didn't know about his family business."

"So, does she know what kind of family her sister is hanging around?" Smith inquired with mild curiosity.

"Well, that's the problem. The sister I met today says her twin, Madeline, disappeared over a week ago. No trace left behind. She's here trying to find out what happened."

"Torrez has been seen with other girls before this one. You said yourself he seemed distant from them. Maybe he just dumped her and moved on. She's probably drinking it off somewhere or maybe she's exploring the other islands."

"I don't have a good feeling about this. Besides, she was out to dinner every night with Torrez. Even when he's had girls around before, he's never had one with him all of the time like that. He was close to her. He was letting her in, getting serious. That's why I asked you to look her up."

"Listen, I'm sorry. It's been crazy here like I said. But do you really think there's something worth looking into here? The girl probably sailed to St. Thomas."

"Something's off. And this new sister—Megan—shows up, and she has no idea what she's doing. She reported her sister missing a week ago, but the police don't know anything. They probably didn't even check into her disappearance until the sister actually showed up here. Torrez could easily be behind this, and we can't ignore a possible kidnapping or homicide over a drug bust."

"We're not just talking about a drug bust, man, and you know it. We're talking about bringing down a notorious murderer and his enormous drug ring. Even if we can prove that Miguel killed the sister, that still won't bring down the big guy. Now, you need to stay focused on the real target, man. As soon as you have the chance to get into the family's network of low life scumbags, take it. We need them to make you one of their own if we're going to bust them," Smith reminded him.

Gabe pushed the idea of the sister already being dead aside. "Come on, man, just help me out. I at least want to look into this a little bit."

Gabe could imagine Smith shaking his head before caving. "What do you need?"

"Find out everything about Megan and Madeline MacKenna you can. Especially Megan, the one sniffing around. I want to know where she is from, all of the background usuals, if they have family, friends, etcetera, and I need to know what hotel she is staying at here on island. And get it to me fast. She's already sticking out like a sore thumb."

"Anything else? You want me to send over some new aprons for that fancy job you've got?"

"Yeah that, and you can kiss my ass."

Smith laughed now, back to chiding his partner. "You just get the job done. And try to avoid getting shot."

Gabe's jaw tensed. A day didn't go by that he didn't regret what had happened on his first case with Smith. He was only twenty-five at the time, and anxious to prove himself as a new DEA agent. Smith had already been working for the agency for five years at the time, and though he'd tried to reign in his new, energetic partner, Gabe had been on a mission to bring down the bad guys.

He'd sparked a small flirtation with one of the girls he'd seen hanging around their target at the time, and she'd trusted Gabe enough to do a little digging. The night she'd agreed to meet him to pass along the Intel she'd been followed. As Gabe had walked across the busy Miami Street to meet her, she'd been shot right as she neared him. And so had he. Smith had come running around the corner as the car had sped off. They'd put four bullets in Gabe and left him for dead. But Smith had raced him to the ER, getting him to the surgeons just in time. They had told him if he'd been a minute later, Gabe wouldn't have made it. One bullet in particular, right in between his ribs, had nearly finished him off. And to date, Smith still hovered over Gabe like he was his guardian angel, always reminding his younger partner to watch his back. And to be wary of who he trusted.

"Make sure you get me the info by tonight, partner. Megan is planning to hand out flyers. If Torrez did do something to the sister, Megan is in trouble. They are truly identical twins, and he's bound to get word she's here before too long. We don't want another sister to go missing."

"You know, now that I think about it. Boss might think the sister could be useful to the op. Maybe the sister is just what we've been waiting for. I bet she could gain access to their operation faster than you. It's happened before. She would just have to wear a wire, she could go in asking questions about her twin, and we would be close by in case she needed us. There's no telling what they might say in front of her. They'd have no reason to suspect she was law enforcement. She'd just be the sister to them." Smith sounded excited.

Gabe thought of the hostile, worried, yet seemingly determined woman he had just met. He knew she would do it if they asked her to. And instead of giving him hope for a speedier end to this mess, the idea of her or any innocent person getting close to the Torrez family made his stomach churn. There was no way he could let it happen.

"Exactly, she'd just be the sister to them, which means they might tell her a lot, but they'd have no reason to keep her alive. The moment she starts asking them questions, they'll kill her for sure. They might go after her anyway, just for being here and asking around about her sister. You know how their operation runs. All threats are taken out. And you of all people know how I feel about innocent people being put in danger, especially after what happened ten years ago. Sometimes I think you don't care about the fact that girl died trying to help us that day."

"That's not fair. I do care. I'm sorry about her. I tried to warn you not to approach her, remember? But more than anything, I don't want to see you get shot anymore. As big of a pain as you are, I'm kind of hoping you live through this case so you can come back and partner with me again, man. If you don't think the sister can help us, that's your call."

"She's not exactly undercover material. Don't think she could pull it off. I'll get the job done."

Smith's tone turned a little defensive. "We'll do it your way for now...The info on Miss MacKenna will be at the drop site at three p.m. tomorrow."

Gabe hung up and started the car. It aggravated him that Megan was out there snooping around like she was. She had no idea what kind of people she was exposing herself to. They didn't like loose ends, and Megan MacKenna was exactly that.

7

Miguel Torrez's cell phone buzzed. He sat with his head resting on one hand, staring blankly ahead as the vibrations moved it across his desk. After two more unanswered calls, he finally glanced down. Noting the caller id, he answered curtly. "*¿Qué pasa?*"

"*Jefe*. I have to tell you something."

"What is it?" He brushed a lock of his chin-length, sleek black hair from his olive-toned, face. His three-day-old beard needed to be shaved. It wasn't like him to hide the good looks he had received from his late mother under a beard, but he was struggling to maintain his normal routine lately.

"The red head is on island, *Jefe*."

Miguel's hand tightened around his phone. "Impossible."

"No, *Jefe*. It's true. I know Trevor told everyone we were supposed to say she'd left the island on a sailing trip if anyone asked. And I had no problem with that, but I knew I had to call you right away. She's not gone, Jefe. I saw her with my own eyes. She's here. I saw her drivin' a rental car."

"Raul. She is not here. Do you need a few days off? To catch up on sleep maybe? I shouldn't have to remind you, but I don't have room for errors."

"It was her boss. I swear. You can't mistake that face."

"I don't know what you are talking about. Trust me, she's not here."

"*Jefe*. Somethin's not right…I swear it was your lady!"

"Are you messing with the product, Raul?"

"No, boss—"

"You know how I feel about employees messing around. Do I need to reevaluate your membership on my team?"

"No, *Jefe*. I'm clean, I swear. I'm not making this up either. It was her. I know it," he reemphasized, with a shaky voice.

"I'm hanging up. I'm only saying this once. I don't like my team trying out the product, and neither does my father."

Miguel tossed the phone aside and turned towards the sofa and chairs where his men sat, glancing over curiously, awaiting his instruction. "The situation was handled just as you told me, right Trevor?"

As his light brown eyes focused on Trevor, Miguel missed the worried look that briefly flashed across Dalbert's face.

"Jus like I tellin' yoh," Trevor said easily.

As Miguel's jaw clenched, Dalbert noted the despair in his expression.

Miguel closed his eyes, shifting to rest his head against the office chair. "I want Raul brought in for a talk."

A small smile formed on Trevor's face. "Consida it done, *Jefe*."

8

"I'll just hold, please. No one returned my call the last time even though I was told someone would," Megan stated sharply. She knew she sounded hostile, but she didn't care. Hostile or polite, it didn't seem to have an impact on the results she got from the police.

She was calling them, again, to see if they had made any progress on her sister's case and to tell them about the item she had found that proved Maddy had left in a hurry. Perched on the edge of the bed in her hotel room, she held the phone under her chin and zipped open her sister's faded, green traveling backpack once more.

It was the only tangible proof of Maddy's stay on St. Croix and, with the exception of the hotel and flight records, the last fragment of evidence Megan wasn't making this up. The hotel cleaning lady who had given it to her had actually mistaken her for her twin. Apparently, she had found it after Maddy had checked out.

It was an old bag that needed to be thrown out, but Megan knew her sister wouldn't have left it behind intentionally. Maddy hung on to all of her stuff, valuable or not. Megan had nicknamed her twin Hector the Collector for a reason. Nothing was even inside. Just half a bottle of sunscreen, some shimmery, coral lipstick, and some t-shirts you couldn't pay Megan to wear.

Even so, as much as Megan wanted to believe it held a clue that could help her find Maddy, more than likely, Maddy had simply forgotten the bag, packing in a hurry. It had probably been under the bed or out of sight. Maddy was typically forgetful, hasty, and not the sort of person to sweep her hotel twice, or once even, to make sure she had everything.

When Megan had walked around the resort property earlier, her hopes had soared for a moment. A server had greeted her, "Miss Maddy!" Her eyes had scanned the horizon for her twin, but of course, he had been calling to her. Megan honestly couldn't understand how people mixed them up. Sure, they were identical twins, but seriously, the two had completely different tastes. They dressed like polar opposites and behaved like opposites.

At the moment, Megan wore a silk, sleeveless Kate Spade blouse, a black, almost knee-length, pencil skirt, and black, two-inch sandals. Her hair was smoothed up into a neat bun. Megan considered her look classy, but Maddy threw around words like, "proper, boring, and snooty," when she referred to Megan's style. Maddy would have been walking around the resort in jean cutoffs she still had from high school, a ripped, rock concert t-shirt over her bikini top, flip flops, if she wore shoes at all, and her hair pulled into a loose braid. Completely different tastes.

Megan had pumped the server for information. Had he known Maddy? Hung out with her? Simply served her a meal or two? Had he seen her with anyone? But she had left the poolside bar empty handed. He had seemed disappointed to find out Megan wasn't Maddy, especially when he had discovered that Maddy and Megan didn't share an easy-going personality. True, Megan was under extreme stress, but her personality wouldn't have been much more agreeable had the circumstances been different. Megan didn't really care. She had accepted the fact, long ago, that Maddy was more fun. Maddy was bubbly, brimming with positivity, and nice to everyone. Megan knew she was a bit cold, and maybe people were right when they said she had a superiority complex, but if her attitude was what kept her out of trouble, then it was fine with her. Maddy was just too nice to people. She trusted everyone, and that was probably why she was in a heap of trouble now.

As she ran her hand over the worn material, Megan realized with much trepidation that even if the police were right and her sister had moved on to another island, she was not going to be easy to track. She didn't even have a credit card. All of Megan's efforts to conform her sister to normal society had been wasted. Maddy couldn't have cared less about credit reports and so forth. She had lived from one moment to the next, always ready for the next adventure.

Megan scolded herself, wishing she would stop thinking of her sister as if she were already gone, impossible to find. She had to keep telling herself Maddy was alive and unharmed. It was the only way this search was going to continue. The police were obviously going to be of no help.

She listened now as a man cleared his voice on the other end of the line. "Miss MacKenna? Dis is Offica Davis."

"Have you got any leads?" Megan blurted.

"I'm sorry Miss. We haven' been able to discova a ting about yoh sista. We know dat she checked out of de hotel, but deh is no trace of ha since."

"But what about the backpack I found? Why would she have left it behind? Couldn't that mean that she was taken from here by force?"

"The hotel staff confirmed dat she checked out of de hotel alone. I'm sorry. But she probably just forgot ta pack it."

"Okay, but what can you do to help me find her? I know she's in danger."

"Without any evidence of a crime and no real leads ta follow, all we have is a missing person. We'll keep lookin' foh her, but she has probably gone on with her travels. Maybe yoh should consida goin' home or ta 'nother island."

"I'm not leaving until I know something."

"Okay, Miss MacKenna. We will contact yoh if any ting come up. We' given de description of yo' sista ta de authorities on de otha nearby islands by de way. Maybe someone will see ha deh."

Megan hung up the phone with a whisper of, "Thank you." She felt so helpless. How was she supposed to find Maddy if no one even believed she was in danger?

A breeze swept into the room, ruffling the sheer, white curtains gently, and sweeping over Megan's skin, causing her to look up. The horizon swirled with reds and pinks as it began it's descent over a calm Caribbean ocean. Such an exquisite picture and one that she never would have seen with her own eyes if it hadn't been for Maddy disappearing like this. She had been sure the police would have found something out by now. But instead, three days into her search, she was really running out of ideas.

She eyed the phone, wondering if she should let Grandma Lynn in on the truth. She hadn't wanted to worry her, so she'd stopped by the retirement home and told their grandmother she had decided to use some of her vacation days and meet up with Maddy.

Grandma Lynn had been so surprised and happy she hadn't been able to contain her excitement. *"Don't even call me or check-in, Meg. Just have fun for a change. You and Maddy haven't spent quality time together in ages. I'm so happy you're doing this. Go and relax on the beach. And tell me all of the details when you get home. If you decide to come back, that is. You never know…Mr. Right might be from the islands, Honey…"* she'd teased.

Megan had rolled her eyes and smiled as she kissed her grandma goodbye. She was always encouraging her to get out there and date again. Guilt filled her a little now as she thought about the lie she'd told. What she would give to be able to vent to Grandma Lynn and tell her what was happening. She swallowed, shaking off the thought. She wouldn't tell her unless she absolutely had to. And she'd give it a few more days at least. If only there was someone she could talk to. Or someone who would help her.

The only person who had shown even an inkling of interest in helping Megan was the messy-looking cook…Gabe. Megan wished she could erase him from her memory. She told herself he was only interested in helping her because he was interested in sleeping with her, something that would never happen. She had sworn off men altogether after her brief engagement, four years earlier, but even if she were going down that path again, which she wasn't, it wouldn't be with a man like him. She had a list of qualities she would look for in a man, if she were so inclined, and at the top of the list would be the word responsible, followed by honest, reliable, and caring. As she pictured Gabe's scruffy beard and t-shirt with holes, she couldn't imagine the word responsible relating to him at all. Of course, she'd judged a man by appearances alone before, and she'd lived to regret it. It was a lot easier to be alone than to let a man in period.

Her ex, Ben, had been a well-reputed DA in Miami. Until the scandal broke. Unbeknownst to Megan, he had been a regular client of an escort service. She'd only just mailed out their wedding invitations when a co-worker had dropped the Miami Herald on her desk, Ben's photo one of many under the headline PROSTITUTION RING BUSTED. The scandal that ensued had nearly destroyed her emotionally, but she was tough. Megan had experienced more crisis in her twenty-eight years than most people did in a lifetime. She recalled how tough she'd been and took a deep breath. She could find her sister alone. She'd do what she had to do.

She decided to check every little zipped up pocket of Maddy's backpack one more time, and her fingers felt a smooth surface. Surprised she had missed it before, she pried at the surface and pulled out an old photo, its edges worn from the years. Her heart tugged at the memory. It was a picture of Maddy and Megan at their grandparents' farm, standing in front of the pond, the first summer after the accident. Their energetic, action-seeking parents had died while mountain climbing the spring they turned eleven. The pain had left a hole in their hearts nearly impossible to put into words.

Their parents had been mountain climbers endorsed by sporting goods companies, and had traveled the world, one extreme adventure after another. They had spent part of the year with their daughters, leaving them with their grandparents while they were away. Then suddenly their parents were gone, faulty equipment in bad weather suspected. Emotional devastation aside, Megan's instinct to comfort Maddy had kicked in immediately. Megan had automatically assumed the role of mother, even though their grandparents had always been there and gotten full custody of them after the accident.

Megan blamed the accident for Maddy's recklessness and also for her unwillingness to do anything remotely rational. The twins had leaned on each other and become even closer after their parents' death, yet ultimately, they had taken two paths, Maddy becoming more spontaneous and Megan always doing the "responsible" thing.

The photo showed them side by side, their arms draped around one another, pale, freckled faces staring solemnly at the camera. The tiny emeralds from their matching necklaces gleamed in the sunlight in the picture. They hadn't smiled much that first summer.

The usual pull of protectiveness reeled through her, and Megan placed her hand on top of the photo as if she could reach into it and grab her sister. A suffocating pain throbbed in her chest. The breeze blew across her, leaving a chill on her skin this time. She watched as the sun grew smaller, disappearing into the ocean. She imagined how scared Maddy must be, wherever she was. She reached up to her neck, rubbing the emerald pendant between her fingers and swore she wouldn't give up searching.

9

Maddy floated through the darkness, slightly aware of a distant drumming sound, reminiscent of a steady heartbeat. Time seemed to stretch on, though she didn't mind. There was something comforting about the blackness. As her thoughts began to come together, she wondered why there were no shining lights or voices reaching out to her. Would she see her mom and dad? She was dead wasn't she?

As if contesting her last thought, a dull throb became recognizable at Maddy's temple. She had suffered her share of party-induced migraines, but this pain was building at an alarming rate and much more intense than any of her past ones.

As the ache began to trickle down her head, moving its way to her extremities, a new sensation crept over her. An odor so terrible hit her at once, and her nostrils flared as recognition registered. Nausea rolled through her as the potent stink of raw fish overwhelmed her.

As a little girl, she had refused to touch the fish she and Meg had caught in their grandparents' pond, only interested in the thrill of the catch, unwilling to deal with the stinky, slimy fish on the hook. But one fish on a hook would seem like blossoming roses compared to the stench that filled the darkness surrounding her.

As her senses slowly returned, Maddy began to panic. She was blind. What had happened to her? As if responding to her unspoken question, the shooting pain in her head became more unbearable. Had she been in an accident? How bad was it? She was obviously breathing if she could smell raw fish, so what was wrong with her vision?

The droning sound became clearer. It was a repetitive thudding noise, but she couldn't place it and frankly didn't care. The aches and soreness were ripping through her arms and legs. She tried to take a deep breath, but as she inhaled, the taste of fabric burned her tongue. She breathed through her nose, hating the scent of the fish, and tried to bite down on the cloth, but it was a futile effort. Her mouth was gagged, dry, and aching. Reality terrified her as she realized she was tied up and lying on her side.

Maddy tried to move her wrists, then her feet, but it was useless. She was bound, gagged, and surrounded by darkness. She slammed her head into the hard surface she lay on and hope surged through her as she saw a smidgeon of light. Realizing her eyes were covered as well, she thanked God that she wasn't actually blind. She moved her face against the floor, ignoring the burn it caused and slowly worked the cover off of her eyes. The light wasn't much but still bright enough to startle her. After a moment of squeezing her eyes shut and open, a trick she had learned as a kid, her eyes adjusted to the dimly lit space.

A few things came into focus: a pair of rain boots, a cooler full of long, skinny, silver fish, and a tool box. Other than that, she couldn't make anything out. As she was attempting to flip her body over to get another view of the space, the thudding sound suddenly registered. It sounded like waves. That was it! She was on a boat. In the cabin of a fishing boat. But why was she there? What had…?

Her heart sank at the memory. She remembered it clearly. She had followed Miguel into the wild only to witness him threaten a man with a gun. She had fled as the sound of gunshots blasted behind her. She'd run as fast as she could, but she hadn't seen the cliff coming. She remembered the waves hitting the jagged rocks as she fell towards them. And that was it. She had no memory after falling into the ocean. Just darkness, until now.

As her mind caught up to speed, so did her pain, but she tried not to think of it. She called up strength from deep down, imagining the ways she could inflict pain on Miguel instead of focusing on the aching burns on her wrists and ankles. What she would give to see him now. She wondered if the coward was sending her somewhere to be executed or if he would have the nerve to pull the trigger himself.

With every ounce of her strength, she shoved herself up a little and managed to turn onto her other side, hoping to shift the pain to other areas of her body. She scanned the space and the alternate view. She sucked in her breath sharply, and her body went rigid. As she gaped at the figure beside her, the roar of the boat's engine and the cloth gagging her mouth barely muffled the scream of terror she unleashed.

10

"We need ta talk, mon."

"My daughter's *Quinceañera* is about to begin. Don't tell me you're having problems getting the girl here, Trevor." Ricardo Rivera stood in front of the small mirror in his home office, adjusting his black and silver striped necktie with his free hand.

"Me contact at Madeline's hotel claim ha sista is on islan' lookin' for ha."

Ricardo stopped fidgeting with the tie.

"*Señor* Rivera?"

"Give her a few days to snoop around. She won't find anything. You made sure of that. She'll leave once she realizes there is nothing to find and no one to help her."

"I don' tink so. 'Cording ta me contact, de sista puttin' up fly'as, interviewin' staff, searchin' de island. She gon catch Miguel's eye soona or lata, an' yoh know he' go afta ha."

"Why? She's a looker, too? Does this guy go after every good-looking tourist type he sees?" He walked away from the mirror, stopping to stare out at the ocean from the large, open window.

"Dat's de ting. Dey identical twins."

"Identical twins?"

"Dat's right."

"Well, this is interesting news, Trevor. I'm glad you brought it to my attention…I wonder what Miguel would do if he found out his number one man was betraying him. I know what his father would do," he finished darkly.

"I tell yoh. I tired o' workin' foh dat family. An' yoh offa was good.

Dat's why I tell yoh bout de gurl, Madeline. I know she some ting special ta Miguel. Yoh tell me ta find his weak spot an' I did. Now yoh plan gon' work."

"We'll see over time how deep your loyalty runs. I haven't seen Madeline with my own eyes yet. You said your guys would have her here four days ago, and you keep sending me messages that there is a delay. I don't understand what the hold up is."

"I sorry, but I had sum problem initially. I had ta fish ha out o' de ocean wit'out lettin' Miguel onta de plan an' not involvin' Dalbert. She wa' unconscious an' needed ha head bandaged from de fall. I had ta leave ha wit me friend fo' a few more days 'for I could get ha on de boat. But every ting been taken care o', and she en route as we speak," explained Trevor.

"And she is alive and well?"

"Ya, mon. She fine."

"Excellent. We need her alive for the plan to work. And about the twin. For now, let's give her a little scare. I don't want her interfering with my plans. Two missing tourists would cause the police to get more involved, and it would be better if she just left. But if she doesn't leave within two days, we'll let her join her sister. I suppose it could make it easier for us to entice Miguel if we had two. It seems he had formed quite the attachment to the girl since you tell me he has never been so upset before."

"So, I send in Marcus, mon?" asked Trevor.

"No. I want this taken care of immediately. Send in Lukas. I didn't bring him here to sit around doing nothing until Miguel gets here. It's time to put him to work. He'll have her packing before night falls."

Trevor barely hid the delight from his response. "Well, guess we considar' de sista officially no' a problem, mon."

Hanging up his cell, Ricardo turned at the sound of footsteps approaching the open doorway.

"*Papá*, my party is about to begin," exclaimed his fifteen-year-old daughter, Alejandra, as she wrapped her arms halfway around his waist. He wore a black suit for the occasion, but also to give himself a trimmer look. He was a burly man through his shoulders and chest, but had taken on some extra pounds in his stomach over the past few years. His dark hair, which was turning gray these days, was cut into a precise and even looking crew-cut, and he had a thin mustache. He appeared every bit the prominent business owner and respected citizen of his city that he was.

"*Sí, mi Amor*," he returned the embrace fiercely and pushed her at arms length to look over his pride and joy in her beautiful, white gown. She had crystal, blue eyes and long black hair. Tears filled his eyes, but he coughed and cleared his voice to hold them back. "You are the spitting image of your mother," the pride in his voice clear.

"*Gracias, Papá*. I miss her so much. I wish she could be here for my party."

"Me too...don't forget though, she's watching over us now. She'll be watching your first dance and crying tears of joy from above. You've become such a beautiful young lady."

"*Ay, Papá*...don't make me cry now. The party is about to begin," she smiled up at her father dotingly.

He grabbed her hand and led her towards the door. "Let's go then. You don't want to see your *Papá* cry either, I'm sure."

As he teased his daughter, he thought secretly about the retribution that was coming to the man who had stolen his wife from him and his daughter. Justice, which police and lawmakers had been unable to give him, would finally be had.

11

Gabe's forehead wrinkled as he read through the Intel Smith had gotten to him. Megan MacKenna was an extremely successful real estate agent who lived in Naples, Florida, the prestigious area of Southwest Florida, where the average home cost around $600,000. She graduated from University of Florida with a business degree and a 4.0 GPA. She had no criminal background, not even a parking ticket. Not only did she pay her bills on time, most of them were set up to withdraw automatically from her bank account.

She was organized in every facet of her life. She didn't have a cent of debt, no student loans, and her credit cards were paid off on a regular basis. She owned a 2000 square foot home in Old Naples, which was small for the average home there. Her home would soon be completely paid off, with one year left on her mortgage. She drove and owned outright a Maserati Gran Turismo, had once been engaged, and every spec of her financial records indicated she didn't travel or do much besides workout at a private gym and go to and from work each day. She shopped online, though records indicated she frequented Naples high-end shoe and fashion boutiques as well. But there were no records of dining out, nightlife, or much of a social life at all. Her monthly bills also showed she paid for her only living relative besides her sister, her grandmother, Lynn MacKenna, to stay at a very nice retirement home in Naples.

From the outside looking in, it would seem the twenty-eight-year old kept to herself. There was an escort scandal her one-time fiancé had been apart of in Miami, but Megan herself, seemed to have it together.

Gabe contemplated that last piece of information. Maybe the scandal had scared her into a life of solitude.

Gabe sighed as he glanced over the report again, wishing he could just make her leave the island. Megan was about to be way in over her pretty little head. Everything the DEA had dug up on the two sisters verified that Megan had been completely honest with him at Captain Sully's. The twins were identical in looks and opposite in behavior.

The missing twin, Madeline, had never owned anything, never gone to college, never had had a job for more than five weeks, and a trail of travel receipts since the age of eighteen, revealed she had been all around the world, basically living out of a backpack as she went. Travel records showed a stop now and then back to her sister's place in Naples, but Madeline never stayed for long.

The report further revealed the tragic, mountain climbing accident of the twins' parents when the girls were only eleven-years-old. The parents had left the twins in their paternal grandparents' care, the MacKennas, six months of the year for their adventure trips. Until the accident, after which the grandparents were granted full custody. The remainder of their youth was spent living in a small farm community outside of Naples in Immokalee, Florida, at the farm their grandparents helped run. Two years earlier, their grandfather had passed away, and Megan had moved Lynn to the retirement home in Naples.

It was easy for Gabe to conclude, especially after the brief conversation in Captain Sully's, that Megan had chosen a calculated, rational existence not like the adventuresome nature of her parents, and Madeline had chosen to follow in her parents' footsteps. Yet this time, her carefree lifestyle had landed her in the company of real bad guys. The kind that killed to protect their lifestyle. If he didn't get this message across to Megan, she could end up like her twin. Missing.

And more than likely, dead.

Gabe noted Megan's hotel and room number, then pulling a lighter from his pocket, set the report ablaze. He dropped the burning papers into the street barrel and made a decision. He was going to pay Megan MacKenna a visit.

12

The rental car's air-conditioner had only been working on the lowest setting since the day before, but as the unwelcome heat wafted in through the open window, Megan realized it was better than nothing. No wonder there were hardly any tourists around this time of year. It was unbearably warm on the island.

"Room numba?"

Megan narrowed her eyes at the man barely acknowledging her through the window of the security hut, his eyes focused on a newspaper in his hands with the name ST. CROIX AVIS. He was one of four security gate personnel at the resort she had met since arriving to the island. Though the other guards hadn't offered her any leads or information that could help her find Maddy, at least they had been sympathetic to the situation.

They had each taken flyers and promised to ask around their neighborhoods for Maddy. Before Megan had left the hotel earlier that morning, one of them, an older man named Jerome, had even said he was putting the missing twin on his church's prayer list. Megan hadn't really prayed in a long time, but ever since Maddy's disappearance, she'd prayed more than she had in her entire life. She'd teared up when Jerome had told her that piece of information. It had helped her have a brighter perspective as she'd gone out to look for her sister for the day.

But as she studied the man behind the kiosk now, she felt depleted of energy and hope. She'd spent the entire day handing out flyers, talking to whoever would listen, and driving all around the island. She'd covered every tourist destination and been to dozens of local shopping complexes and businesses. No one, not a single soul, had recognized her or the photo of Maddy.

Maybe it was just her frayed nerves or her exhaustion, but suddenly the unfriendly security guard was truly irritating her. The fact that he was still asking her for a room number at this point was too much. The resort was practically deserted, and he kept acting as if he didn't know her. Of course he knew who she was. She was the woman who kept annoying him about her missing twin sister. Megan gripped the steering wheel and gave him a tight-lipped smile, though he wouldn't have noticed as his head was buried in the newspaper.

"I'm in room 604," she answered politely.

He didn't even glance at her before hitting a button that automatically raised the security barrier. Heat rose and blushed Megan's cheeks. "I hate to bother you, again, but are you sure you don't remember any details about my sister's stay here, sir?"

Irritation swept his face as he dropped the paper into his lap and gazed between the open security gate and Megan. He let out a slow breath. "I tell ya every ting I know, Miss MacKenna. Yoh sista wasn' here more den a couple days. Den she tek off wit a couple of guys I neva seen befor. Probably tourists she met at de bar o' sum ting."

"And you still don't remember what these guys looked like? Nothing? Please, I'm getting desperate here…I have to find her."

If she had touched a cord of sympathy it wasn't apparent. "I let ya know if I 'memba any ting," he answered coolly before pointing toward the open gate.

As he picked up his newspaper again, her eyes swept over the title. "What about that paper? Do you think they'd let me run an ad in it about my sister?"

He lowered the paper an inch. His eyes met hers for a moment as he shrugged. "Maybe."

He lifted the paper back up, ending the conversation. Megan groaned inwardly and stepped on the accelerator, driving away from the hut and through the gated entrance.

Four days in St. Croix and she hadn't turned up a thing, other than an old backpack. Megan drove the windy path towards her bungalow building, rather isolated from the amenities area of the resort. It was quite peaceful with Bougainvillea plants, Hibiscus bushes, and coconut palms decorating the landscape. Megan couldn't identify much beyond that, but there were certainly a variety of tropical flowers to admire.

The scent from Gardenia blooms drifted towards her through the window, reminding her of Grandma Lynn. After Grandpa Kyle had passed, Grandma Lynn had refused to move in with Megan. She'd said she was single and too young to be looking after an old lady. Though Megan had tried to convince her otherwise, Grandma Lynn's stubbornness had won in the end, and she'd started looking for retirement homes. When Megan realized she couldn't sway her grandma, she'd insisted on paying for her to be in the best home she could find, and one that had a garden.

Grandma Lynn had always had a soft spot for gardens. She'd tended to a small one on the farm years ago. The retirement home they'd settled on had an enormous garden, and most importantly, it had Grandma Lynn's favorite flowers…Gardenia. She claimed the garden was her place to find peace. As Megan rounded another curve, she noted the variety of blossoms, red to pale pink. Perhaps that's why Maddy left. It was too quiet and peaceful for her sister's taste.

Megan parked in front of the bungalow and climbed out of the junky, little car, as she was referring to it now, resisting the urge to kick it. Though the air-conditioning wasn't working at full power, it had offered some relief from the island temperature. Even though she'd tried to dress weather-appropriately with a short, thin cotton dress, the humid air seemed to reach out to her and settle over her at once, sending a drop of sweat down her temple. Out of habit more than anything, she wiped the sweat away before it could ruin what was left of her make-up. She sighed aloud. She didn't just miss her Maserati. She missed her office and her house. Her routine. She missed her life.

Maybe the police were right. Maddy had just left on a whim. It was something she had a reputation for, for Heaven's sake. Megan wondered if she should just leave and go back to her life. Maddy would probably show up with some ridiculous story and a new tattoo before she knew it. After all, how was she supposed to find her sister if no one had seen or heard of anything bad happening to her? All facts pointed to what the police were saying...

Maddy checked out of her hotel, and no one had seen her since.

Of course, she still had questions...Who were the guys she had left the hotel with? Maddy could have gotten involved with a man, but had she left St. Croix with him? It was a definite possibility. Her twin was probably sun tanning on a booze cruise somewhere in the British Virgin Islands by now. Still, before she had left Naples, Maddy had been sober for nearly sixteen months. Had she given up on sobriety?

As she climbed the steps to her bungalow, Megan tried to convince herself the theory was true. She would go home and wait for Maddy to show up with her new tattoo and tale of sailing the Caribbean islands. Then, she would try, yet again, to convince Maddy to get a job and stay put. And they would have the same old argument about why Maddy refused to act more responsible.

As she pondered her twin's recklessness, a hand clamped over her mouth, and her arms were pulled into captivity.

Everything went dark.

13

Megan was drowning. Blindfolded. This wasn't how she was supposed to die, she thought mournfully. Her sobs were aiding in her death, allowing more water in to suffocate her.

Strong, iron-like hands, clenching her neck, held her upper body securely under the water. Rushing water poured into the tub next to her submerged head, making an eerily hollow sound, accompanying the heartbeat that was hammering in her head. The tub was the only place she could have been transported to in under ten seconds of her capture.

Her mind told her to kick, to fight for her life, but her limbs couldn't move against the cement-like force of her killer. She had been tied up, blindfolded and dunked into a tub full of water in less than ten seconds.

All of a sudden, by the nape of her hair, she was yanked from the tub, the steel hands of her captor still in place, holding her what felt like inches above the condemning water. She gasped for air, her throat and lungs on fire. She choked up the fluid and fought to replace it with deep gulps of air. Just as she thought she might be able to catch a real breath, her captor plunged her head down. She couldn't help the scream that escaped her mouth as the water covered her head once more and consumed her lungs.

As she fought the killer's death grip, searing pain shot through her arms, back, and legs. She wondered if this is what they had done to her sister. Surely, she would die this time. No goodbyes. No more Maddy. No more responsible, structured life. It probably served her right to die this way. She had prided herself in her good credit, wealth, and respectable citizen status for too long. It would be some cruel cosmic joke for her to die at the hands of a criminal in a bathtub on an island that tourists barely frequented.

Her captor seized her from the deathly waters, toying with her emotions. Was she to live or die?

Megan spit up water as she fought for air. "Please," she cried as she was forced downwards.

She sucked a breath as the water hit her chin. One-two-three-four… She tried to count as she was drowned this time. She lost count as her impending death approached.

Images of her last farewell with Maddy flashed through her mind. Megan hadn't hidden her displeasure from her twin upon the announcement she was quitting yet another job and flying to the Virgin Islands for vacation.

Megan had asked her twin, disappointment full in her voice, "What do *you* need a vacation from? Your whole life has been a vacation."

Only looking sad for a moment, Maddy had recovered in a flash with a smile for her twin. "Ah, come on Meg…You're gonna wake up one day, and your life will have passed you completely by. Why don't you take a break from the daily grind and come with me? It'll be like when we were kids…carefree times. We'll laugh, dance, go to the beach. Meet some cute locals. Seriously, Meg, life's unpredictable. We could die in two minutes. Don't you want to do something spontaneous and have some fun before it's all over?"

Megan had taken her sister's hands and kissed her cheek before replying. "I think you're having enough carefree times and fun for the both of us, baby sis."

Maddy had pulled her twin into a hug and laughed as she replied. "Hey, you're only sixty seconds older. And that's still not an excuse for you to act like you're sixty years older. You need to start dating again, Meg. Not all men are lying cheaters like Ben."

As Maddy headed for the office door, Megan had called out to her.

"Wait, Maddy." Her expression turned serious. "Promise me you'll be careful…and check in with me."

Maddy winked and blew a kiss across the room. "I'll even send photos, Meg." With that one last promise she had taken off on another adventure.

Ironic, cruel world it was turning out to be, Megan decided. After all of her efforts to do the right thing and live responsibly, unlike her parents and sister, she was going to die, just like her sister had joked about, without having lived.

A sudden pull at the rear of her head, yanking her from the water, had her snapping out of her deathly euphoria. She vomited this time. Fighting between chokes for bits of air, she wanted to tell her captor to just go ahead and get it over with. Kill her already. What was he waiting for? Yet she couldn't stop choking.

Her captor tugged at her hair. "I have a message from my boss," he said, his accent distinctly European.

"Leave St. Croix, immediately," he stated. This time she recognized that his accent sounded German.

She found her voice, figuring there was nothing to lose even though she was still held tightly in his grip. "Where is my sister?"

There was no response as her head was plunged under. When she resurfaced this time her captor spoke, his voice cold. "Your sister is gone. Leave the island now, or you'll end up the same as her."

She felt his hands picking her up now and was stunned the next moment as something hit her temple. As she fell into the water, she recalled Maddy's last words of wisdom. *We could die in two minutes.*

She wished she could take it all back and tell her sister she'd go with her on vacation. Maybe then, she could have at least had some fun with the closest friend she had ever had before she died. *But it's too late now.* And she slipped away.

14

Gabe got through security at Megan's resort easily and followed the windy path to her bungalow. He had her room number, which narrowed down what might have been a more extensive search, but he would have found her eventually. The resort wasn't exactly at maximum capacity. In fact, it was seemingly vacant, but that would change as high season began in four weeks time.

He saw her rental Ford and parked his car next to it. He climbed the steps to her door, raised his hand to knock, and froze. It was standing open a couple of inches. Irritation flickered through him. How in the world was she supposed to stay safe if she couldn't even close her door?

He decided that was something else he would suggest to the aloof red head as he gripped the handle and knocked loudly on the open door. "Miss MacKenna," he called out.

He waited out of respect for her privacy, though his fingers itched to push the door completely open. "Miss MacKenna, we spoke yesterday. It's Gabe."

When there was still no response, his curiosity outweighed his politeness. He pushed the door ajar and took one step into the room. "Miss MacKenna, it's Gabe Sanchez. We met at Captain Sully's yesterday."

As he spoke he walked into the front hall, taking in the room. It was decorated with Mahogany hand carved furniture, gold lamps and door handles, and the aquamarine painted walls displayed Caribbean landscapes. White ceramic tiles covered the floor, and sheer curtains opened to a patio revealing a view of turquoise waters. Memories of his youth began tugging at his mind, but the nostalgia was interrupted as his next step made a familiar, but out-of-place noise. He looked down, his eyes widening as he noted the puddle of water he'd stepped in. His stomach ached, and frantic thoughts raced through his head as he followed the water towards the bathroom door and pushed it open.

"No," he said in a desperate whisper. Images from ten years ago flooded his brain, and suddenly he was wondering if he should've told Megan the truth about the Torrez family and her sister's involvement with Miguel. He brushed the regret aside and hurried to her.

She was floating in a tub of overflowing water, duck tape wrapped around her head, covering her eyes. Her ankles were crossed and tied, and her arms were bound behind her. Blood ran down her temple, staining the tub and the knee-length sundress she wore a light, murky brown. Her mouth was slightly open, the water threatening to cover her lips as she sagged dangerously close to the rising water.

"Don't be dead," he ordered, turning the faucet off and grabbing the unmoving figure from the water. He carried her from the bathroom, placing her on the king size bed.

"Megan, wake up." He went to work and pulled the tape off of her head as quickly as possible. He turned her on her side, hitting her back and sighing as her breathing deepened. He unwrapped her wrists and thanked God when he felt a strong pulse.

He tore the bindings from her ankles next, then propped her up against the pillows. He patted her face lightly, hoping to awaken her from wherever she had gone.

"Come on, Megan." His eyes focused on the head injury now even as he spoke. If she had a concussion, she'd need to go to the hospital. He hurried to the bathroom, grabbed a washcloth and doused it with clean water, and raced to the bed. He wiped the blood at her temple, and sighed with relief as he studied the cut and knew it wouldn't need stitches. It did, however, look like a knot had formed at her hairline, and was already quite red and swollen.

"Megan, wake up," his voice was more desperate than ever. He knew if he called for an ambulance, he'd have to flee in a hurry or become a suspect in whatever had happened to her. The police could jump to the wrong conclusion and might even try to link him to the missing sister, seeing as how they didn't even have a suspect or a starting point in the case. And now that Megan had been attacked, his gut told him whatever had happened to Madeline had to be linked to Torrez. And if Gabe were to be questioned by the police, someone in Torrez's operation would likely hear of it, and that wouldn't help his own investigation at all. Headquarters needed him to remain under the radar.

Gabe dabbed up the blood around her cheek and pressed his other hand lightly to the other side of her face. "Megan, *come on.*"

Her eyelashes fluttered, a moan started in her throat. As she began to cough lightly, Gabe pulled away, surveying her cautiously. Her eyes squinted and then widened in disbelief as she woke up fully.

"You?" she cried, her expression fearful. "Get away from me."

"And here I thought I was going to be thanked for being a hero," he muttered, relief filling him. "Welcome back, Miss MacKenna."

15

Anxiety shot through Megan as she tried to think straight over the hammer of her heart. The scruffy cook, Gabe, who she had been struggling to keep off of her mind, had attacked her? She never would've suspected him, but she couldn't explain why he was standing in her room. She glanced longingly at the hotel phone and wondered if she could get to it before he stopped her. She willed her aching limbs to life and lunged for the phone on the bedside table. Her fingers grabbed the cord, but he got to the phone first.

"Why didn't you just finish the job in the bathroom?"

His expression changed from annoyance to concern. His grip remained tight on the phone as he hovered beside her. "Megan, I don't know what happened here, and from your current condition it looks like you barely survived the attack, but you've got to believe me. It wasn't me."

"Then, what are you doing in my room?" Her grip around the phone cord remained firm, as though holding onto it she still had a lifeline. She searched the room for her purse, knowing it contained her cell phone, but unsure of what had happened to it after she'd been attacked. Maybe it had fallen outside of the room.

"I wanted to help you look for your sister. I knew you wouldn't call me, so I decided to volunteer my services in person."

He continued to explain before she could vocalize her doubt. "Look, you seemed really shaken up at Captain Sully's. Then, I saw the flyers on my shift today. You must have come back to leave them when I wasn't working. The flyers had the hotel front desk number listed as a contact, plus your cell number."

"But the hotel front desk would not give my room number out. They assured me of that." Her hands tugged at the cord, but he wouldn't release the phone.

"I don't know who you're going to call right now, but I can promise you this…If you are calling the police to report me as your attacker, they are going to throw me in jail and not investigate the matter further. They might even make me a suspect for your missing sister's case."

"Well, maybe that's what I want them to do," she moaned, as she released the phone cord and lifted the cloth to her aching temple.

She watched as he set the phone down and took a step back, placing some distance between them. He held up his hands. "Megan. I'm here to help you. I was just trying to be nice. And like I said, you were definitely upset the other morning, and I just couldn't stop thinking about it. I figured I'd offer to help. But if you don't want my help, I'll go."

"You still haven't explained how you got through security or found my room," she accused.

"Well, I told the security guard, who really wasn't even paying attention, by the way, that I was going to the restaurant to eat dinner. Then, after driving around the property for a few minutes, I spotted your rental car. I recognized it, of course, from when you were at Captain Sully's. I decided to try the bungalows closest to your car, but then I saw the door partially open, and curiosity led me here. I was going to explain to you the dangers of leaving your door open when I realized you were already in trouble. The water pouring out all over the floor led me to the bathroom where you were about to go under the running water and drown. Now, aren't you glad I got here when I did?"

"Is it supposed to comfort me how easily you got past security and tracked me down?" she asked condescendingly.

He tossed his hands up. "The guard didn't seem overly concerned with securing the place."

Megan couldn't argue that point. "But why would you want to help me find my sister? You don't even know me." Her mind raced on. Were men so desperate for dates around the island they'd track a woman down to her hotel room? Could he sincerely be interested in helping her find Maddy? Or did he secretly know Maddy?

"You're right. I don't know you…"

"Just tell me if you met my sister. Don't lie to me. Do you know what happened to her?"

"No. I never met her."

Her cheeks flushed. She wondered what he was keeping from her. "Then why would you come here to help me?"

"Isn't that what you're asking people to do? To help you? Is it so hard to believe that I want to help, *just to help*?"

Megan took a deep breath. He had no idea how hard it was for her to trust people. But he had a point. She'd all but told people her room number with all of the flyers she'd passed around. Maddy's words came back to her now. *All men aren't lying cheaters like Ben.* Maybe he was telling her the truth. Good Samaritans still existed. Maybe. Still, the fact of the matter was, Gabe wasn't the man who had attacked her. She'd woken up too terrified to think clearly.

"I know it wasn't you," she said after a moment. "I couldn't see him since he blindfolded me, but there's no mistaking his voice and accent."

"How so?"

"It was distinctly different than yours. I think it was German."

"German?"

"Yeah. I'm pretty sure. I mean I took Spanish in high school, but I'm sure it was a German-sounding accent," Megan said tightly, resituating the cloth on her temple.

She observed him as he seemed to drift. One hand reached across his abdomen, a finger rubbing lightly across the fabric of his shirt. As his finger lingered over his ribcage, she wondered what on earth he was thinking about now. She still wasn't sure what his intentions were. She'd met a lot of people over the course of her career. She felt like she could read people, and as much as the rational part of her mind told her someone who wasn't in law enforcement wouldn't be much assistance to her in her current situation, she really didn't perceive him as a threat. But there was something off about him. Something didn't add up.

Or maybe he'd been straightforward with her about everything, and she was simply irritated at herself for letting him interfere with her train of thoughts more often than she'd have admitted to anyone over the past couple of days. She had tried not to notice his strong arms and legs, his callused hands and athletic build at Captain Sully's, but seeing him now, standing in her room, she was struggling not to think about him in that way. He'd cleaned up a little. His blue cotton t-shirt was stain-free and the khaki shorts only had a few ragged edges. His black hair was pulled in a short ponytail like the last time she had seen him, and he still hadn't shaved the beard. But even so, he really was very handsome.

She squeezed her eyes shut at the thought. The hit from the German man had definitely done more damage than she'd realized. Otherwise, she never would've let her mind wonder on so long about his appearance. The man needed to shave, cut his hair, and buy a decent pair of shorts. Without holes or torn edges. She opened her eyes, to find him watching her. She hoped her cheeks weren't bright red, and forced herself to sound calm. "So you just want to help me," she said cautiously.

He shrugged. "Call me crazy. I had a feeling you could use some help."

Megan pondered that last bit, but decided that even if he were holding something back, he had saved her. She would thank him and send him on his way.

"Well, I wouldn't normally thank a strange man for coming to my hotel room, but," her sentence trailed off as the memory of the water suffocating her returned. Her bottom lip began to quiver.

Gabe's voice was tense, yet soft, when he spoke. "Do you want to tell me what happened? I mean, if it's not too hard?"

She figured the smart thing to do was ask him to leave and then call the police. She'd leave out the part about him finding her. She felt certain he was not her attacker. But it wouldn't hurt to tell him what happened. "I was almost to my room when a hand clamped over my mouth, and it happened so fast. I was blindfolded and tied up. He must have been waiting in front of one of the other rooms because I didn't see him."

She tilted her head in confusion. "I don't remember unlocking my room. I think he had already opened it. But how?"

"Maybe he used your key. It was fast, like you said, right?"

She nodded. "Yeah, but there was already water in the tub when he forced my head under. Right when he pulled me inside, he started drowning me." Her eyes widened with fear. "Do you think someone at the hotel helped him break into my room?"

"There's no telling. The important thing is that we get your head looked at and get you safely to the airport."

"You expect me to leave?"

"Well, I was going to offer to help you find your sister. But after coming here and finding you like that…You said it yourself, Megan. He tried to drown you. You're not safe here."

16

"But I need to tell the police what happened. This proves something happened to Maddy."

"Megan, I'm not trying to discourage you, and you should tell the police everything, but why don't you phone them from the airport? They can make a detailed report over the phone I'm sure. They can come investigate the hotel room after you're gone if they want. Your safety is more important."

"If you're worried about being one of their suspects, don't. I'll wait until you're gone, and then I'll call them. I won't tell them you found me. I'll tell them I woke up on my own. And they'll trust me when they see me like this." She gestured towards her blood-stained dress and wet hair. "They'll start taking me seriously. They'll really start looking for Maddy," she said optimistically.

Gabe sighed. "Megan. Even if they believe you, which sure, they will, how has your experience been with the local police so far? Do you think they'll just dive into your case and solve it?"

"I admit they haven't been very helpful, but that will change. With this new evidence, they'll do their job," she replied smugly.

"Yes. But will they be able to keep you safe? What if they can't determine how this guy broke in? Where can you stay on the island that you'll really be safe? And you're right. After what happened to you, I think it's safe to assume it is linked to your sister. Why else would they hurt you? Did he say anything to you? Can you remember?"

"Oh, I remember, alright. He held me under water over and over... Every time he pulled me up, I started choking and trying to breathe and then he'd push me under again. I tried to talk to him, but he'd only push me back under. I swallowed so much water. I couldn't breathe," she paused.

Gabe noted her eyes filling with tears. His instincts urged him to comfort her somehow. To sit down beside her, like he would any other victim he'd speak to, but after two steps he made himself stop. He didn't want to alarm her any further. And since she had no clue he was DEA, she'd make the assumption he was trying to hit on her. And even though he didn't want it to be true, he had to admit there was an attraction there. A blind man would've been attracted to the woman, even with her frigid exterior.

She cleared her throat before continuing. "After awhile I threw up. I guess I blacked out for a minute. I remember thinking about my last conversation with my sister."

Her shoulders slumped, and Gabe imagined they must have argued. But he didn't push her. He waited patiently. "I was sure he planned to kill me. Eventually, he spoke. He said he had a message. He told me if I didn't leave St. Croix immediately, I'd end up the same as my sister."

Gabe's heart rate picked up. It sounded like a professional. Without a doubt, the sort that the Torrez family would work with. Not only did he need to get Megan off of St. Croix; he needed her to go to the airport immediately. Maybe Torrez placed a tail on her. Someone could be watching from outside of her hotel room. And if she didn't heed their advice, he knew they'd kill her. The fact that they'd given her a warning surprised him, and it made him uneasy. They might be waiting outside the door for all he knew.

Gabe wasn't sure how to get through to her, but he had to try. He sat down on the edge of the bed, a few feet away from her. He glanced over to see tears streaming down her face. "And then he hit me, and I passed out," she stuttered the last bit and suddenly she was sobbing. He'd been waiting on her to breakdown. He was surprised she'd kept it together as long as she had.

He hopped to his feet and went to the bathroom to retrieve a box of tissue. As he handed it to her, he took the bloodstained cloth, and surveyed her wound. It looked better already, though still very swollen. As she let the tears pour out, he caved and sat down right beside her. When she didn't protest, he gently patted her back, hoping to calm her down. The sooner he could get her to the airport, the better. After a few minutes, she dabbed at her puffy eyes and nose, and she seemed to relax.

Gabe pulled his hand away from her and placed his palms together in front of him. He tilted his head towards her. "I'm sorry about what happened to you. I'm sorry about your sister, too. But let me drive you to the airport. We can stop at the hospital first to make sure you don't have a concussion. We can even go by the police station if you'd like. I'll just wait outside while you file the report. And then I'll drive you to the airport. I know you don't know me, but I'll feel a lot better when you're on a plane, heading to the States. I'll stay with you until you are safely onboard and on your way. I won't let anyone come near you. Promise."

Megan raised a brow at him, as if sizing him up.

He smirked. "What? You don't think I can protect you? I stay in shape. I'm kind of strong…for a breakfast cook." He lifted his arm and flexed his triceps, obviously trying to make her smile, but as she studied his very sculpted arms, an uncomfortable look returned to her face. Gabe cringed. He shouldn't have pointed out his strength. She'd be thinking of how he was obviously capable of hurting her, even though she said she knew he hadn't been the man to attack her. He attempted to reassure her. "It wasn't me. I didn't hurt you."

Her eyes met his. "Yeah, I know."

He couldn't read her now. Her stare was blank. Her eyes still seemed upset, but she didn't seem to perceive him as the threat. He coughed and got to his feet. "So, can I help you pack? Or do you want me to wait outside your door? I promise I'll get you safely to the airport and onto a plane unharmed," he concluded, his head shaking decisively.

She straightened her shoulders, looking away from him when she replied. "I'm not going home yet, Mr. Sanchez. This proves that someone knows about Maddy and that something bad happened to her. She didn't just start island hopping like the police think. And I'm going to tell them that."

"Okay, so tell them, and then leave," Gabe urged. "He said you'd end up like your sister. Megan, I'm not trying to scare you, but that doesn't sound good. Just tell the police everything and then leave the island. They found you once. They could find you again."

She ignored him and went on. "He never said that she was dead. He said I could end up like her, but he never said that she is dead," hostility crept back into her tone and expression as she stared at him now, daring him to refute her.

"But," he began.

"I *know* she isn't dead. You wouldn't understand. But we're twins, and we sense each other. We're connected. We've always been, no matter the distance between us. I'd feel it if Maddy were dead. And she's alive. I'm certain."

Gabe exhaled slowly. "First of all, it's not Mr. Sanchez…just Gabe."

"Thanks Gabe. I mean it. Thank you for coming here and finding me." She stood up, squaring her shoulders as she faced him. "But I think I can get to the hospital and to the police station alright if you want to go now," her tone defiant.

"You're not thinking clearly," he shot back.

"Maybe not."

"Maybe? Someone tortured you to scare the hell out of you so you will leave, he easily could have killed you, and you think you should stay? Even if your sister is alive, can't you see that whoever has her isn't playing around? These people aren't afraid to kill to protect their secrets. You have to leave. It's not safe here."

"What do you know about these people? And how do you know it isn't the one man alone who did something to Maddy? What do you know?" she accused.

Gabe gulped. That had been close. His expression softened as he stepped closer to her. "Nothing. But you hear about crimes around the island sometimes. And when I found you like I did, it scared the hell out of me…" He wasn't lying about that part either, which didn't sit quite right with him. Since when did he have a weakness for damsels in distress? He'd been avoiding relationships and women like Megan, who deserved more than he could offer, for years. The truth was his work and his determination to bring Torrez down always came first. But if he didn't know any better, he'd think he was already forming some sort of attachment to her. Maybe he'd been stuck on an island for too long.

Megan tilted her head up, haughtiness in her stance. "Thank you for your *concern*, for me Mr. Sanchez," she said dryly.

Gabe's fingers balled into a fist. The woman was something else. She assumed he was only helping her because she was beautiful. If only he could tell her the truth about the Torrez family without blowing his cover. Her looks had nothing to do with his interest in keeping her alive. "I admit. You're beautiful. And if circumstances were different I would probably not be encouraging you to go home, but you need to get on the next plane out of here. He could find you again. He warned you to leave the island. He got into your hotel room."

She pursed her lips together. "That's a valid point. I need to switch hotels after I go to the police."

Gabe groaned, tossing his hands up. "What will it take for you to leave? Do you think the man who tried to drown you was joking? That was just the messenger, like you said," he blurted with an exasperated breath.

She narrowed her eyes at him. "I told you. I am not leaving. Period."

Gabe shook his head. "What do you think will happen the next time they find you?" he asked quietly.

Megan reached for the pendant chain, rubbing it lightly as she gazed towards the window. "Our parents died when we were young. Our grandma isn't in the best of health. Maddy is all I've got left. I can't leave." She hesitated, a myriad of expressions crossing her face. "I can't believe I'm about to ask this. But if you're finished trying to convince me to leave, I could use your help."

His brow lifted, but he didn't say a word.

She raised her chin, her tone casual. "Do you know of any hotels I could stay at that wouldn't be the most obvious place for someone searching for me to look?"

Gabe folded his arms across his chest. "You mean, you're willing to accept the help of a guy like me?" He'd seen the way she'd been assessing him, from his old ripped t-shirt to his beard, from the moment she'd laid eyes on him. She had to be desperate if she was willing to ask him for help. Of course, having one of Torrez's hit men send her a message had to have terrified her more than she would admit. And even if she wouldn't say it in so many words, she knew she needed help. And Gabe was the only one willing to help her.

She visibly tensed, but stood her ground. "This simply means, Mr. Sanchez, that I'm accepting your original offer to help me find my sister. If you could just point me in the right direction for a different hotel, I'd appreciate it. I mean, if the offer to help me still stands," she said coolly.

"And if it doesn't?"

Her gaze sought his, but she quickly concealed her panic, appearing confident. "Then I guess that's your cue to leave."

"Well, Megan…," he began, "I guess you could thank my mother, God rest her soul, for raising me to have a good sense of right and wrong. I'll try to find another hotel for you, one where no one would think to look. But I have one simple request."

"Which would be?"

"Stop calling me Mr. Sanchez. It's Gabe or Gabriel."

She let out the breath she'd been holding and shook her head curtly. "Okay, Gabe."

His mind began racing over all of the things Smith was going to say to him if he found out about any of this. He'd just gotten himself in too deep. And there was no turning back.

17

Miguel slammed the shot glass onto the bar top, ignoring the curious looks from a couple a few stools away. They may have come to the waterfront bar to enjoy tropical drinks as the sun set over the ocean, but they could move to a table if he was ruining their ambiance. This was his bar. Or his father's at least.

Georgie appeared in front of him within seconds. "Would you like another round, boss?" asked the twenty-four-year-old bartender. His nose and cheeks were bright red, sunburned from another day at the beach, no doubt. The young transplants from the mainland arrived in droves just before high season began, hoping to land the ideal jobs to maintain their habits in paradise. Between bartending, surfing, drinking, and entertaining tourists, it was a perpetual spring break for guys like Georgie. He'd landed his job at Miguel's dockside bar in Christiansted two years ago, and unlike many of his peers, he'd remained on island year round ever since, unwilling to risk losing his job to another transplant, even during the off season. Working in the heart of town on the waterfront meant year-round business and good tips for a bartender like Georgie.

"Another Cuervo shot and a frozen Pain Killer while you're at it."

Georgie grinned, his pearly white teeth shining brilliantly against his cherry-red, sunburn. "So, it's been one of *those* days, boss. Don't worry, I'll fix you my special Pain Killer, and you'll forget about your troubles in a flash." His blonde ponytail whipped his cheek as he turned around.

Miguel didn't reply. He knew no matter how much alcohol he poured into his system, he wouldn't be forgetting his troubles any time soon.

He could not stop thinking about Madeline. Losing her had been the most difficult thing he had experienced in a long time. He couldn't sleep. He felt angry and depressed. The alcohol and pills weren't soothing his pain either. When Raul had reported that he had seen Madeline alive, Miguel's heart had nearly stopped beating. The surge of hope he had automatically felt was quickly replaced by devastation and anger. Of course, she wasn't alive. She had been gone for over a week now, and she would be gone, forever.

"Here you go, sir. Kiss your worries goodbye," said Georgie, placing the drink before him along with the Tequila shot.

Miguel nodded at Georgie and took a big drink of the Pain Killer, waving the bartender away with his hand. He wasn't in the mood for company. He wanted to drown in his sorrows alone. He was remembering Madeline.

She hadn't been like any of the other women he'd dated before. She was carefree, adventurous, and easygoing yet excited about life. She was gorgeous, and best of all, she had trusted him. People weren't known for trusting him. Not even his own father did. And Madeline had been the first woman, with the exception of his mother, who had ever trusted him.

Sure, he hadn't exactly told her the truth about what he did for a living, but he figured she would have warmed up to it eventually. But he hadn't had the chance to tell her. When she had reacted the way she had to his discussion with Benny, a dealer who had stolen from the Torrez family, his father's henchmen, Trevor and Dalbert, had done what they get paid to do. Protect the family interest. It all had happened so fast.

Miguel had thought for sure they would have brought Madeline back so he could talk to her and give her a chance to remain quiet, but to his surprise they had returned empty handed. Trevor had immediately launched into a story about how he'd phoned Victor, who had ordered him to take care of Madeline immediately. Being the thorough and loyal thugs that they were, they had obeyed Miguel's father and killed her without so much as giving Miguel the chance to say goodbye.

Miguel downed the shot now, welcoming the warmth it released through his system and the accompanying buzz. He took a pill out of his pocket and swallowed it down. He needed all of the help he could to try to forget the pain, even for just a little while. But his mind returned to the day in the woods. He hadn't even gone back to look at Madeline's body. He had wanted to remember her the way she had looked alive.

Miguel could hardly look at Dalbert and Trevor, his so-called "assistants", after they had killed Madeline. They wouldn't have cared even if they had noticed the grief in his eyes. Everyone knew they were paid by Miguel's father to keep a close watch on him and report his every move to the real boss. His father wanted him to help run the family business, yet he couldn't trust him to do it without Dalbert and Trevor. Yes, as long as his father was breathing, Miguel would be supervised by the duo of grim reapers.

His father's cruel hand had raised him and though he'd grown numb to most of the atrocities his father had committed, and had even taken his share of lives for his father, he couldn't understand how his father could so easily murder women. But Miguel had seen firsthand how his father operated. He saw no distinction between gender when it came to dealing out death, and he treated each kill in a strictly business-like manner. Miguel knew his father would kill him if he ever crossed him. Being his son would do nothing to protect him. That's why he'd been able to kill Madeline so easily. He knew Miguel would never question his authority or decisions. If only he could stand up to the man. But what did it matter now? Madeline was dead.

As he wiped a lone tear away, he thought of his cold, uncaring father. The man had taken everyone he had ever loved away from him. He finished the cocktail and stood up from the bar stool, swaying slightly. Maybe it was time to visit the old man. He found Dalbert's number on his cell phone and pressed send.

"Yeah boss?" answered Dalbert, automatically.

"I need you and Trevor to keep an eye on things for a few days. I'm taking a little trip."

18

As the boat slowed, the roar of the engine diminished and abruptly cut off. Waves tossed the vessel up and down, and Madeline prayed the body not far from her would stay where it was and not roll onto her. Her mouth was as dry as the desert, and her limbs throbbed from being bound in an awkward position. She told herself to think positive, but as more time passed it became increasingly difficult. They hadn't offered her food or water, or even checked on her at all. Her sundress was soaked through with sweat, and her legs were sticky from when she'd seen the body earlier and lost control of her bladder.

Footsteps pounded on the deck above, sending echoes into the cabin. She eyed the stairwell, leading up top, noting the spike in her pulse. She hadn't met her captors yet, or even seen them, but she assumed they would be Dalbert and Trevor. She hadn't feared them before the woods that day. Sure, she had never really liked Trevor, but she hadn't been afraid of him. But everything was different now.

As two sets of feet descended the three-foot stairwell, the hair on her neck stood up. Chills covered her body.

Maybe Miguel had ordered them to kill her out in the middle of the ocean.

As they came into view, she lowered her eyes, dropping her chin to her chest, hoping the men hadn't noticed how her blindfold had moved up to her forehead. She had never seen them before, which made her even more terrified. If it had been Dalbert or Trevor, she could've at least tried to bargain with them to let her go. A wave of nausea rolled over her, and she squeezed her eyes shut, praying they wouldn't kill her.

She braced herself, preparing for them to grab her, but though they'd begun talking a mile a minute in Spanish, it must not have concerned her. No one touched her. As the conversation she couldn't understand even one word of went on, she decided to risk sneaking a peek.

Barely opening her eyes, she noted the two men and the gun one of them had tucked into the back of his jeans. They were hovering over the body a few feet from her on the floor, struggling to lift it up.

The dead body, she thought with a shudder. It was a smell, along with that of the fish, which would stay with her forever. She didn't know much about bodies, but she knew from the odor this man had been dead at least a couple of days.

As one of the men tightened his grip on the body and began to turn, facing her direction, she shut her eyes. She held her breath, hoping they would leave her alone. As they continued speaking, seemingly oblivious to her, her thoughts drifted to the cliff.

How long had it been since she fell? Where were they taking her? Why had they stuffed her in a fishing boat with the man Miguel had killed? After seeing his face initially, she'd searched her memories of the day in the woods, and now she was sure it was the same man Miguel had been hitting.

She stole a glance again, shivers running down her arms as they heaved his body up to the deck. Miguel, the charming, handsome man she had been dating for three weeks, had murdered someone. Someone who had begged for his life. *No one betrays me*, Miguel had said. How could she have spent three weeks with a murderer and not picked up on any bad vibes?

But she had felt like something was off. She'd suspected all along that Trevor wasn't a good person. And when she'd asked Miguel if Trevor and Dalbert were his bodyguards, she'd known better than to accept his story about how they were his assistants. They were his assistant hit men it turned out. Maddy groaned as she went over the facts. That day in the car, she'd been thinking about Miguel's strange behavior. She'd felt a gut instinct that something wasn't right, and instead of waiting in the car until Miguel returned so she could break up with him on their date, she'd trekked into the woods after him.

She wished she could tell Meg how sorry she was. If she'd taken her twin's advice, she never would've gotten herself into this mess. Meg always said she was too trusting of people, and it turned out she was right.

And now she was tied up in the bottom of a fishing boat waiting to be the next dead body.

She wondered if Meg was looking for her or if she just assumed she had started partying again. Maddy wouldn't blame her twin for thinking the worst. She was probably too busy with work to really care about Maddy not checking in. Unless it had been more than a week.

Maddy honestly had no idea how much time had passed. Had she been unconscious for days? From the constant hunger pains in her stomach, she knew it had been awhile since she fell from the cliff. And if a week or more had gone by, Meg would have to be worried. The boat rocked as another wave hit, and Maddy's hopes diminished. She was in the middle of the ocean it seemed. Even if Meg was looking for her, how would she ever find her?

A loud splash jolted Madeline out of her dreary thoughts. The sound brought an image to her mind, and she screamed into the cloth gagging her mouth.

As she imagined the man's body sinking into the ocean depths, her heart sank with it. Tears she didn't know she had left, ran from her eyes. No one was going to find her. She'd be fish food. Like the pour soul they'd just thrown overboard.

19

"Listen, Megan, if I were you, I'd check out of the hotel and drive straight to the airport. That way, you'll at least be seen doing what the man who threatened you told you to do."

"Seen? You think he's watching me?" Megan's voice strained as she placed her toiletries bag into the open suitcase on the bed.

Gabe gave her a skeptical look from where he was perched by the sliding glass patio door. She made a mental note to work on sounding brave if she was going to keep up this charade. Sure, she'd told Gabe she was fine and that she was not leaving the island, and yes, she knew she had to stay and find Maddy. She wouldn't give up. But still...A strange man had almost killed her, and as much as it made her angry and even more determined to find Maddy, it also left her petrified. And she didn't want Gabe to know how scared she really was. All she needed him to do was find her a different hotel. She didn't even want the police to know where she was staying. Revealing her current location had nearly gotten her killed, and she wouldn't make that mistake again. But Gabe could find her a place where no one would think to look for her, at least at first. Then he could go back to his life, and she'd pray the police could help her find Maddy. Especially, since she had proof Maddy was in danger now.

He stepped away from the window and tilted his head, contemplating. "He told you to leave. He might be watching to make sure you do."

"If he's watching me, he'll see you, too, when you leave. What if he goes after you?" She blurted.

One side of his mouth curved up. "Don't worry about me. I mean, I'm touched. But I'll be fine."

Megan's cheeks heated, and she turned her back to him, picking up a stack of freshly folded blouses she'd taken off hangers. She pressed them into the suitcase. "I'm not worried about you," she said flatly.

She heard a small chuckle, but continued to ignore him. The truth was, she wasn't really worried about him. She was worried about herself and the decisions she was making. First, she'd decided to stay, in spite of a warning from the man who'd nearly drowned her, then, she'd opted to delay her police report so that Gabe wouldn't be questioned, and finally, she'd asked Gabe, a regular guy, a breakfast cook, to help her get safely to a new hotel room. Asking him to find the nearest beach bar or restaurant would have been one thing. But asking him, a guy she knew nothing about, to assist her was another.

It was more than that though. By asking him to help her and not just relying on the police, she was trusting Gabe. She could hardly believe it herself, but she had the strangest feeling she really could trust him. And even more than that, she felt safer having him there while she packed. Even if he wouldn't know what to do if the man came back.

She placed a pair of capris in her suitcase and inwardly sighed. Regardless of how much safer she felt having him around as she went through her post near-death experience and a rollercoaster of emotions, she knew she needed to get to the police and get rid of Gabe Sanchez as soon as possible.

Ever since she'd met him at Captain Sully's he'd been distracting her too much. Of course, by showing up to help her, he'd probably saved her from drowning. And again, in the back of her mind, she wondered if he had told her the truth. Had he really shown up to offer her help? Out of the kindness of his heart? She stole a glance at him, and quickly turned away. She wasn't sure what to think about him. For now, concentrating on Maddy was more important.

Her plan was to go to the police after she checked out and tell them everything. Except the part about Gabe saving her. She'd changed her clothes and was only going to carry the murky, bloodstained dress to show them. She would ask the resort to leave the room alone for another day at least so the police could investigate the room if they wanted to. Gabe thought she should drive to the airport first in case anyone was watching, but Megan wasn't sure how much that would help. Going straight to the police seemed logical enough.

"Are you almost ready?" he asked, interrupting her thoughts. "We should agree about a couple of things before we walk out that door."

She spun around to see he'd wandered to the front door again and was glimpsing out of the eyehole. When he turned around, she saw the anxiousness in his face. "What do we need to agree about?"

"The plan. I think you should check out of the hotel and drive to the airport first."

"But—"

"No buts. That's the safest part of the plan. Unless you'll change your mind and get on the next plane off the island." He finished with a frown, giving Megan a disapproving look.

She felt her irritation return. He had no idea what it was like to be in her shoes. Maddy needed her to keep looking for her. She couldn't get on a plane and leave. "How do you know what's best? Did they give you this sort of training at Captain Sully's?"

"I haven't always worked in a grease pit," he replied, defensively.

Megan wondered where he had worked previously, or what his history was in general, and was about to ask when she thought of Maddy. Here she was arguing with the one person who was willing to help her a little, and Maddy was in the hands of people who could be hurting her...Like the man who'd attacked Megan. *Please be alive, Maddy.*

She took a step towards Gabe. "I'm sorry I said that."

"It's fine. You have a lot you're dealing with."

"I appreciate your help, Gabe. I just want to find Maddy. Tell me what the best plan is." She sat down on the end of the bed next to her suitcase, folding her hands together.

"I'm taking you to the airport and putting you on the next flight home."

"No. I told you I'm staying," she said firmly.

He sighed now, and gestured to her suitcase. "Everything packed?"

She nodded, and watched as he zipped it closed. Once he set the suitcase on its end, his eyes met hers. "First, you check out by yourself. I'll be in my car, keeping a safe distance. I'll make sure no one is following you. Tell the front desk you're headed to the airport to leave and that the police might look at the room after you're gone. Tell them to call your cell phone if any information about your sister comes up."

"Okay, that's fine, then what?"

"Then you drive to the airport."

"In case someone is following me?"

"Yes."

"Where will you be?" Megan wished her voice didn't sound so concerned.

"After you leave the hotel property, pull over and let me pass you once I catch up with you. I'll lead the way to the airport."

"And what then? We just drive to the airport and wait a minute so it looks like I'm leaving? Then drive to the police?"

"No, once we get to the airport, I want you to turn your rental car in and walk to the terminal for departures."

"I feel like you're not listening to me," she said sarcastically.

"Don't worry. I know you aren't leaving St. Croix yet. But it has to look like it in case anyone checks. If you turn your car in and they follow up, they'll assume you must have left."

"So what then? Get a new rental car from a different agency?"

"No. I'll pick you up near the baggage claim. I'll take you to a medical clinic to get your head looked at, and then to the police. I'll wait nearby while you talk to the police. Then, when you're ready, I'll get you to a hotel where no one would think to look for you. Hopefully, anyone serious about finding you will think you're gone after you go to the airport. It'll probably be a couple of days before they figure it out. As long as you lie low and try to blend in a little. You have a hat by the way?" he asked, looking over her hair.

"Yes, I have a hat. And your plan sounds fine, but where is the hotel?"

"There's one right by my place. Oh, and I wouldn't tell the police where you are going to stay. I hear things sometimes, and some say that criminals on island have eyes and ears everywhere...even in law enforcement."

"Comforting. But considering how easily that man found me, I agree. I won't tell anyone where I go next. So it's near your place?"

"Yeah, and it's not nice...not like this hotel, but no one would suspect that you would go there next."

"Oh great, it probably has those centipedes I heard about."

Gabe shrugged. "Well, it may have a few, but it's not the bugs you need to worry about now. It's the people who want you dead."

Megan swallowed a lump in her throat, and picked up her purse. "Perfect," she mumbled.

"Oh, and you'll need cash for the hotel I'm taking you to. You don't want to leave a credit card trail if you can avoid it."

She nodded, feeling the anxiety return as they headed towards the door. "I've got cash on me." She paused in the entrance. "But how am I going to get around? I'll need another car..."

Gabe picked up the suitcase, and winked at Megan. "Meet your new chauffeur, Miss MacKenna. If you want to get another rental car in a day or two, I'll take you to a different place to rent one."

"Assuming I'm still alive in two days?" she asked with a smirk.

Gabe smiled, but it didn't reach his eyes. "I know I can't convince you to leave, but Megan...please stick to the plan."

A few minutes later, she glanced in her rearview mirror as she headed towards the hotel's main entrance to check out. As much as it comforted her that Gabe was willing to help her get safely to the police and to another hotel, and then help her get around for a couple of days until she could rent a new vehicle, something tugged at her mind.

He seemed quite comfortable with planning her best exit strategy. Was he really just a regular guy, helping her because it was the right thing? Maybe he hadn't been interested in her at all, like she had initially suspected. Maybe he was keeping something from her.

As she pulled into a parking space, her frenzied thoughts overflowed. "I don't know if I should trust him." She squeezed her eyes shut and sent up a desperate prayer. *Please help me find my sister.*

20

"What were you thinking?" Smith all but growled into the phone. "And what about hotel security cams? Even if you wore a hat and sunglasses, the police will be looking for you if they review the footage. You should've stayed away."

Gabe understood his partner's hostility, but he hadn't had a choice but to tell him. He needed Smith to do some digging into the guy with the German accent. "I spotted the cameras when I walked her to her car. This guy, whoever he is, is professional. He took them out. Besides, I'm only helping her find another hotel. She refuses to leave. You should've seen how I found her. If I don't at least point her in the right direction, she'll be dead before sunrise."

"But you tried to warn her. It's not on you if she gets killed now. Don't let one woman's reckless decision drag you into a mess you don't need."

"Did you hear me? They will kill her."

"Why did you go to her hotel in the first place?"

"I wanted to try to convince her she should leave it to the police and head home."

"Uh-huh. Maybe you've been on that rock too long, man. You sure you don't have a thing for this chick? This isn't like you to deviate from your plan."

"I'm not deviating from the plan. And no, I don't have a thing for her. I just don't want to see another person get killed by the Torrez family. And I'm sure they're behind this. So, technically, that makes Megan part of my business now. You'll need to tell the boss."

"How do you know it's related?"

"This is right up their alley. A girl goes missing, probably because she saw something they didn't want her to, her sister shows up and starts asking questions, and then they send a professional to scare her."

"Don't you think, if it was one of the Torrez guys, he would have killed her?"

Gabe sighed as he spotted Megan's rental car following him around another bend in the road. "That part is off, you're right. But maybe he didn't want to draw too much attention to himself. If he'd murdered her straight away without giving her a chance to run, he'd risk the police launching a full on investigation. Two missing sisters? After all of the attention Megan has stirred up with the flyers?"

"And you're certain it's connected?"

"The man who attacked her told her to leave or end up like her sister. Maybe Maddy saw Miguel or his father do something. Whatever happened, you can bet they got rid of her. I wish I could get Megan to understand that, but I can't really tell her anything that would convince her without revealing my identity."

"All of this is risky, man. Have you thought about what I said before? You could come clean with her, and bring her into the assignment somehow. You know, like we talked about."

Gabe thought about how the DEA might place a wire on Megan and ask her to approach Miguel and his father. "I don't know about that yet. Let's see what we can find out about this guy with the accent first. I'll track him down, and see where it leads. I want to keep Megan out of this as long as possible."

"You really think you can hide her for long? I've seen the photos. That red hair, those looks…Are you sure your sympathy level for this girl isn't related to some sort of island fever? When's the last time you even had a conversation with a good-looking woman?"

"Look, you know how personal this case is to me. I've spent twenty years waiting for the opportunity to bring this guy down. You and I have spent the better half of a decade following a trail of bodies, all dead for one reason or another because of the Torrez Empire. I'm not going to screw it up over a pretty girl."

"So you admit, there's an attraction?"

Gabe heard the humor in his partner's voice and shook his head. "Can you look into Austrian or German men traveling to the island and those nearby recently? Or see if any pop up on any of the agency radars? Maybe there are some living here or on nearby islands that have a record."

"Contact me again in twenty-four hours. I'll see what I can find."

"Thanks."

"We haven't discovered any Germans on Torrez's team so far. Maybe he's a new guy?"

"Could be."

"Just remember what you've accomplished so far. You've laid the groundwork for months now. And you were even starting to gain the trust of that guy Raul. He could be your way into the family circle."

"Maybe. But he's low on the totem pole. Hasn't been in their circle of trust himself for too long. Listen, I know things have gotten more complicated, but it goes with the territory."

"Complicated? Yeah, that's one way to put it."

"It's fine."

"She stands out. How you plan to keep her hidden? How long are you gonna help her?"

"I don't know. One day at a time for now. But I've got a few ideas."

"Just remember, if anyone sees you helping the sister, you'll have a price on that pretty head of yours."

"Aw, I didn't know you were sweet on me honey."

"Screw you."

"Seriously, how long have we been partners?"

"Long enough to know that even though you really are a big pain in the ass, I don't want another partner."

Gabe knew his partner was worried he couldn't be around to watch out for him. He was stuck reliving the incident from a decade ago. "Hey, I'll be home soon enough and when this is all over with, I'll show you how to make a killer omelet for Kate. She still hanging around?"

Smith groaned. "Barely. She's high maintenance. Maybe if I cooked for her it would help."

"Maybe…I told you, man, you'd better step up your game. She could do a lot better."

Gabe chuckled as he listened to Smith curse him out before hanging up. But his smile disappeared as his thoughts returned to Megan. He needed to convince her to go home. He just wasn't sure how he could without telling her the truth.

He watched her through the mirror. She had both hands gripping her steering wheel tightly. She was probably a nervous wreck driving on the left side of the road and trying to deal with everything that had already happened. If only she understood how much danger she was really in. He had a feeling she was too stubborn to see reason, which meant keeping her safe would be that much more difficult for him. "Here's to me keeping you alive, Megan," he whispered.

21

Victor Torrez watched from a front window as the automatic iron security gate opened then shut behind the black sedan as it pulled into the semicircle driveway. Two of his perimeter Pit Bulls approached the vehicle as his only child stepped out of the car he had sent to pick him up from the airport.

Miguel waved the dogs off with a simple command, and started towards the front entrance of the cliff side Botany Bay estate. Though there was the usual cockiness in his stride as he walked up the marble steps to Victor's main St. Thomas residence, his face needed a shave, and he was swaying just enough for Victor to notice.

Miguel was dressed in a yellow linen button down and dress pants, wealth evident in his clothes from his designer shades all the way down to his loafers. Victor knew behind the sunglasses, his son's eyes would be red, from a combination of liquor and prescription drugs. Perhaps Miguel was on the family's number one source of income, Cocaine, as well, but Victor would remind his son of abusing his power if that turned out to be true. An overdose of the stuff was, after all, what had killed Miguel's mother.

Or so Victor had told Miguel.

Miguel took off his sunglasses as he entered the front foyer and surveyed the row of his father's bodyguards with annoyance. "Could I speak with you *in private*?"

"Not even a hello? Something certainly must be troubling my only child."

Miguel rolled his bloodshot eyes. "I need to talk to you."

Victor gestured down the hallway. "Come, let us speak in my office, *Hijo*."

Miguel glanced at two young women sitting on a white leather sofa, scantily dressed and sipping from Martini glasses, in the palatial living room to the right of the main entrance. "Keeping good company as usual I see," he droned.

Victor led the way, casting a glance over his shoulder. "Is that why you're here? You ran out of whores in St. Croix?"

Miguel grabbed the back of his father's shirt and threw him towards the wall, narrowly missing one of the prized collector paintings. Victor's bodyguards were there in a split second, prying him off. They shoved him hard against the opposite wall. Victor smoothed the wrinkles out of his shirt. He prided himself in his luxury clothing even more than his arrogant son.

He raised an eyebrow at Miguel after adjusting his shirt. "My, my, did I hurt someone's feelings?"

Miguel spat his words now. "Madeline was not a whore. And you killed her."

Victor pursed his lips. "Let him go." The bodyguards released Miguel at once, and Victor walked a few more feet, opening his office door. "Come inside. Let's talk about your problems."

Miguel followed his father into the private office and began pacing the white tiled marble floors. From the bulletproof balcony doors, there was a view of the infinity swimming pool below, with the ocean visible just beyond. The entire estate was secure, from video surveillance to security fences and gates, to the armed men and patrolling Pit Bulls. Victor took no chances with his protection. A lot of people wanted him dead. His journey to wealthy drug lord had left a fair amount of victims with mourning families behind.

Victor knew of pain and suffering. He had grown up barefoot and starving on the crime-ridden streets of *La Perla*, one of San Juan's most dangerous neighborhoods, while his mother had attempted to provide for him. Victor had been six-years-old and had watched from a tiny, roach-infested closest the day she died, overdosing on her pimp's heroin. He'd never known his father, and his mother's pimp had offered him his first job, running heroin to his slew of working girls, shortly after her death.

It had been a nightmare childhood, but because of it, he had made something of himself and created a powerful empire. No price was too high to pay to get to where he was today. And no one was worth losing his hard-earned life over. Not even his whiny, spoiled son.

Victor hated that his only child had turned out to be so weak, and he blamed it on his late wife, Maribel. She was never able to conceive after Miguel, and by that point, Victor had decided he didn't want any more children. He'd learned it was easier to control strangers. He could buy the kind of loyalty he needed. And Miguel had turned out to be such a disappointment.

Miguel's mother had spoiled him. Babied him. But Victor's empire didn't have room for emotional babies. It was the main reason Victor had to have Miguel watched and supervised by Trevor, Dalbert, and the rest of his St. Croix crew. Miguel was too weak to make the appropriate decisions to protect his father's interest. Though Miguel had proved himself useful now and then, he always disappointed Victor when it came down to it. Miguel never would have ordered the hit on Madeline. She had been exposed to incriminating evidence and would have made an excellent witness for the DEA, FBI, or any other agency after Victor. Even if they'd only busted Miguel, they'd have been one step closer to nailing Victor, their most desired target.

Victor took a seat on one of the large, office ottomans, and kicked up his feet on the stool. "I'm told you've been partying for days, Miguel."

Miguel shrugged indifferently at his father's statement. He pulled out a pack of Marlboros and a lighter from his shirt pocket. He lit the cigarette, inhaling deeply. "I'm not here to talk about whether or not I've been drinking too much."

"It's not just the alcohol that concerns me. You know I don't tolerate anyone abusing the products we handle. It's one thing to party once in awhile, but I hear you are barely functioning. And I saw you stagger up my steps. I see your eyes, your appearance. You look like hell. I don't want you to become reckless, *Hijo*. It's what killed your mother. When she couldn't conceive anymore, she buried herself in her habit. Such a sad thing to witness."

"Funny, *Padre*, that I never saw this side of my mother that you speak of. But maybe she buried herself like you say because she wanted to escape from your heavy hand. Maybe it helped her deal with the pain."

"Your mother was a cokehead, among other things, and if I raised my fist to her from time to time, it was only an attempt to straighten her out. I knew she would kill herself with drugs. She was too weak."

"It was a mistake to go away to Miami for school like you insisted. Mother would have been okay if I had stayed to protect her. And you made me go. As if I weren't prepared to work for you at the time. Why did you really send me away?"

"I wanted my son to have the education I wasn't able to have. You'd think you would be more grateful."

"Are you sure? You didn't send me away so you could kill my mother?" Miguel stopped pacing and focused his glare on his father.

Victor was shocked his son was suddenly so perceptive. Or maybe it was an alcohol or drug induced enlightenment. Miguel was just fishing. There was no way he knew the truth. "*Hijo*, in spite of your desire to blame your junkie mother's death on *me*, the one person who has always been there for you, I didn't kill her. She did that all on her own. Such a sad person she was."

"She was fine when I left for Miami, and I never saw her do any drugs. It's impossible for me to believe she suddenly became a junkie while I was away."

"It's the truth. You weren't here. She started using as soon as you left. You were gone for four years, Miguel."

"But I came home to visit. Mother was different, yes, but it was because you were scaring her too much. How could you ever have laid a finger on her? She was such a fragile and sweet woman."

"You should have seen your perfect mother when she was high on her precious drugs. It was repulsive."

"And yet, you spend your time with women half your age, drunk and doped up on drugs you give them. Kind of hypocritical, if you ask me," Miguel pointed a finger in his father's direction.

"I'm entitled to whatever I desire. And there are no real women left for me out there. Not since…" Victor's sentence trailed off as he stared into space. His expression was somber suddenly as he sat silently, deep in thought.

"Since who? Mother?"

Victor snapped out of his thoughts and turned his attention back to his clueless son. "Forget about it, Miguel. Are you done venting to me about your little girlfriend? Do you want me to send you on a vacation or something? You need a break from your duties here? It's fine, *Hijo*. Trevor and Dalbert can keep things together for me while you are away."

Miguel snubbed his cigarette out in the ashtray on the desk. "I came here because I wanted to hear it from you. I want you to tell me why you had to have Madeline killed. I loved her. *I told you* I loved her. You did it to show me again how much you despise me, didn't you?" Miguel slammed his fist onto his father's desk.

Victor stared, unblinking, into his son's eyes. "I ordered the hit because you got careless Miguel, and you let her see something she wasn't supposed to see."

"But I could've talked to her, reasoned with her. She was different than any other woman I've known."

"You hardly knew anything about her. You only knew her for a couple of weeks. She would've turned you in to the authorities for sure. She thought you were a local business owner, not a killer."

"Madeline was special. She would've listened to me, I know it." A tear ran down Miguel's face. He sat down on his father's sofa, seeming to give up on his arguing.

"I did it to protect you, *Hijo*. That's the difference between you and me. I will kill to protect my life and interest. You're too much like your mother. If you want to remain part of my business you ought to really think about that. Do you have the stomach to kill those who get in the way when necessary?"

"I already do that for you. Wasn't that what I was doing when Madeline screamed and ran away?"

"That was different. That was a low-life thief, stealing from my supply. I'm talking about people, for example, you get close to, like this Madeline. You couldn't have pulled the trigger, I know you." Victor's voice was heavy with disgust.

Miguel dried his eyes and stared hatefully at his father. "I'll never be able to share my love with a woman will I, Father? You'll always be there to kill the ones I get close to. Just like you killed my mother."

Victor sat silently, staring down at the floor. He couldn't argue with his son any longer. He was reliving the night he had killed Miguel's mother. He had choked the life out of her after he had drugged her heavily. He had felt stronger after killing her. He had felt high with the rush of power it had given him. And that rush had eventually led to the death of some other disappointing women.

Of course, his Maribel hadn't been a junkie. She had been a scared, little coward, unable to have more than one disappointing child and an annoyance to live with. He'd tried to keep most of his business a secret from her, but inevitably, she'd discovered the truth. She had been appalled by Victor's business antics and had simply been in the way.

After nineteen years of marriage, she had tried to convince Victor to end his life of crime. Unfortunately for her, her guilty conscience from simply witnessing some of her husband's wrongdoings had gotten her killed. Victor had been relieved to get rid of her.

Miguel stood up from the sofa, and opened the office liquor cabinet. He pulled a bottle of tequila out, taking a swig. He clutched the bottle and started for the door. "I'm going to my room now. I'll go back to St. Croix in a couple of days. You don't have to worry about me being in your way here. I knew I wouldn't get any answers from you, *Papá*."

Once his son was gone, Victor walked to the balcony, inhaling the fresh scent of ocean air and studying the expanse of his property with pride. He considered the slippery path of self-destruction his son seemed to be on. If Miguel couldn't pull himself together and do as he was instructed, Victor couldn't afford him on his team. He had fought, cheated, and killed to get where he was today.

No one was going to take it from him. Not Miguel. And not a tourist who saw something she shouldn't have.

22

"What if Maddy's in there?" Megan stared from the passenger window at the rundown, apartment buildings, clustered together with clotheslines decorating tiny patios and chickens running around the property.

On the drive from the airport to the medical clinic to the police station and now to her new hotel, she had listened to Gabe's easy banter about some of St. Croix's history and his island knowledge. She'd taken a mental note of everything he shared, deciding any tidbit of information she should file away in case she could use it on her search for Maddy.

After he'd followed up on his promise to get her to the police station, she'd decided to go ahead and ask him a little bit about himself; like where he was from. He'd seemed a little thrown off by her interest, but he'd revealed a few things about himself. He was supposedly a native to St. Croix. But when his parents had died, he had moved off island with his grandma, a Puerto Rican woman. He hadn't mentioned where they'd gone, now that Megan thought about it. He also hadn't mentioned how his parents had died, but he'd quickly moved the conversation along. He said he'd only come back to St. Croix recently because he was trying to sort out some things from his past, but he hadn't elaborated.

Again, though she felt like he'd told her the truth about his origins, she sensed he was keeping something from her, yet she knew firsthand how losing your parents felt, so she decided maybe the mention of his parents' death had made him uncomfortable talking about himself. In the grand scheme of things she figured it didn't matter. Now that she had filed the police report and the police seemed genuinely convinced she was telling the truth about Maddy, she wouldn't be seeing Gabe much longer. He said he would give her a ride here and there until she rented a new car, but honestly she had decided severing her ties with him as soon as possible would make the most sense for both of them. The more she thought about the man who had attacked her, the more she realized she didn't need to drag a regular guy like Gabe into her problems.

But first, she'd let him get her to a new hotel. The police had offered to help her find a place, but what Gabe had said earlier about criminals having eyes and ears everywhere, even in law enforcement, had made her hesitate. She'd told the police she would come to them if she found anything. And they had agreed to contact her via her cell phone if they made any kind of discovery.

The long drive around the island had revealed some beautiful sights, like the sun setting over ocean scapes, hills, lush foliage, and even crumbling historic sugar mills. Gabe had explained how parts of the island had kept their names from the island's plantation days, such as Estate La Grand Princesse, which he had driven through moments ago. And then of course, the drive had shown Megan some of the many lower income areas of St. Croix.

"I guess you don't spend a lot of time in the projects back home? Where is home anyway?" Gabe asked, keeping his eyes ahead as he drove through the evening traffic of Christiansted.

Megan sensed his tone and jumped to her own defense. "I'm not judging."

"Alright."

"Not completely. I admit, it kind of throws me off guard a little how the island is so beautiful in some areas and quite developed and then you drive me by blatant poverty stricken areas and…"

"You have a thing against poor people? You never answered me either. Where are you from? I told you when you asked me the same thing," he pointed out.

"I don't have a problem with poor people. Maybe poverty though."

Gabe spared her a look, seemingly confused, then turned forward.

"I live in Naples, Florida. I moved there to work for a financial firm with my business degree, but I quickly got pulled into the real estate market when I realized how lucrative it could be. Business is good there for commercial real estate agents, especially. Ever heard of Naples?"

"Sure have. I have relatives in Fort Lauderdale. I'm familiar with the Sunshine State. Naples is a very wealthy area."

"Yeah, it is, but I've only been there since I graduated from college. I was raised in a rural area outside of Naples, called Immokalee. Have you heard of it?"

"Actually, I have…not exactly a destination for the rich and famous, like Naples."

"Exactly. A poverty stricken area, complete with an abundance of projects. My mom would've followed Dad anywhere, and she did. They were high school sweethearts and they wanted out of Florida. They backpacked everywhere and got into mountain climbing of all things. Along the way, Mom got pregnant with Maddy and me, and from what my grandparents told me, they went back to Immokalee when money got tight and things got too hard caring for us twins. So my grandparents started pitching in, and the next thing you know, Mom and Dad are testing out equipment for people who were trying to get their companies up and running. They ended up investing everything they had, sort of partnering with different enthusiasts like themselves. And Maddy and I got left on the farm with our grandparents."

"That must have been hard, not seeing your parents often."

"It was, but we got used to it. Their quest for adventure always came before us. And then they died on one of their trips." Megan hesitated, staring at her hands as she recalled the pain.

Gabe cleared his throat softly.

"Since the company they were partnering with was a startup and none of them had thought to plan for an emergency and have life insurance or anything, my grandparents had to bare the financial strain of taking care of two pre-teen girls. So they did the only thing they could to survive so child services wouldn't take us from them. They started working extra jobs, and they put us to work, too. They did their best, and even with Maddy and I working after school, weekends, and summers with them on the farm, let's just say putting food on the table was a group effort that didn't always pan out. So when I left for college, which I got to with an academic scholarship I worked my butt off to get, I never forgot that life…"

Gabe turned to her as he waited for the stoplight to change. She could see his eyes in the street lamp shining above his car. He seemed genuinely interested. She hadn't spoken of her past with many people. Still, he seemed like he wanted to know. "And I made a vow to never end up there again."

He nodded. "Gotcha." A half smile formed at his mouth. "I guess ending up with me as your new friend wouldn't be something you'd write home about. I bet Naples doesn't have projects, like Immokalee or St. Croix."

"Like I said, it's not poor people. I come from that. It's the situation. And I rose above my circumstances. And I'm not about to judge you. You're the only one who has really offered me any help. Besides, there aren't exactly people to write home to. I live a rather isolated life."

"Isolated?"

Megan smiled. "Well, that's my term for it. Maddy always says it's a boring, lonely life." Her heart jumped to her throat, her brow wove together. "I wonder where she is."

Gabe tilted his head in her direction, his face somber. "Stay positive. Maybe you were right about going to the police. You never know what they might find now that they have more evidence."

Megan gestured behind the car. "I know how it sounded when we drove past the last projects. But I only meant, that now that you've driven me around some of the island that I didn't see on my own excursions, I feel even more overwhelmed. Maddy could be anywhere. And what if she is in one of those projects for example? If I go knocking, door to door, will anyone talk to me? So far, I haven't gotten any information about Maddy from anyone I've asked."

"I don't know, but I would imagine that if your sister has been kidnapped like you suspect, she's probably being held by people with money and power."

"Why would you assume that?"

"Just guessing. You hear things about crime rings and drugs around the island. Maybe your sister got mixed up with the wrong people."

"She doesn't even drink anymore."

"Anymore?"

Megan paused, remembering how she'd doubted her sister when she had told her she'd changed and abandoned her partying ways. Something had happened to her sister in Amsterdam. But Megan hadn't wanted to hear about it. The truth is, Megan had never really been sympathetic to Maddy's problems. It has always felt like Maddy had brought her problems on herself.

She glanced at Gabe. "Yeah, supposedly she quit partying altogether, which was huge for her, considering the past ten years of her life. She'd been sober for at least sixteen months when she left the last time."

Gabe shrugged. "Maybe she fell off the wagon."

"But she never did drugs before. At least, I don't think she did." As soon as she said it, she realized she really didn't know what Maddy did before.

"Now that you've gone to the police and told them what happened, they'll handle the investigation from here. If they need to search in the projects or the rich neighborhoods, they will. You just need to stay out of sight. Or leave. Like I keep telling you to."

"As soon as I find Maddy, I'll be happy to go," she replied definitively.

She noticed his hands tense around the steering wheel, but for once he didn't argue with her refusal to head home. As they turned down a cobblestone street, reaching the interior of Christiansted, Megan took her hat off. It was dark enough, she figured, it wasn't really that necessary.

But Gabe reacted at once. He reached across the car, picked it up and placed it back on her head. "Keep it on."

"It's dark out now."

"Doesn't matter. Have you looked in a mirror? Your hair is very noticeable," he lowered his eyes to her face now. "Not to mention your face," he added under his breath.

The way his tone had changed when he studied her, made her heart speed up. But she couldn't waste time trying to figure out what was so alluring about him or why her temperature spiked when he complimented her. She cleared her throat. "Fine, I'll keep the hat on," she said with a sigh. "But it just seems like a very touristy look. I only packed it thinking that if Maddy was just ignoring my calls and I found her, I'd take a day to go to the beach with her before I headed back to reality. I sunburn so easily." Her tone sank as she surveyed the century old buildings, some in a state of disrepair, and noticed a couple of homeless, barefoot men sleeping on the sidewalks. Maddy could be anywhere. They could be passing the building she was in at that moment for all she knew.

"I know it's a tourist look, but I'll get you a baseball cap tomorrow. For now, just keep that on until I get you to your new room. That beach hat could save your life. The second one of the bad guys, whoever they may be, recognizes you, they will come after you again." He sounded worried now and focused his gaze out of the front window of the car as he drove.

"I know how you feel about me staying here. You don't have to sound so disapproving. It's my life."

He snapped his head towards her, his expression dark. "It is your life. I just hope you know what you're doing, that's all. But what do I know? I'm just a fry cook trying to help some crazy real estate agent out a little."

Her temperature rose once more, but not in a good way. "Crazy? No, I'm not crazy. Anything but. I'm responsible, I pay my bills early, I am organized, sensible, and the only thing that could get me to leave my very rational and meticulously organized life behind right now to come to this rock, is my totally wild and reckless twin sister. She's the crazy one. I think you would like her much better than me as a matter of fact. You seem like her type." Megan scrunched up her nose as she said the word type.

Amusement crossed Gabe's face. "But not yours, huh?"

Before she could reply, he went on. "My point is, keep that hat on. At least until you get inside the new room. I'm not sure how I'd fight off the guys looking for you if they spot you while you're with me," he added.

Megan readjusted the hat, stuffing her thick, long locks under the hat as much as possible. "Better?" she asked with a defiant tone.

Gabe pulled the car into a spot on the side of the cobblestone street and looked at her. "Well, you still stand out, but we can't exactly reverse the artwork God did with your face now can we?"

Megan's pulse picked up, but she couldn't let him know how his praise was getting to her. Men flattered her often. So what was it about Gabe Sanchez? She didn't have time to figure that out. She rolled her eyes. "I told you, *Mr. Sanchez*, you are my sister's type. Definitely, not mine."

"Just stating the obvious, Megan. That hat is only going to help you blend in so much. If you know what's good for you, you'll stay inside the hotel room all day tomorrow. I'll give you my cell number. If you need anything, just call. My shift ends at two. And I can take you around the island to ask more questions if you really want to. Maybe letting me do some of the asking might help you get some answers."

"Why do I have a feeling, you'd just tell me to stay in the car while you asked the questions?"

"Not a bad idea." He reached for the door handle and hesitated. "Stay put. I'll be back in a minute with your room key."

She handed him her cash. "You won't be long?"

"No. Lock the doors when I get out, okay?"

Megan nodded, gulping down her anxiety as he disappeared through the dark streets. Everything he'd said to her seemed rational enough, and she knew he was right. But she'd been planning her next move ever since she'd filed her latest police report. She hadn't told Gabe everything the police had said.

They believed Megan's story and had promised to look into it, but they had said the likelihood of finding any evidence regarding Maddy's disappearance wasn't high. They simply didn't have the physical proof they needed. Not even a missing purse, wallet, or cell phone to show them she'd been in an accident. Only the threat of a mystery man with a German accent, who Megan couldn't even identify because she'd been blindfolded.

Megan knew she could always go home and try to get the FBI or some other government agency to assist her, but what if her sister didn't have much time left? What if they were planning to kill Maddy? She refused to give up, and she was running out of time.

Tomorrow, she'd make a bold move. She'd do anything to find Maddy, and she knew exactly what she had to do.

23

Gabe spied the clock on the wall and hurried through the last two tickets he had to prepare. Sweat soaked through his t-shirt. The combination of the tropical heat in October and the eight burner gas stove and
ovens were suffocating. But he worked through it and focused on his
job. He was the king of breakfast food: omelets, French toast, sausages,
pancakes, hash browns, grits, salt fish and more. And then there was the
lunch menu: stewed chicken, boiled fish, Callaloo, and of course, fried
plantains, to name a few.

His grandmother never would've believed it possible. If only he could
share with her the details of his case. But she didn't even know where he
was, much less what his cover assignment involved. Smith was checking
in on her at her retirement home from time to time, but his partner
knew better than to divulge any case info to family.

He imagined closing the case, heading home, and telling her about
his cooking skills put to use. After the murder of his family, she'd taken
full custody of him and relocated the pair to her cousin's house in Fort
Lauderdale where she'd insisted on teaching him to cook. She had tried
to teach him everything she knew in the kitchen, but he had been reluc-
tant to learn as a teenager. She'd finally insisted he master two of her
favorite Puerto Rican dishes, Lechon, or roast pork, and Mofongo,
cooked plantain mashed with garlic and meat or seafood. Since taking
the job at Captain Sully's he'd widened his expertise. He'd been a quick
study. He knew keeping the job would help him stay under the radar
while he tried to infiltrate the Torrez family.

For the three years she'd taken care of him before he left for college, his grandmother had loved teaching him to cook. She'd hover beside him, sharing stories of his ancestors, speaking in Spanish only, as she never wanted him to forget the native tongue of her side of the family. She had moved from Puerto Rico to St. Croix as a young woman, where she'd met his Crucian grandfather, who died from cancer before he was born. She'd teased Gabe about his mediocre knife skills and had shown him how to make uniform vegetable cuts. She would say she was teaching him so he could have another skill besides basketball, but he'd always figured she was so sad from the deaths of her daughter, his dad, and her granddaughter, that her time cooking with him had been therapy for her as much as him. Looking back, he wished he'd appreciated the gesture more at the time. But he'd been a stubborn, grief-stricken teenager, determined to find a way into law enforcement so he could bring his family's murderer to justice.

His grandmother had warned him against building his entire life around revenge, yet she had always supported him. When he'd earned his academic scholarship and left his basketball dreams behind to go to college in Chicago, she'd been proud. During his time away, earning his undergraduate degree in Criminal Justice and then later his Master's, she'd visited him as often as she could. And when she hadn't been able to, she'd sent him care packages with baked goods she'd prepared.

Though she worried about his line of work and the danger he was in, she'd always been supportive. She would've paid for Gabe to go to college, but he had insisted on paying his own way. His grandmother had kept his parents' house all these years, and because it was a private home on the beach, she had made a lot of money off of it by hiring a real estate company to lease it as a vacation rental. But she had never wanted Gabe to come back to St. Croix. She was terrified that whoever had killed the rest of the family might somehow have heard about Abigail's younger brother being in the house that long ago night. The police had kept it quiet, but his grandmother had decided to leave St.

Croix at once, just in case Gabe was in danger.

She didn't know his current case was related to the same drug ring that had gotten Abigail hooked. But she had known off and on for years how he had worked on related cases in Miami. He hadn't wanted to worry her when he left, so he hadn't mentioned the connection. Still, he figured she suspected the truth.

When he'd said goodbye to her before going under, she'd told him she would keep him in her prayers, but that she wished he'd make his peace with the past and leave it behind. She was afraid he'd never be happy if he didn't let his pain go. Maybe she was right.

But he knew he was exactly where he needed to be for the moment. And now, Megan had shown up, and he felt like he had to help her even though he knew he was risking his cover. He hated feeling so torn. Smith was right. She'd gotten in his head a little.

During his nearly eleven years with the DEA, Gabe had thrown himself into each case and been on numerous short-term undercover assignments around the U.S.A. and it's territories. Every time he was on an assignment, no matter where he found himself, Gabe thought of his family's murder and the connection to the Torrez family. But he had never let anyone consume his thoughts like Megan was. He couldn't stop thinking about her. The desire to protect her was overwhelming. Even though he knew Smith was right about the danger he was putting himself in, he had decided to follow his gut on this.

He'd been thinking about it all day. After work, he'd see if Raul was ready to introduce him to Miguel, but then he was going off of the radar for a few days. And he was going to help Megan. He would convince her to leave, or at least try. And at the very least, he'd keep her safe for a few days and ease his guilt about not telling her what he knew about her sister's involvement with Miguel.

Gabe set the plates under the heat lamp, where they were quickly picked up and carried to awaiting tables, and he tossed his apron into the dirty laundry basket as he checked the time. Raul, true to form, would be heading to the convenient store up the block in five minutes, and Gabe wanted to run into the petty criminal today. But first he had to tell his shift manager, Jack, he was taking a few days off.

He walked up to the guy, a transplant from the mainland, who was sitting on an overturned crate beside the walk-in refrigerator. Gabe figured Jack would easily replace him for a few days, but he gave him an apologetic look anyway. "Remember when I started here, boss, I said I might need a few days off before season hit to regroup?"

"Yeah, that was three months ago, dude. You never mentioned it after that."

"Well, the time has come. I could really use a few days now."

Jack gave him an easy grin. "Man, you've got timing. I just hired a new guy to train for season. It's cool with me. We've got you covered."

Gabe grinned. "Perfect. I'll be back soon enough."

"Sure, man. Where you rushing off to anyway? This is about a girl, right? You finally putting yourself out there?"

Jack and the rest of the crew had been giving him a hard time for weeks about how he never dated. Gabe figured he would leave him with a partial truth. "Met a cute little island hopper recently, and well let's just say she's a lot easier on the eyes than you, boss."

"Okay, okay, dude, I get it now. Enjoy your mini vacation. And bring her by so we can meet her, man."

Gabe winked. "See ya, Jack."

"Peace, man."

A few minutes later, he spotted the skinny, tattooed frame of Raul. He wore a gray tank top with jeans, and he was walking with a limp down the cracked sidewalks of the street.

Gabe jogged to catch up with him, drawing back as he noticed Raul's swollen black eye. "What happened to you, man?"

Raul shrugged his shoulders and kept walking. "A misunderstanding with management you could say. No big deal."

"Speaking of your management, when are you going to take me on that job interview I was asking about?"

Raul came to a stop and scowled at Gabe. "Look, man, my boss isn't exactly in the best mood lately if you catch my drift, and I don't think he's hiring new help. You're gonna have to keep frying eggs for awhile. Now, sorry, but I've got a situation to deal with, and I need to go."

"Maybe if he meets me he'll give me a job. Just set up a meeting for me," Gabe pressed.

"Listen, I might have, say two days ago, but he is going through some heavy stuff lately. He's been a little…unpredictable. Besides, he's not even around. Word is, he's been visiting his old man. No telling when he's coming back." Raul scanned the area nervously. He seemed really worked up about something.

"Okay, man, maybe when he gets back, we'll have this conversation again. Are you sure you don't need any help with your situation? I'm off work for now." It was obvious something was bothering Raul, but Gabe wasn't sure how much he would tell him.

"No man, I just need to go. Hey, wait a sec…" He pointed across the street at a man sitting in front of a stand selling fried empanadas. "You see that old guy sitting over there?"

Gabe glanced at the old guy, then Raul. His eyes were roaming all around like he was nervous. "Yeah, I see him."

Raul shook his head vigorously and licked his lips. "Good. I'm not going crazy. I can't be going crazy. I know what I saw, right?"

Gabe raised his brow. "Yeah, Raul. I guess so."

Raul spun on his heel and staggered down the block. Gabe stepped into an alley to watch. A moment later, a black Ford Explorer pulled in front of the smoke shop Raul had stopped in front of, and a man Gabe recognized as Miguel's employee called out from the window. Raul looked pale as he walked over to the vehicle and climbed in. Gabe ducked out of sight as the SUV drove away, this time with Raul in it. He wondered what had spooked Raul. Whatever it was, it couldn't be good.

24

Megan slowed her pace as she started down another street in the tourist shopping area of Christiansted. The sun blazed in the afternoon sky, seeming to drain her of what was left of her energy. She lifted a plastic bottle of water to her lips and drank the remainder, tossing it into a garbage bin as she continued her search. She'd been in so many shops; she'd lost count. Her bold plan to find her sister hadn't panned out like she had hoped. With each step she took, she wondered if the man who had threatened her would jump out of an alleyway. So far, since leaving her hotel hours ago, she hadn't turned up any new clues, but she was still alive. That had to count for something. Still, she felt so frustrated. She thought her plan had been good.

Her hand tightened around the strap of her sister's olive colored, SAK purse that was draped over her shoulder and across her body. She had packed a few of Maddy's things before leaving Naples, thinking her twin might need a clean pair of clothes, knowing she'd never wear any of Megan's, but also thinking that dressing like Maddy could be helpful in tracking her down. And regardless of how identical the twins were, Maddy's style was completely different than Megan's and anyone who knew them, would know the difference. Megan had to believe that someone on the island had known her sister. She'd been there for three weeks before she disappeared. Determined to play the role of her sister, Megan had formed her plan and carried it out.

As soon as she'd finished texting Gabe early that morning that she was going to take his advice and stay inside the room for the day, Megan had started getting ready to leave. She hated lying to him, especially since he'd gone to the trouble of getting her a different hotel room and even dropped off dinner for her the night before, but she didn't have a choice. These were desperate times.

Megan had left her hotel, dressed to the T, like her twin would have. She wore a pair of Maddy's faded and torn blue jean shorts, over a red bandana patterned bikini with strings that tied around her neck and trailed towards her waist, just like Maddy. She'd covered it with a white, logoed Jimi Hendrix tank top with thin straps that crisscrossed below the neck, and selected some of Maddy's beaded bracelets and large, silver hoop earrings. She had styled her hair into a loose French braid that wove sideways around her head, leaving some hair down around one side of her face. It was one of Maddy's signature hairstyles. Unfortunately, Megan hadn't been able to talk her gypsy twin out of the two tattoos she had gotten three years ago while she was vacationing in Thailand, but thankfully, she had been able to convince her to get them on parts of her body where clothing could cover them up.

When Maddy had made a rare overseas call to check in with her twin and tell her about her plans to be tattooed, Megan had pleaded with her to conceal the tattoos just in case she ever decided to join the real world and get a steady job. Maddy had laughed at her sister. "Okay, I might get the tattoos in places I can keep covered up, just in case we ever decide to play switch-a-roo on anyone ever again, like old times…But I will not get a steady job. Me? Tied like a captive to my job, like you, Sis? Forget about it, Meg. I'm a free bird, like Lynyrd Skynyrd said." Maddy had promised to send photos of her ink job before hanging up.

Megan wished Maddy's newest tattoo were the biggest thing she had to worry about right now. But the cut, slowly healing on her temple was a reminder that this was monumentally worse than a little tattoo. She had meant it more than ever earlier that morning when she had said, "Lord, help me," with her heart pounding in her chest as she trekked out into town dressed as her twin.

Before returning to the tourist shopping area, Megan had taxied it to a local complex called Golden Rock, one of the areas she hadn't previously checked on her searches. She had wandered around the supermarket and also gone into a pharmacy. To anyone familiar with Maddy, Megan would look identical today, the charade fool proof. But evidently, no one recognized Maddy or Meg. The entire day had been a waste of time.

Once in the taxi, she had stared aimlessly at her cell phone for a few minutes. There was no one for her to call and talk to. She couldn't call Grandma Lynn without upsetting her, and she had cancelled all of her appointments at home and handed her clients over to her co-workers. She had told her coworkers the same thing she'd told her grandmother so they had said they weren't calling her. Everyone had agreed that Megan needed to enjoy her vacation. It felt strange not listening to the beeps and rings of her phone constantly.

She'd contemplated calling Gabe, who she knew was working, but she figured he would only have yelled at her if she told him the truth about what she had done. After a few minutes of indecisiveness, she'd asked the driver to take her to the tourist shopping area. She knew Maddy liked to pick up souvenirs and knickknacks from time to time, so she decided to peruse the shops and chat with the employees.

But as she strolled over cobblestone streets, her eyes swept to each dark alley, where she wondered if the man from her hotel might be lurking, and she felt defeated. She wondered if she should head to the hotel and call the police to check on their investigation, when she spotted a store sign she hadn't gone into yet. Familiar goose bumps popped up on her arms, and she spun around, searching for Maddy. But her sister wasn't there.

She turned towards the sign. ISLAND GEMS. Maddy didn't typically buy jewelry unless it was cheap, but something told her to go inside the store. Maybe Maddy had been in there. She rushed across the street, oblivious to her surroundings as she pushed the door open and strolled inside.

Her eyes swept the store, taking in the variety of jewelry cases lining the store and the clerk dressed in an attractive red sundress. She smiled at Megan. "G' aftanoon."

Megan took a breath and formed a tightlipped smile. "Good afternoon." She forced her feet forward and approached the nearest jewelry case. What was she looking for anyway? She'd been in a dozen shops today, and no one had seen Maddy. And if the woman recognized her, it wasn't apparent in her expression.

"Are yoh lookin' foh som'ting in particula'?"

"Well…," Megan wanted to talk, but her mind was still racing over the feeling she'd gotten. Perhaps it didn't have anything to do with the store. Their chills had always linked them to each other when something was wrong. What if something was happening to her sister at that exact moment?

"This one is our most popula' bracelets. Do you have a Crucian hook, Miss?" Megan pulled herself from her thoughts and forced herself to look at the bracelet the clerk had set before her. It jogged her memory, and she suddenly recalled why. She'd seen one just like it on her waitress, Celia, from Captain Sully's. Below the one in the clerk's hand, there were a variety of the bracelets in the case. There were gold ones, silver, thick and thin, and a variety of latches designed to hook them together, most of them with a u-shaped latch. Were the circumstances different, she might have tried one on, but she wasn't there to shop.

She cleared her throat. "Actually, I'm looking for someone. She—"

Megan stopped short. In the case to the right, something caught her attention. She bent down, pressing her hands to the glass, pointing wildly at the pendant.

"Find som'ting yoh like?" asked the saleswoman, coming closer this time, obviously recognizing Megan's sudden interest.

"Where did you get this one?" Megan never took her eyes off of the necklace, her hands were pressed down on the case, her fingertips straining to get closer.

The woman seemed confused by the question. "We buy our jewelry from a variety o' companies and jewelry designers. Would yoh like ta see it?"

"Yes." Megan looked up now, staring into the woman's eyes. "But where did you get *this* necklace?"

She unlocked the cabinet and retrieved the necklace, carefully setting it down on the glass counter. The small, green emerald pendant glistened up at her, the worn gold chain trailing away from the gem. It was identical to her own, and she would recognize it anywhere. "I don' know Miss. It came in recently, I know dat. It certainly is unique."

Megan touched the emerald pendant lightly, trying not to let the tears that were forming fall. It didn't mean anything. It couldn't mean anything. Finding Maddy's necklace did not mean she was dead. She wouldn't still be getting goose bumps or sensing her if she were dead. But finding her necklace was not a good sign. Megan swayed a little and grasped the corner of the counter top to steady herself.

"Miss, are yoh okay?" the attendant asked. "Yoh need ta sit down?"

The woman's words sounded muted and distant. Maddy had lost her necklace and somehow it had ended up here, in this random jewelry store. She was not dead. But why wasn't she wearing her necklace?

"Miss, canna get yoh some watah?"

Megan looked back to the woman, trying to form words, but her tongue felt heavy.

"Miss?"

Megan felt her heart beating out of control. She mustered her strength. "How much is the necklace?" she managed to say.

Megan knew the actual value couldn't compare with the sentimental value, which made her pulse race all that much faster. Maddy would never have parted with the necklace willingly.

"Tree hundred dollars."

Her face contorted with anger. "This isn't worth three hundred dollars. You should hand it to me. It's my missing sister's necklace. It's stolen," Megan leaned across the counter as she spoke.

The woman seemed startled for a second, but recovered. She shook her head adamantly. "I tellin' yoh, dis isn't stolen property. Perhaps yoh like ta look at som'ting mor' affordable? May I suggest our Larimar collection? It's a Caribbean specialty and quite exquisite."

Her hand reached for her own necklace, and once in her grasp, she held it up. "I have its twin. This necklace is my sister's, I assure you. Now, where did you get it?"

The clerk seemed genuinely confused. "I'm sorry I canna help yoh Miss. De owner of da store is off island right now. Maybe yoh should come back 'nother time and ask him."

Megan handed over her credit card. "Give me the emerald necklace."

The woman took the card and turned to a credit card machine. Megan signed the receipt, never taking her eyes from Maddy's necklace. The clerk reached for a box and bag to wrap it in, and Megan shook her head.

"Just give it to me," she whispered, holding her palm open. As the cool chain fell into her open hand, she felt chills run down her spine. She'd finally found a clue. And now everything was worse.

She exited the store in a rush, blindly crossing the street and taking off in a jog. She didn't know where she was going, only that she had to get away from the store. She lost her sense of direction but just kept moving. She took street after street, turn after turn and then stopped abruptly.

The smell of urine hit her nostrils as she took in the bleak alleyway, empty beer bottles cluttered around the ground, and the homeless shelter built from old boxes. She pivoted and stopped in her tracks as her heart slammed to her throat.

"Maddy?"

She shook her head. "No, it's me."

A scowl darkened his face and he rushed her, pinning her to the alley wall. "What in the *hell* are you doing, Megan?"

He reeked of grease and fried food. He looked like a wild man with his dark baseball cap, his unshaven face, and faded, old clothes. He fried eggs for a living, and he had chosen an underdeveloped island in the middle of the Caribbean to live. It made no sense that she should feel something for him. But in all her terror, she couldn't feel anything but relief as he glared at her.

"What are you doing?" Gabe demanded.

"I found her necklace." As she choked out the words, the relief faded to despair.

She buried her head on his chest and sobbed.

25

Megan was hysterical, and in his arms, and though Gabe knew he should be angry at her, the feel of her was seriously testing his self-control. He imagined wiping her tears away, stroking her hair as he held her, and murmuring to her that she was safe with him. As she leaned into him, her head on his chest, his blood pressure skyrocketed.

But his training kicked into gear, and he tucked his irrational ideas aside. He needed to treat Megan like any other woman he might help. He could analyze his growing concern for her another time.

In the back of his mind, he had been wondering when Megan would completely break down. After the attack in her hotel room, she'd pulled herself together a lot faster than he would have expected. He had attributed it to her stubbornness. She was simply too concerned with finding Maddy to care about her own safety or the fact a man had tortured her. She'd recovered right away because her entire focus was on her sister. But something had broken her down now.

He wanted to ask her a million questions. Why was she dressed like her twin? Why hadn't she stayed in the hotel room like she'd promised? Was she certifiably insane? Trying to get killed? But he added it up quickly. She'd wanted to pretend she was her twin to see if anyone recognized her.

If he weren't so worried about keeping her alive, he might compliment her for the idea. If she'd been working with his team, they easily could have asked her to do something like that. To be bait. But his agents weren't keeping her under surveillance or following closely in undercover vehicles to protect her. That was up to him. But if she was going to lie to him, he wouldn't be much help.

Posing as her twin had been a bold, but reckless move. But he'd wait a minute before giving her the lecture she deserved. He was momentarily feeling relieved she was still alive. Anyone could've seen her and tried to go after her. He'd almost been back to his place, when he'd spotted her jogging down the streets. He'd thought for a minute that it was her twin.

He let her cry. He didn't move. He just let her lean into him and sob. *I found her necklace*, she'd said. He hadn't realized Maddy wore a certain necklace, but apparently Megan was sure she'd found it. His ten years and counting of experience with the DEA and the many cases he'd worked had his thoughts going to the worst place possible. From the present condition of Megan, he could see she was thinking the worst, too. As much as he hated to think it, maybe this discovery would convince Megan to go back to Florida.

After a moment, he decided to see what she'd tell him. "Megan, what necklace did you find?"

She tilted her head back, peering up at him. Her face was bright red, streaming with tears that seemed to have no end. "It's Maddy's necklace. It was for sale in a jewelry shop. She never would have taken it off. Willingly."

"You're sure it's hers?"

Megan's head nodded as she wiped tears away. "Yes," she whispered. "I have the matching necklace." She reached for her neckline and held it up for him to study. "They were our birthday gifts when we were little girls. We never take them off."

Gabe's thoughts ran ahead. If Maddy's necklace had ended up for sale, he had to assume the worst. But he didn't want to frighten Megan any more considering her state. "Can I see the necklace you found? Is it in the store still?"

"I bought it. I tried to ask questions, but they said the owner wasn't on island. They told me to come back and insisted it wasn't stolen. I have to tell the police."

"I agree. Can I look at it though? Just to make sure it matches?"

Megan pulled the necklace from her pocket and opened her palm. Gabe took it and held it beside Megan's necklace. He swallowed, making sure to keep his voice steady. "Yes, you're right. It's a match alright. Where did you buy it?"

She shook as she sobbed into her hands, mumbling to herself. "Megan? Do you remember where you bought it? Try to remember."

She leaned into him, and her breaths came out in gasps. He glanced in either direction, unsure of how to help her. He wanted to yell at her and tell her how reckless she'd been. If only he could stick her on a plane out of here. As she trembled, lost in her tears, he sighed. There was no use trying to talk sense into her when she was so upset. He patted her back ever so lightly. "It's OK. Just breathe. We need to go. I'll drive you to the police station, OK?"

When she didn't reply, he took it as agreement. He tugged his hat off and placed it on her head. She didn't argue, just continued to cry. He shifted her sideways and in the hook of his arm, he held onto her, as he guided her down the alley and straight for his car.

She cried the entire drive to the police station and only responded with a nod of her head when he asked her anything. He was really starting to worry about her. He wasn't sure how long she might go on like this. He wondered if given her state he could convince her to leave St. Croix.

After a short call to Smith to ask him to look into Miguel's whereabouts, he surveyed the surrounding areas. If anyone had followed them, he couldn't spot them. He waited patiently, watching from across the road for her to come out of the police station. Evidently, they weren't too busy because after only fifteen minutes, she appeared in the entrance and staggered down the steps. He pulled his car out and she climbed back in, her face pale with grief.

"Did you tell them everything?"

She nodded in response, still quiet. Though her tears had seemed to slow down drastically, her face was puffy, and her eyes were desperate. What was she planning in that head of hers now? He'd find out for sure. But first, he had come up with a solution for her immediate breakdown. He glanced over as she sat silently beside him while he drove. She stared blankly out of the window. "Is that a swimsuit you have on under your clothes?"

She surprised him when she responded aloud. "Yeah. I wanted to look exactly like my sister."

"That was a bold move. And a very dangerous one, too. I've never seen you dressed so casually. I thought you were your twin. Anyone who has seen her would've bought it."

She gazed over at him, and he could see new tears welling up in her eyes. "Why would her necklace have been for sale, Gabe?"

He kept his voice steady. "It might've been stolen. What was the name of the store, anyway?"

"Island Gems."

Gabe felt his stomach drop. ISLAND GEMS was one of many local businesses owned by Victor Torrez.

26

The driver opened the Escalade door, and Ricardo stepped out onto the dirt drive, adjacent to the worn down-looking storage shed. That's where his captive would be waiting. He surveyed the isolated area, noting the main house, a poured concrete block, ranch-style, about fifty feet away. He kept it furnished and clean, though he rarely went inside the house.

The ocean was a quarter of a mile away, and the property was private thanks to the citrus trees that lined the borders in rows and the tall privacy fences he'd added after purchasing the bank-owned farm. Overgrown brush and rusted farm equipment from the previous owner were scattered around here and there, which Ricardo had decided to leave in place as well. From the outside looking in, no one would know how he had built a couple of prison-style cells within the crumbling shed and fortified the walls. Hardly anyone knew Ricardo had purchased the old citrus farm, and those who did knew better than to mention it to anyone. Only a select few knew Ricardo's actual intentions for the property, specifically the shed. Outside the city limits of San Juan, the property was the perfect place to hide someone. The perfect place for revenge.

Trevor pushed the shed door open and sauntered over, smiling at Ricardo. "*Señor* Rivera, so nice ta see you."

"I see you've finally gotten your affairs in order. I was beginning to worry."

"No worries, mon. I take the flight over dis aftanoon to check on tings. And jus' like I said, my guys got her here."

"How is she doing?" Ricardo joined in step with Trevor as they headed towards the small building. Ricardo knew Madeline had arrived a day ago, but business matters had made the trip impossible for him sooner.

"She ha no idea where she is or what she is doin' ya. She tink Miguel is behind dis. She very angry wit him."

"That's fine. Keep her in the dark about why she is here."

"*Señor* Rivera?" Trevor stopped abruptly in front of the door. "I was in St. Croix earlier today, and one of Torrez's guys says dat he saw de redhead, de sista dat is, walkin' out of a hotel in Christiansted. He tink dat it is Madeline, of course. If he's right, then she didn't heed the warning from Lukas. I need ta know what you wanna do bout it."

"Did he tell Miguel what he saw?"

"No. Miguel still in St. Thomas, but he want to tell him. But Miguel beat him up last time, so it wasna hard fa me ta convince him ta keep quiet. I tell him dat I would personally deliver da news to Miguel, so dat he could spare himself 'nother beatin'. If Raul had any sense he woulda taken ha picture or someting fa proof, but luckily fa me, he not so smart."

"Why wouldn't the sister have left? Lukas promised me he didn't hold back, and he said she returned her rental car and left St. Croix. She must be clever if she outsmarted him."

"Or maybe she's gettin' some help, *Señor* Rivera," Trevor rubbed his chin.

"Who would help her? I thought you knew everything that happened on St. Croix, Trevor. It's one of the reasons I hired you."

"Sorry mon, just an idea, of course. I'm sure she's not getting any help. She's jus got a death wish apparently. So do yo wan us to kill ha?" Trevor asked the question without emotion, as if he were bored with the topic.

Ricardo ignored the small churn in his stomach, and felt his fingers reaching for the antacids he kept in his pocket. He sighed, as he came up empty. Of all the times to run out. He wasn't used to talking about murder as if it were no more significant than the weather.

"No, but I can't have her messing up my plans. I want her out of the way. Just bring her here…alive. As soon as we're done here, make arrangements to get her. I'll decide what to do with her later. My plans coming to fruition are more important than anything else for the moment."

"Ya, mon. I'll even let Raul help locate ha. He'll do whateva I ask."

"Trevor, are you sure Miguel isn't suspicious of you?"

"No, mon. Miguel is on 'nother planet wit his mournin', and I been very careful every step of da way. No one knows I'm workin' fa you now, *Señor* Rivera."

"Good. Now, I'd like to see our new guest."

Trevor opened the door to the shed, and they stepped inside. A makeshift sitting area had been thrown together near the entrance. Luis, a skinny guy with short brown hair and crooked teeth sat beside a card table that had a portable TV perched on top. A small worn couch and a cot were the only other furniture, and a cooler was placed near Luis's feet. Dirt floors lined the shed, and the lighting was low, with just a couple of lamps in the corner and a lantern. The windows had been covered up, except for two, higher up on the walls, so hardly any light entered the space. In the rear, the prison cells lined the room on opposite sides, and a small outhouse style toilet was near them.

Luis looked up briefly, nodding his head at Ricardo, then resumed carving a piece of wood with his pocket knife. Ricardo didn't exactly trust him. Or the woman Trevor had hired to stay in the house and cook a few meals when asked to and help them out for the days ahead, but since committing a crime of this magnitude wasn't something he had experience with, he'd allowed Trevor to be in charge of hiring dependable help. Recruiting Trevor had taken some time, but it had been worth the wait. Trevor had worked for the Torrez family for years, and he knew the ins and outs of the criminal world. If Trevor said they could be trusted, Ricardo believed him.

Ricardo walked to the prison cell, straining to see the girl. Trevor held up a lantern, spilling light over her body. She was curled up on one side, unmoving on the dirt floor. Her hands and feet were bound in front of her, and layers of dirt and grime covered her face, arms, and legs.

"She's filthy. It's hard to imagine she's good-looking," Ricardo remarked.

"Mon, she still wearin' da same clothes she ha da accident in, and she been tied up fa days. We haven't exactly offered ha da spa treatment, but we gave ha wata to drink. Besides, she need to be in dis condition fa the video."

"Why is she still tied up?" Ricardo figured the bars were suitable enough to contain her. She appeared very fragile from where he was standing.

"Luis, *el cuello*," Trevor hollered.

Luis peered up for the second time and tilted his neck, gesturing towards the scratch marks with his knife. Ricardo glanced from the scratches to Madeline. "She did that?"

"Ya, mon. We had ta tie her up 'gain."

"Are you sure she's alive? We haven't even made the video yet."

"I tellin' ya, she fine, mon."

"Well, let's get this over with. I have a meeting to get to after this."

"Right away, sir." He snapped towards Luis. "Cámara, ahora, Luis."

As the doors to the prison opened, Ricardo stepped inside. He bent over the woman and tilted her head towards him, examining her face. Through the smear of dirt, he recognized her exquisite looks. Her hair was the color of fire with dark hues melded throughout. No wonder Miguel had been so enamored. Her eyelids fluttered open and her hazel eyes met his, instantly filling with fear.

"I must say, even in your condition, you are quite ravishing," Ricardo murmured.

"Go to hell," she whispered.

"I'm headed there already. But I'm taking a few people with me."

"Where is Miguel?"

"Miguel isn't here...yet. But don't worry. You'll see him soon enough. First, you're going to help us make a video."

"I won't. And I don't want to see him ever again...unless it's to kick his ass."

Ricardo was amused by her determination but needed to hurry things up. "I'm afraid you have no choice. You are the star of the video, sweet Madeline."

"Don't say my name like you know me. You're just another thug like Miguel and Trevor," she accused.

"I'd love to tell you a little more about myself. I know a lot about you already. And your sister. It would only be fair for me to open up about myself. Perhaps after your debut video has been made you will join me for dinner one evening. Of course, we would have to clean you up. You smell awful." Ricardo wrinkled his nose as he stood back up, releasing Madeline's head.

"What about my sister? You keep her out of this. Let me out of here already! Please," she finished with a sob.

He shook his head. "Just accept it, Madeline. This is happening, and you can't do anything about it. I look forward to dining with you. And seeing what Miguel loves so much about you...after you're cleaned up."

Hostility filled her expression. "I would never eat dinner with you."

Ricardo glanced over at Trevor, who was instructing Luis on where to stand with the camera. "I've changed my mind about staying, Trevor. I can't stand the smell of her. Or her lack of manners. Call me when it's done."

"Ya, mon." Trevor entered the prison now, reaching for Madeline, but she jerked her body and slammed him in the shins with her bound feet. Trevor lost his grip on her, and fell to his knees.

Ricardo hesitated by the cell entrance. "Are you sure you can handle this Trevor?"

Trevor jumped to his feet, grabbed Madeline by one arm and pelted his fist into her jaw. As she rolled away, moaning, Trevor turned to Ricardo. "I can handle it."

"Make sure you don't permanently damage that pretty face. I might be able to overlook her lack of respect after she's been cleaned up."

"Ya, mon. I'll let ya know when we finished."

"Thank you, Trevor."

Trevor reached for her again, as Ricardo pivoted and headed towards the door. He ignored her frantic screams and walked into the sunlight. He spared his driver a glance as he opened the door to the vehicle. "I need you to pick me up some antacids."

As the Escalade lurched forward, he retrieved an old photo from his wallet. His wife had been an exquisite beauty also. But she had been taken from him. Victor Torrez would soon be paying for his crimes.

27

Megan's frame was hunched lifelessly in the passenger seat.

"Listen, Megan. I know you're breaking down. But get out of the car. This won't solve all of your problems, but I promise it will help you feel a little bit better."

Megan straightened her back and gazed beyond Gabe's frame, where he stood holding the passenger door open. They'd detoured from the main road and driven down a seemingly vacant gravel road and pulled into the oceanfront cove just moments ago. He'd walked behind the car, opened the trunk, and shortly after opened her door, wearing a pair of dark blue swim trunks and the same t-shirt. He had a pair of faded beach towels in his hands.

On the drive, her tears had kept falling, and she felt worse than she had in her entire life. Not even her parents' death could top the despair she felt now, wondering what had happened to her twin. Even the police officer had seemed grim as he'd filed the official missing persons report after Megan had told him about finding her sister's necklace and even shown it to him. When she had asked if he thought the police could find who had taken her sister since she'd given him the store name where the necklace had been for sale, he had actually shrugged. *"People have a tendency to keep quiet around here, even if they know something…But we'll be asking questions."*

Gabe tapped on the roof of the car, and Megan knew she should respond. "Why would you bring me here?" Her distraught eyes met his for a moment before turning back to the cove.

The stretch of snow white sand curved a mile or so down and was enclosed by a variety of seashore vegetation, mostly shrubs of Seagrape, with green, leathery leaves, and varieties of Palms on one side. A pool of pristine water, the most breathtaking turquoise color she'd ever seen, lapped gently against the shore, and no one was around. It was like a photo out of National Geographic, but all Megan could think about was Maddy.

"Saltwater heals wounds...all kinds. Haven't you heard?"

"My sister's in trouble. Maybe being tortured by thugs as we speak. I've wasted the past hour crying. And now the police seem to think the worst about her. But I need to pull myself together and keep looking for her. I have to. I appreciate the gesture. I'm sure you didn't know what to do with me. But you can take me to town. I can't go swimming right now."

"I know you don't want to do this. This place is sort of a local secret. It's safe. And no one will be here in the middle of the week, this time of year. Just get in and get out if you must. But get in. If nothing else, it will help your tears dry up so you can get back to the search. I realize you're not going to stop looking for Maddy, and I don't blame you for that. But I saw you had the swimsuit on and when you couldn't stop crying for the past hour, I thought about what my grandmother would say."

Megan raised an eyebrow at him. "This is what your grandmother would suggest? Has she ever had a sister go missing?"

His hand tightened around the car door. "No, but she's lost loved ones too soon, and she knows about suffering and loss. She'd tell you to get in the water. She'd tell you there are healing properties in salt water and that it will refresh you, if nothing else, to help you keep going."

Megan sighed, reaching for his hand. As he pulled her up, she noted the jolt of electricity that shot through her limbs with his touch. She didn't want to feel anything for him. She wanted to think about her sister. How could he undo her like that with the simplest gesture?

She withdrew her hand from his and turned towards the ocean. The fresh sea scent enveloped her and the breeze swept over her skin, awakening her senses. She spared Gabe a glance. "Your grandmother sounds like a special lady."

Gabe nodded, "She is." Closing the door to the car, he motioned for Megan to go before him towards the beach. "Ladies, first."

"I suppose she taught you a few manners, as well," Megan said under her breath.

Gabe caught up with her as she peeled her flip-flop sandals off and started down the beach. "On the weekends, this place is kind of busy, mostly locals, but during the week, it's like our own personal beach. There's only one house up the cliff there, and it's mostly for season vacation rentals." Megan glanced up, peering into the hillside, barely seeing the roof of the home.

"I go to the beach every once in awhile back in Naples, you know. But not enough to keep an extra swimsuit and towels in the trunk of my car," she glanced at him as she spoke.

"I like to be prepared. This island has some amazing beaches. And I'm sure the ones in Naples are nice…but it's not the same as the Caribbean waters, I promise."

"What's this place called, anyway?"

A funny look, definitely sentimental, washed over his face. "Haypenny Beach," he said softly. Before she could dig further, he grinned. "Feel that sand between your toes? Just enjoy it for a moment. You never know when rain showers will pop up this time of year. You should go for a swim while you can."

With that, he dropped his shoes, the towels, and car keys into a pile on the sand, and tugged his t-shirt over his head. She caught her breath as her eyes scanned his torso. She told herself to breathe, but couldn't feel any air coming in. His stomach was sculpted, his solid chest spanned to his muscular arms, and there was a scar across one side of his ribcage. He looked like he'd stepped off the cover of Men's Health magazine. He pulled the band holding his hair out, dropped it onto the pile, and waves of black hair fell to his shoulders. He gave her a clipped nod, then ran into the water.

Megan paused, staring after him, torn between awe, annoyance, and curiosity. He wasn't anything like she'd initially suspected the day he had first approached her table at Captain Sully's. She'd thought for sure he'd be wild, reckless, and always on the lookout for his next good time, but he'd been nothing but helpful, seemingly calm, and genuinely nice. And though she felt for sure he wasn't out to hurt her, she sensed there was a world of pain and struggle below his teasing surface. But she had the feeling he wasn't about to open up to her. And as much as she appreciated everything he'd done to help her, the question still nagged at her mind…Why was he helping her?

She set her shoes down beside his and watched him diving through the water. After a moment he resurfaced and floated on his back, letting the waves rock him gently about. A peaceful expression rested on his face, and she let out a sigh.

Maybe he just felt sorry for her because he'd lost his parents, too. Maybe he was just a happy-go-lucky guy, with a painful past, taking it one day at a time…Sort of like Maddy.

At the thought of her twin, Megan took off Gabe's baseball cap, tore her shirt over her head, and yanked her jean shorts off. She unraveled her braided hair and dropped the hair tie on her clothes. She'd get in the water and go for a swim so Gabe would take her to town. She needed to continue her search. And maybe the water would cool her body temperature down. Watching Gabe run shirtless into the water had been too much. Maybe the salt water would cure her of her interest in him she mused. She dropped her sister's purse on top of her clothes and walked to the shoreline.

She waded a few feet in, instantly welcoming the caress of the warm, salty water. She pressed a hand to her emerald necklace as fresh tears stung her eyes. The waves coaxed as they swept against her shins, beckoning her to come closer. She felt the tension seeping away as her feet stepped further in. When she was far enough out, she dove headfirst under. She swam through the water, coming up on occasion for air, and after awhile she turned over, like Gabe had done earlier.

She gazed up at the blue Caribbean sky as she floated, and exhaled away some of the pain. Gabe's grandmother was right. There was something healing in the water.

28

Gabe gave her some space. He watched from a good thirty feet away as she drifted, occasionally flipping to dive under again. He prayed she would come to her senses and decide to go home, leaving the investigation to the police. Though he knew the police might not find much, especially if Torrez was behind Maddy's disappearance, he knew Megan would be safer if she left.

He'd hoped to talk to her about it after she left the police station, but when she'd climbed in the car and kept crying like she had, he realized she needed to let it out. And then suddenly, his grandma's old school solution to just about everything ailing a person hit him. Let the salt water do its thing.

In the car, Megan had argued there were better things to do with her time, and he had silently agreed, but his thinking was that her getting on a plane would be the better thing to do. And after dealing with the stubborn woman for a few days, he realized she wouldn't do that. But he figured trying to help her calm down, by making her go for a swim, would allow him the chance to try, once more, to convince her to leave.

Of course, he hadn't factored in the part about being so close to Megan while she was in a swimsuit. That hadn't been easy to process. The woman was breathtaking *with* her clothes on. One glance at her in the bikini had him wondering if his partner was right. He was in too deep, and unbeknownst to Megan, she was distracting him from his assignment.

Everything Smith had said to him was replaying in his mind. The longer Megan stayed on St. Croix, the better chance that someone would see her, and the threat from the German man would become a reality. Knowing what he did about the entire situation not only had Gabe feeling guilty, it had him convinced it was his duty to protect her while she was on St. Croix. The situation was getting more complicated by the minute, especially with his undeniable interest in her. When he'd taken her by the hand to help her out of the car, her touch had sent a spark through his body and he'd fantasized about pulling her into his embrace. That was so unlike him. It was unprofessional. The sooner she left, the better. He had work to do, and Megan getting killed would haunt him forever. He had enough ghosts to deal with as it was.

Gabe went under once more, relishing the feel of the salt water. His grandmother's advice had helped him as well. It was time to try to talk some sense into Megan. He waited until she started to walk out of the water herself, and once she did, he followed close behind. His heart rate accelerated at the sight of her in front of him, but he reminded himself he had a job to do. And getting distracted by her would be an amateur move. He caught up with her and grabbed the towels. He shook them out and tossed her the one with the least amount of sand on it.

"Thanks," she said lightly, then proceeded to wrap the towel around her body, and turned to look back at the ocean.

He dried off quickly, then stepped beside her. "Want to sit down for a minute?"

Her shoulders lifted and fell, and he plopped down where he was, resting his elbow on his knees in front of him.

She sat beside him and exhaled slowly. "I meant, thanks...not just for the towel. But for making me get in."

"No problem. It was as much for me as you."

"You been having a rough time lately?" she asked with mild sarcasm.

"Yeah, ever since you showed up, I've been a little stressed out, trying to keep you out of trouble," he replied with a small laugh.

Her expression sobered. "Trust me, I understand. I've spent the past seventeen years trying to keep my sister out of trouble, and evidently I've failed."

"I know a little more about that than you'd imagine," he admitted.

She gazed over and up at him curiously. "I understand not wanting to talk about the past. I hardly talk about my parents dying. Only with my grandma some."

"Does your grandma know you're here?" he prompted. Maybe if he could convince Megan that her grandmother needed her safe, she'd go home.

"Yes."

Gabe frowned. Apparently, that wasn't going to help further his case.

"But she doesn't know the truth," Megan confessed.

Gabe gave her an enquiring look. "Go on."

"Well, she's my only living relative…besides Maddy. And I didn't want to worry her. I told her I was finally taking a vacation. She's been on me to take time off for years. She was so relieved when I told her, I couldn't change my mind and tell her the truth. I haven't seen her that happy in a long time."

Gabe chose his words carefully. "Don't you think your grandmother would want you to make your safety a priority at this point? And for you to go home and continue the search for Maddy from there? You could contact every government agency under the sun. St. Croix is a United States territory. You can go about this in a safer manner, Megan. What would your grandmother say if she knew the truth?"

"I've already left messages with every agency I could. But she'd probably say all of the things you're saying."

"So, you'll go home?"

"Is that the real reason you brought me here? To talk me into leaving?"

"I'd be lying if I said it didn't have something to do with it. But I really did bring you here so you could get in the ocean. I hated seeing you like that. You stopped crying, didn't you?"

She studied him, and he felt his pulse beginning to rise. Her hair was drying in waves around her face. The sun had blushed her cheeks and the ocean had visibly relaxed her. She was calmer than before. Serene almost. Smith came blaring into his thoughts as he looked at her lips. Maybe he'd gotten too much sun himself.

After a few seconds, she glanced down. "Can I ask you something?"

Anything, he thought. He kept his face blank. "Sure."

"What did you mean when you said you could understand more than I'd think about trying to keep someone out of trouble?"

When he didn't reply, she went on. "I don't mean to pry, but ever since we met, I get the feeling you aren't telling me everything. I understand what it's like to lose your parents. I keep thinking maybe that's what it is…You don't want to talk about the past. But I'm curious I guess."

Gabe saw the sincerity in her eyes and decided he could part with a little more of the truth. Especially, if it would help her make the right decision. The decision to leave St. Croix. "You know how I mentioned my parents dying?"

"Yeah."

"Well, that same night, my sister and her friend died, too."

Gabe watched as his words sunk in and Megan's face blanched. "Was it an accident?"

He shook his head. "No."

"They were murdered?" She asked the question so softly, he barely heard it.

He intertwined his fingers, turning his head towards the ocean. "Abigail was my older sister. When she was fifteen, she became addicted to heroin. I was twelve at the time. My parents were wealthy and respected in the community. They did everything they could to cover up their daughter's addiction and tried to get her help. But she wouldn't…or couldn't take it. I watched it destroy our family, but I was young and so naïve. I kept trying to save her. Every time she came home to steal more money from Mom and Dad, I'd try to convince her to stay or give rehab another chance. But it never worked. The night they were murdered, I was upstairs in my room, trying to sleep. I was so excited about my basketball tryouts the next day, I wasn't thinking about my addict sister or our family drama for once."

Gabe glanced over at Megan, whose eyes were wide as she held onto each word. "Anyway, I heard all of these voices downstairs and started to investigate. Before I got too far, I saw them hurt my dad. Abigail was there with two guys, one was her boyfriend, the other I didn't know. My dad saw me and motioned for me to get out of there. I was sure he wanted me to call the police, and that's what I decided I'd do. But I didn't make it to the phone in time."

Gabe felt Megan's hand cover his own, squeezing it. He swallowed. "I have this reoccurring nightmare about that night. Even after twenty years. The police never closed the case. Abuela knew I would be in danger if we stayed, so she took me, and we never came here after that. I guess that's why I keep trying to convince you to leave. I don't mean to sound like your sister is gone. I only know how the justice system here failed me. Bad people do bad things, and sometimes it's not easy, or possible, to stop them."

"I'm sorry about your family, Gabe."

"It's fine. It's been twenty years."

"And you're still looking for your family's murderer, aren't you? That's why you came back here isn't it?"

"In a way, I guess. I'm looking for something."

"Thanks for sharing that with me. I know it couldn't have been easy. I won't tell anyone what you told me. I can tell you don't talk about it often. Is this beach one you came to with your family? Is that why you seemed sentimental when I asked about the name?"

"You're perceptive. Yeah, once upon a time, we lived in that house up on the cliff."

She shuddered. "My parents died in an accident. I can't imagine if my family was murdered. You seem pretty together for someone who's had to deal with so much. Some people would've decided to give up. I think it's amazing you haven't stopped looking for answers."

"Most people wouldn't call that amazing. They'd call it a waste of time."

"I wouldn't."

She pulled her hand away and dropped it in her lap, fixing her eyes on the water. "Megan, I'm not trying to scare you, but not just because of what happened to my own family so long ago…But I've heard things about crime around the island. And something happened to your sister, you know that now for sure. What will it take for you to leave and let the authorities look for Maddy?"

"I'm not leaving without her."

She stood up, brushing the sand from her towel. He rose to stand beside her, watching her closely. Her mind was racing again he could tell.

She stepped towards him. "I won't ever stop looking. We might have a lot more in common than I ever would have suspected."

He felt his heart racing in his chest and told himself to step backwards. She was leaning entirely too close to him. The way she was looking up at him had him confused. If he didn't know better, he'd think she was drawn to him. But she'd made it quite clear there was no attraction between them, at least on her part. He was her sister's type. She'd told him twice. Not that he was keeping track. He was the one with an attraction to her. And he intended to get over it, and soon.

He focused on his words. "The difference is, I don't have anything to lose, Megan. I've spent twenty years trying to find answers and it's robbed me of actually living. I'm thirty-five now. You're a lot younger. You have the chance to walk away before things get worse here. Don't make the same mistakes I've made. I'm frying eggs day in and day out. Looking for answers on a cold case. You have a life back in Naples. And a grandmother waiting for you to come home."

"I'm twenty-eight-years-old. I can make my own decisions. And you have a grandma, too, as I recall." She lifted a hand, resting it against his chest. He wondered if she could feel his pulse beating. It was speeding up by the second.

"She understands the choices I've made."

"You're wrong about one thing."

"How's that?"

"I don't have a life back in Naples. Maddy was right about me. It took her disappearing for me to accept the truth…I don't have a life at all," her voice hitched.

He took a deep breath. "It's not too late for you to fix that."

"Maybe not," she said noncommittally.

Her gaze moved to his mouth and he told himself he was hallucinating even as she leaned up on her toes and kissed him. As her lips brushed against his, all of the rational reasons he could come up with to end the kiss faded away. And then a murmur escaped her mouth, and he caved. He leaned down, letting his hands wrap around her waist and pulled her closer. Her hands slid up his chest and around his neck, and his heart nearly exploded. He let the kiss go on longer than he should have, and after a moment, he forced himself to be realistic. Megan MacKenna wasn't his. She was kissing him, yes, but it was probably as a result of being tortured by the German man, finding her sister's necklace, and her near nervous breakdown. And if he was going to keep her alive, he needed to treat her like any other person on a case. But as her fingers wove into the hair at the nape of his neck and her lips parted a little more, he lost his concentration.

Before he could bring himself to end the kiss, she pulled away. His breathing was ragged, and a surprised expression covered her blushing face. "Sorry about that. I don't know what I was thinking." Embarrassed, she retreated a step.

Gabe didn't want to alarm her. He wished he could tell her the kiss was fine. It was amazing. But he couldn't. He needed to get her to the airport. Away from St. Croix and away from him. "You probably just got a little too much sun," he blurted.

Megan seemed to be in a daze. She picked up her belongings and started towards the car. "Yeah, too much sun," she mumbled. "Can we leave now?"

He noted the sudden sharpness in her voice. His thoughts were frazzled. *Focus, man. It was only a kiss, and you need to keep her alive.* "So I can take you to the airport?" he called out, jogging to catch up with her.

"No. I may have gotten sun poisoning or something, but I'm not leaving St. Croix until I find Maddy. You can drop me at my hotel and go back to your life though. I've probably interrupted it enough already."

She had no idea. "Oh, I'm beginning to get used to it."

As she cast him a dry look, he unlocked the car and opened her door for her. As he walked around the vehicle, his thoughts returned to Smith. His partner may have been right. Maybe he was allowing his attraction to Megan to mess up his focus. The sooner she was off of St. Croix, the better for both of them. He would ask Smith to help him convince Megan to return to Florida. Whether she was ready to or not, he was going to make her leave.

29

Maddy awoke to a throb in her head that traveled from her beaten, swollen eye and shot throughout her broken body. Panic swept over her as she recalled how the rope slashed against the flesh of her wrists and ankles, binding her to the chair, and the moment the red light on the camera had illuminated. As unwelcome memories flooded her thoughts so did the realization she had survived.

They didn't kill me...yet.

She shuddered from the reminder of the inevitable. Though his face had been covered with a ski mask, the pleasure in Trevor's eyes before he had raised his fist to punch her confirmed her biggest fear: He would have no problem killing her. She willed herself to think of something other than the bloodlust in his eyes and focused on her immediate situation.

From the hard dirt floor of her prison, she took a slow steady breath and was struck by the overwhelming stagnant, musty air. It made her think of the livestock barn at the farm her grandparents had worked in Florida, minus the strong scent of animals. She and Meg had been brought up helping out on that property, and the scents, among other things about farm life, would never leave her memories. Yet, the unrelenting heat of the small space was unlike any she had felt before. And Meg had been with her at the farm. Coping with the aftermath of their parents' accident had been tolerable with her sister. But the walls of her prison would never see Meg. Maddy was all by herself, and she was entirely to blame.

The throbbing at her temple seemed to grow, and she wished for

Excedrin. Or a bottle of the Cruzan Rum Miguel enjoyed so much. It had been sixteen months since her last drink, but offered the potent island rum right now, she could imagine herself guzzling it. Maybe it would numb the pain and soothe her increasing fear.

What were they going to do with her? Why had they filmed her beating? And who was the video intended for? Was it a ransom? Maddy was as broke as it got. Why would anyone kidnap her for a ransom? The only person she knew with money was Meg, but how could these people, whoever they were, know about Meg? As her thoughts came back, she remembered how the older man had mentioned her sister. They knew something about Meg, but even so, Meg was well off, but she wasn't super rich. There had to be another reason.

Time and again, Meg had warned her about serial killers and psychopaths she read about in novels or saw on episodes of Dateline. Women were kidnapped, sold as sex slaves, killed on camera for psychopaths, she had heard it all. If she knew which scenario was hers, perhaps she could try to accept her fate. And if Miguel wasn't behind this, as Trevor had informed her with a smug expression, then who were these people?

She hadn't understood the Spanish Trevor, and his sadistic sidekick, Luis, had spoken throughout the filming, but she had stopped caring when the potent taste of blood had filled her mouth. Crying had seemed futile after that. No matter how she screamed or begged Trevor to stop, he'd kept going. His calloused hands on her neck had squeezed until she was sure she would die. Maddy was the star of their show, but clueless to their intentions and had turned to prayer, begging for an out of body experience. At last the small red light on the end of the video camera had faded away, and so had she.

Maddy's ribs ached, and she felt the sting of cuts across her face and body. But she wasn't dead. She vaguely recalled Trevor's hot breath on her ear at one point whispering to her before she fell unconscious, that if she survived, they might feed her and clean her up. Had that happened, or was she imagining the memory? She wasn't sure how much time had passed since she had eaten, but more than anything, she craved water.

She fought through the pain and pushed herself up to a seated position, shocked to discover her hands and feet were no longer bound, though the rope-burn lingered. With her palms pressed to the ground she edged closer to the front of her prison and peered through the bars with her uninjured eye. No sign of Trevor. Luis was at the table drinking beer, focused on a small TV screen. Maddy figured it was just her luck she would get guarded by the man whom she couldn't communicate with. Her mouth felt like it was made of cotton balls. What she would give for a drink of water.

"Hey, Luis," she croaked.

If he heard her, he made no indication of it. She tried again. "Excuse me, I'm thirsty. Can I get some water, please?"

He cast an annoyed glance over his shoulder and turned back to the TV screen. Maddy's voice dipped with desperation. "Por favor, can I get some water?"

He still ignored her.

"Luis, agua. Por favor!" she pleaded.

He twisted around in his seat. "Cállate!"

Maddy's voice hardened. "Agua. Agua, por favor!"

Her tone must have struck a chord. Luis got up from the table and retrieved a bottle of water from the cooler. He stalked over to her cell and stopped, clearing his throat as he looked down at her. "Quieres agua, bonita?"

Maddy's heart sped up as their eyes met. "Sí, por favor."

He shrugged his shoulders and unscrewed the bottle cap. Maddy's hopes soared as she waited for him to give her the water. It would make the hell she was living somehow bearable, if just for a moment. Luis knelt down on the other side of the bars and reached the bottle through, but inches before Maddy could grab the bottle, he stood up. With the flip of his wrist, he poured the water out on the ground near his feet.

"No, no, no," Maddy protested, trying to get closer to the water. But it was too late. The water soaked into the ground, mixing with the dirt, just a foot out of her grasp.

Luis's snicker squashed out all hope left. "Cállate, mujer."

He tossed the empty bottle through the bars and trekked to his chair in front of the TV. As it rolled towards Maddy, she clutched onto it. Her lip quivered as the plastic touched her mouth. A single drop fell onto her chafed and bruised lips.

A tear slid down her cheek and stung as it hit one of her cuts. "Please, God, please send…" A sob escaped her lips, and she wiped another tear. "Send someone to find me." She moaned as her head clouded with reality and overall despair. "I'm so sorry, Meg. I'm sorry."

Maddy curled into a ball and closed her eyes tight. She had never been so scared in her life.

If only she had listened to Meg.

30

Buckets of rain beat down on the streets, causing drainpipes and gutters to overflow and steam to rise from the pavement. Through the windshield wipers beating frantically back and forth, Gabe noted the closing up of shops as the business day drew to an end and nighttime bars and restaurants opened. His stomach rumbled, reminding him he hadn't eaten since his break earlier that morning at Captain Sully's. He glanced over at Megan, realizing she probably hadn't eaten either. Maybe that's another reason she'd kissed him. She'd been weak from lack of food...

As the rain fell, his mind drifted. He toyed with the idea of not feeding her. If it meant she'd kiss him like *that* again...He'd never been so attracted to someone. He knew it was wrong. He had a strict policy against long-term relationships. He was too focused on solving his family's murder to give someone like Megan the type of love she deserved. It hadn't been an issue before. Sure, Abuela and Smith had teased him for the past few years especially that he needed to let go of the past and give a relationship a chance. But he'd never met anyone he'd want to risk losing himself and his life's purpose over. Ever since the night his family had been killed, he'd known what he had to do. So he'd stuck to his plan to bring Torrez down, regardless of the cost.

But Megan was an unexpected development. There was something there. Yet he knew he couldn't act on his feelings for her. This was new for him. It scared him. If she hadn't ended the kiss, would he have been able to?

He shook the thought off. Fantasizing about the kiss wasn't good for either of them. He needed to protect her. And ever since they'd left the beach, she'd been a little awkward with him. He figured it was because of how he'd reacted to her kiss. He hadn't said anything other than, *You probably got a little too much sun.* If he'd told her the truth, that she had nothing to be embarrassed about because he wanted to kiss her, it wouldn't have made the situation any easier. At least she wasn't sobbing anymore.

"Have you eaten today?"

"I had a granola bar this morning on my search for Maddy."

Just the opening he needed. The woman might have knocked his socks off with her kiss, but she was too stubborn for her own good. If he could make her see how rash she'd been, maybe she'd leave. So he could stop worrying about her. "You mean your reckless stunt? When you were supposed to be staying in the room?"

The corner of her mouth tilted up. "Come on, it was a good plan... in theory."

Irritation flickered through him. "If you were trying to get killed."

She smirked. "I'm just trying to find Maddy."

Gabe focused on the road, watching as tires splashed water across the roadway. It was a true Caribbean downpour. She'd been too upset earlier for him to question her. He wanted to know more. Any of the dozens of Torrez men could have seen her parading around as her twin. "You never told me where you went today, exactly."

He spared her a glance. From her expression, he could tell she was keeping something from him. "Megan...where did you go?"

"Oh, around. I mean, when you saw me, I'd been in over a dozen tourist shops downtown. And earlier, I was in more of a local area I think. But don't worry, no one recognized me," she said defeatedly.

He tried to ignore her disappointment. If someone had recognized her as her twin, they could've taken her. And he wouldn't have had a clue that she'd even left her room or known where to start looking for her. The more he knew about her day, the easier it would be to see how much she had jeopardized her safety. If her hotel had been compromised, he'd need to move her. "What sort of a local area? You walked there from the hotel?"

"No. I took a taxi. The driver suggested it, and I realized I hadn't looked there yet. I think it was called Golden Rock."

"You went to Golden Rock?" his voice was anxious.

"Yeah, I went to a grocery store, called PUEBLO, I think. And to a pharmacy."

"That is definitely not a tourist area. Definitely local," he huffed.

Megan folded her arms across her chest. "Well, that was my point. My sister would have hung out at local places. I was trying to think like she would."

"Next time you decide to do something like that, I'm going with you."

Megan tilted her head towards him. "Why? Aren't you tired of helping me yet? You've got your own agenda to get back to, right?"

Gabe's eyes darkened. "Why can't you understand that I want to help you stay out of trouble?"

"Just because it's the right thing to do?" she shot back, hostilely.

"Why, yes, as a matter of fact."

"I suppose I could thank your grandmother for instilling such a sense of decency in you, too?"

Gabe's blood pressure elevated as he noted the haughty arch of her eyebrow and her condescending tone. Here he was trying to keep her alive, and she wasn't even a little concerned about the danger she'd put herself in earlier. "Well, sure, I'd give you my grandma's address if I thought you'd leave St. Croix. You can go thank her in person."

"From the man who has spent twenty years looking for answers," she muttered.

"I've learned a lot along the way."

"I'm sure. But as I said earlier, I am a grown woman. And I know you're trying to make sure I don't make the same mistakes you think you've made, but let it go. My sister hasn't even been gone for two weeks yet. And now that I've had my mini breakdown, I am thinking more clearly. I have to find her. I would sense if she were gone. There's no doubt about that. I am the only one who truly believes she is alive, and I refuse to tuck my tail and run."

"Even with men trying to drown you in bathtubs?"

"Thanks for the reminder."

"It should be the only thing you're thinking of right now. If he finds out you're still here—"

"Enough, Gabe. Just drop it," she interrupted.

He grasped the steering wheel tighter, his mind raced with worries. He really needed to get Megan to leave so he could get back to his case. The thought of keeping her alive without blowing his cover was becoming too stressful. And even though it might be the easiest way to get her to understand how much danger she was actually in, he could not tell her the truth. Not yet. Maybe not ever.

As he neared the hotel, he considered all of his options, finally deciding that the most practical one, since she refused to go home, would be to get her to a different island. Specifically, St. Thomas, where he could drop her at the undisclosed FBI office. That's where Smith could help. He could get their FBI contact in St. Thomas on board. With everything she knew now, including the discovery of her sister's necklace, they'd have enough to open a missing persons investigation. He'd worry about her roaming around St. Thomas, since Torrez senior was based there, but he trusted the local FBI team. They'd keep an eye on her and maybe even convince her to go home and leave the investigation to them. And even if she were to explore St. Thomas, there was year round cruise ship traffic coming in and out on a daily basis, so she could blend in much easier out on the streets. If he could just get her to St. Thomas, he'd never even have to tell her who he was. He prayed it would work. He could keep up his cover, get her safely into their custody, and return to St. Croix to bury himself in busting the Torrez Empire.

He'd call Smith, so he could make contact with the local FBI team and let them know they were headed that way. It wasn't the best plan, seeing as how he actually had to get her to St. Thomas, but it could work. He'd make it work. She would be much safer. And most importantly, she wouldn't be sticking out like a sore thumb when a professional hit man might be searching for her.

"So, are you dropping me off at the side entrance again, so I can sneak up to my room?"

"That's the idea. I think it's best if you avoid the front entrance so fewer people who work there will notice you. Honestly, it would be best if we at least switched your room tonight and maybe even hotels. In case anyone came asking questions today about you."

"If you think it would be wise, that's fine," she replied easily.

Gabe glanced in her direction to see if she was messing with him. "It is?"

"I know we don't see eye to eye about every move I make, but I understand you're trying to get me to make better decisions about my safety. If you think I should switch rooms or hotels, I will."

She was being awfully agreeable all of a sudden. She looked amicably back at him and he turned ahead, satisfied she was accepting his advice for a change. Maybe she wasn't trying to get killed. Maybe getting her to St. Thomas would be easier than he thought. "I do. And I think you should eat, so—"

He slowed the car, watching a familiar pair of guys descending the front steps of Megan's hotel, talking as they hurried away. As he watched them disappear into the alleyway, he turned the car in the opposite direction.

"Gabe? What's wrong? I thought you were dropping me off."

"Megan, this morning when you left your hotel, where did you pick up that taxi? Did you have the hotel clerk call you one?" His voice was low and steady.

"Um…no, actually I just came out front and flagged one down."

Gabe's heart slammed in his chest. "I think someone saw you leave the hotel."

"How do you know?"

"Remember how I told you earlier I'd heard some rumors about some of the local crimes and people involved?"

"Yes," she replied, her voice tight.

"I just saw two of those people walking down the steps of your hotel. I don't know if it is related to you, but I need to make sure it's not."

She tilted her head to peer out the back window, then back to him. "Shouldn't we call the police?"

"And tell them what? Your breakfast cook friend, who they don't even know is helping you, saw some guys that look like local criminals leaving your hotel?"

"Well when you put it that way, it doesn't sound like the best idea."

"I'll take your room key. I'll get your stuff, and you can stay at my place for tonight." As soon as he said it, he saw her face blushing and he regretted it. "I'll sleep on the couch. Or you can stay in a different hotel. I just want you to be safe."

She nodded, scrutinizing the streets around them. When she didn't speak, he went on. He didn't want to tell her what he was planning, but he needed to get her tucked away someplace safe ASAP. "I'll leave you at my place for now, while I go investigate. When I get back, if you're uncomfortable, I'll get you to a hotel."

He could hear Smith telling him not to let her stay at his place, but Smith wasn't there. And he had no idea how much danger Megan was in. If Gabe could just keep her alive and get her to St. Thomas in the morning, he could focus on his assignment.

After a few turns, he veered the car into a small gravel drive that wove behind a small apartment building. True to island weather, the rain shower stopped abruptly as he steered the car down the drive. Fortunately, the covered space he parked in was only a few feet from his door. He turned the ignition off and turned to Megan. He reached for her cap and tugged it over a stray lock of red hair. He climbed out of the car, shuffled to her side and took her hand, quickly leading her to the door.

Once inside the small studio apartment, he locked the bolt and nudged her towards the sofa. "Have a seat."

He went right to his dresser in the corner and retrieved a set of dry clothes and a dark baseball cap, bending over to grab a pair of steel-toed boots. He went to the bathroom, changed within thirty seconds and placed a few supplies he might need in his pant pockets, and trotted over to Megan. "Can I have your room key?"

She handed it over without a word, and Gabe could almost read her frenzied thoughts. She was worried about him. But he'd be worried about him, too, if he were her. He was, after all, one of the only people trying to help her. He tucked the key into his pocket.

"I won't be gone long. Make yourself at home. There's water and some food in the fridge. Lock the door behind me. Do not answer the door for anyone but me."

"Gabe, wait."

He paused beside the door. "Yeah?"

"Are you sure this is a good idea? What if that German guy is there? What if they found out my room number?"

He didn't want to tell her what he suspected. There was no reason to alarm her further, when he had gotten her to agree to wait at his place for him. Here, he knew she'd be safe. There were iron bars covering the windows, and there was a good bolt on the door. "I'm just going to ask the front desk some questions. And I'll get your stuff and check out. Just to be safe. I'm sure no one is there."

She stood up from the sofa, her face worried. "OK. But Gabe, please be careful. That guy was really scary."

"No worries. Bolt the door behind me."

She nodded, and he left the apartment. He took off down an alley in a jog, splashing in puddles of rainwater that had collected here and there. He was only a couple of blocks from the hotel if he took the alleyway. His gun was tucked into his ankle holster, hidden below his jeans. He'd talk to the front desk if needed to, but first he'd go directly to Megan's room, where if his instincts were right, he'd find a hit man, with a German accent.

But this time, Megan wouldn't be the one walking through the door.

31

With each step further down the mildew scented corridor, adrenaline rushed to Gabe's extremities. Seeing Raul walking away from the hotel with one of Torrez's recently hired men had to mean they'd found her. But of course, they wouldn't handle the job themselves. Torrez would want to be sure none of his team could be linked to any investigations that could pop up. So like before, he'd send in a professional. A contract killer.

He'd taken the side entrance, and since the hotel wasn't equipped with security cameras, hadn't been overly concerned with being seen. But he kept his cap low over his face. He paused on one side of the door as he prepared to go in. Whoever was waiting, would be expecting Megan alone. And if the threat he'd given Megan the day before had been true, then the man was preparing to kill her. Gabe's pulse quickened as he pushed the thought aside. He'd go in, find out who the man was working for, more than likely one or both of the Torrez men, and handle the situation.

His fingers flexed around the gray and black gun in his hands. He counted down silently, concentrating on his job. He slid the keycard in and out, and pushed the door open, his weapon drawn and ready to fire.

The moment his foot crossed the threshold, a huge figure torpedoed into his side, and he lost the grip on his gun. Arms wrapped around his waist and tackled him to the ground. Gabe reacted at once and pushed his attacker off and rolled away. He staggered to his feet and turned to search for his weapon right as the man's fist pounded into his jaw. He took a hit, then dodged two more as the man swung out, fast and hard.

He pivoted and spied his gun a few feet across the floor. As he started for it, the man punched him in the gut, taking Gabe's breath away. Though he was stunned from the blow, he made himself move. He had to take this guy down.

Gabe focused on the man and spotted his opening and landed three solid jabs in his ribs. He wasn't sure if he was doing much damage, as the man's ribs and stomach felt like a steel cage to his fists, but threw one punch after another. When he thought of how Megan could've walked into the room instead of him, Gabe pounded even harder...uppercut, jab, cross. He watched the blood spray from the man's face, and he knew he was breaking him down.

Just when he thought his opponent was subdued, a blade appeared in his hands. He swiped in anger at Gabe, and the six-inch knife narrowly missed Gabe's waist. Sweat trickled down his body. The man kept slashing, his skill not as impressive as his strength. But the man was powerful. In the corner of Gabe's eye, he glanced at the gun, lying useless beside the bed, but the man was blocking him just enough. If only he could get to it before the knife stabbed him.

His stalker stepped closer, raising the knife. Gabe ducked, missing the blade by a hair from his torso.

"Who do you work for?" Gabe demanded.

The man gave a cold smile. "You won't live long enough to find out." His voice was thick with an accent. German or Austrian. Megan had been right. On the bed, Gabe noticed the duct tape, and he realized it had been intended for Megan. "Did Miguel send you here? Victor? You were going to hurt her again? You'll pay for this."

The man grunted as he lunged forward, wielding the knife towards Gabe with murder in his eyes. Gabe jumped out of the way but not enough. He moaned as the knife tore through the skin of his upper arm. Too close, he thought. "Tell me who you're working for," Gabe repeated.

The stranger wiped blood away from his nose. "It's too bad you didn't send the girl in here. I was looking forward to the time alone I was going to spend with her. I wasn't sent to kill you, but now I have no choice."

Gabe coiled his leg and drove his foot with a sidekick into the stranger's chest, knocking him flat. He jumped over his attacker's body and reached for the gun. His fingers stretched forward, but he was yanked in reverse the next moment by his neck.

The man wrapped an arm around Gabe's torso while the other descended towards his stomach. Gabe used his free hand to push the lowering blade away.

Sweat trickled down Gabe's face as he watched the knife hover inches from his chest. He thought of his grandmother telling him to stop chasing the past before it was too late. Then he thought of what might have happened if Megan had opened the door instead of Gabe. Every ounce of him wanted to protect her. No one would hurt her. He wouldn't allow it. Seconds before the blade slashed into his belly, adrenaline surged through him, and he moved over a couple of inches.

It was all that it took. Gabe shrugged the weight of the man off of him and watched as he collapsed to the floor. Blood saturated the man's shirt as he clutched the knife in his stomach.

"Do you work for Torrez?" Gabe tried again. It was his last chance.

The man's eyes glazed over as his chin drooped to the side.

He was dead.

32

Within minutes, Gabe had left the room, after he made sure there were no obvious traces of him left behind. He'd swept over the room to wipe his prints and been relieved to see the meticulously organized Megan had left all of her belongings zipped up in her small suitcase, stashed in the corner of the room. Not a drop of blood had hit her bag. The floor, on the other hand, was another story. But he wouldn't need to worry about that.

He'd used a new burner phone he'd carried in his pocket to take a photo of the dead hit man's face. He'd lifted the man's fingerprint with the small reel of tape he'd brought and taken a photo. He'd sent the photos to Smith, then phoned him briefly, filling him in on what needed to be done. He'd worked fast. And been thorough.

Smith would send a cleanup crew at once to get rid of the body because the agency had no choice but to keep Gabe's cover intact. They'd get rid of the body before Torrez or anyone could come looking for their man. Gabe had taken Megan's bag but opted not to check her out. She'd paid in cash under a fake name, so they wouldn't have a paper trail to show she'd been there. She would just disappear before they could send someone else to take her out. More than ever, Gabe wished he could tell her the truth, so she could realize the gravity of her situation. These people wanted her dead. But he couldn't break his cover. All he could do was keep her safe and get her away from St. Croix. Gabe had killed their hit man, but they'd send more until the job was finished. That's how Torrez worked. All threats were taken out. Period.

Gabe knew the higher ups in the DEA wouldn't be thrilled he'd intervened and left a body for them to dispose of. But if the hit man was connected to the Torrez family, like Gabe suspected, they'd probably take the disappearance of Miguel's girlfriend and the threat on Megan's life a little more seriously. Gabe worried that they'd want to talk to Megan and ask her to approach Victor wearing a wire, but he wouldn't let them. His plan to get her to St. Thomas was the best way to keep her safe for now.

He felt a headache coming on as he hurried down the obscure alley, realizing how quickly the man would've killed her. The thought of her dying filled him with anxiety he hadn't experienced in ages. If he'd turned down the street a moment later, he wouldn't have seen the guys leaving her hotel. It had been too close. Things were escalating, and it frayed his nerves. He pulled a new burner from his cargo pocket and dialed Smith. He'd already destroyed the one with the photos after sending them.

Smith was expecting one more call and picked up immediately. "Everything's in place. Cleanup guy is en route."

"Thanks," Gabe spoke softly, slowing his pace.

"But I'm not happy about this."

"I figured."

"What's your next move, Mr. Fry Cook? Do you even know? Are you gonna call me tomorrow with another dead body you need taken care of? What's happening, man?"

"I know you're pissed."

"Do you? Because I'm pretty sure you don't know how much."

"I saw a bad situation getting ready to unfold, and I handled it. You would've done the same."

"Maybe."

Gabe held back a laugh. He knew Smith would've reacted the same. He was only angry because once again, he couldn't watch over his partner. "I only came out with a nick. No worries."

"Does this nick require stitches?"

"Not this time."

"So what now? We could send some agents to approach Megan, and you could walk away if you wanted. Or you could come clean with her if you convinced her to wear the wire."

"No. I have a plan actually. I took a few days off work, so I won't be missed. Tomorrow morning, first thing, I'm getting her out of here."

"Where are you taking her?"

Gabe lowered his voice to a whisper. "To our pal Hartford's office."

"The FBI office on St. Thomas?"

"Yep. I think dropping her there and walking away is the safest solution so I can focus on my job and she can get the help she needs. She's got enough evidence for them to open an official investigation now."

"That's the best thing you've said in days. I'll contact Hartford and tell him your plans. They'll be ready to help her."

"Thanks. Did you find anything out about our guy?"

"Yeah, Miguel's been at his dad's place for a few days. A lot of people coming and going, but he hasn't left at all."

"Is there any chance they have the sister there?"

"Surveillance hasn't seen her. They've seen lots of women but not her. But it doesn't mean she's not there."

"I'll check in when I can."

"Take care of that nick, OK?"

"OK."

"And—"

"I know, I know…try not to get shot."

"Exactly. If I had hair, it would all be gray, thanks to you."

"Just doing my part."

"Speaking of your generous heart, where was Megan while you were handling the situation?"

Gabe paused a little too long. Smith sighed. "You're kidding me. At your place, man?"

"Just for one night."

"Uh-huh."

"I didn't have a choice. He would've killed her. I have to go. I'll check in soon to see if you've identified the guy."

As Gabe hung up, he lifted the suitcase onto one shoulder, and picked up his pace the rest of the way to his apartment. He would try not to obsess about how the hit man could have attacked Megan instead of him. Or how his feelings for her were clouding his concentration and making him panic. He'd tell her whatever she needed to hear so she'd agree to go to St. Thomas in the morning. All he had to do was get through the night. Once he reached the door, he gave it a light tap and called out in a soft voice to Megan. "It's Gabe."

The door opened at once, and he ducked inside without a sound.

***

Trevor's newest recruit pulled out his cell phone. He scuffled past the apartment he'd seen the man with the suitcase go into but noted the number.

Trevor answered right away. "Talk ta me."

"Hey T, after Raul and I got her room number for you, I went back later to watch her hotel room like you said to see when Lukas and the girl left. I might have been too late. I didn't see them leave, but I saw some guy I don't know leave with a suitcase. And I followed him to an apartment not far from the hotel."

"Did you get his photo?"

"No, I didn't think to."

"Neva mind. But you neva saw Lukas or da gurl?"

"No. Do you think this guy was helping Lukas?"

"I don know. Lukas hasna checked in yet. Meybe he already left wit ha. But I didna know he had a partna for dis one."

"What should I do now?"

"Watch da guy. Follow him whereva he go. First thing in the marnin' I'll tell ya wat ta do. I'll track down Lukas."

"Sure thing, boss."

When he hung up the phone, he sighed. Of course Trevor would want him to sit outside all night and watch some man's apartment. He circled back to the alley and found a dumpster to lean against that would allow him a view of the door. He tugged his hat down over his face and pulled a joint from his jacket pocket, lighting it in the shadows.

He took a long drag and exhaled it slowly. Being one of Trevor's new recruits meant he had to take every undesirable assignment until he proved himself. Thunder rumbled in the distance. A storm would roll in soon, making the alley all that more uncomfortable. But he had to prove to Trevor that he could handle anything he gave him. It was the only way to make it onto the Torrez team. The money would be good, and his kids would consistently have food on the table. A rat crept into view a few feet away, gnawing on leftover food that hadn't made it into the dumpster. He took another hit off his joint. It was going to be a long night.

33

Megan stared at the cut on Gabe's arm, and a shiver trailed her spine. "Your arm. What happened?"

"It's just a scratch. I was walking down a dark alley. I couldn't quite see where I was going." Gabe locked the dead bolt and placed the chain across the door. He strode over to the bathroom and set her suitcase down. Turning to her, his eyes widened. "Are you alright?"

"Yeah, I'm just on edge. What happened? Did you talk to anyone at the front desk?"

"Yeah. It's a good thing I saw those guys leaving the hotel. The front desk said they were asking about you."

She nodded because she knew it made sense. She'd strolled out in the open that morning in plain view. Someone had seen her. But her anxiety was increasing by the second. "Well, that's not good. But at least they weren't in the room waiting for me."

She noted how Gabe's jaw tensed and wondered what he hadn't told her. "Were they, Gabe?" She glanced at his arm again. It was a sizable scratch if she'd ever seen one. "Did they do that to your arm?"

"No. But there is something else. The front desk said another man came looking for you today. With a funny sounding accent," his voice was strained.

"Funny?"

"I asked them if it was German and they agreed it probably was."

Megan's stomach did a flip-flop. She crossed to the sofa and sank into it. "That's definitely not good," she said weakly. "Do you think anyone followed you here?"

"No. I think the threat is gone. For the moment."

Her mind had been racing the entire twenty-three minutes he'd been gone. "I wanted to ask you something. Earlier, when you saw those guys in front of the hotel you said they were local criminals. How do you know who they are?"

He tossed his hands up. "I've heard things since I've been back. I've been looking into the past to find some answers of my own, like I told you. One of those guys for sure has been involved with a well-known crime family. Which is something I realize I need to talk to you about now."

"What do you mean now? Why didn't you mention this well known family before?" she demanded.

"Everyone knows about the Torrez family. Even the police. It's just that no one gets in their way. I didn't mention it because I didn't see any reason they'd be connected to your sister's disappearance. They are mostly known for their drug activity."

"Smuggling?"

"Yeah."

"Well, if that guy works for the family, and he was asking about me..." her heart rate picked up. "Then they must be the ones who have Maddy. We have to tell the police."

"Believe me, I'm sure the police already consider them a suspect, but that's the problem. No one has ever been able to pin a crime on them. They're powerful. Connected. Capable of pointing people in the other direction."

"How do you know all of this?" she asked, suddenly suspicious again. Why did it always seem like Gabe wasn't telling her everything?

"It's common knowledge they run the drug trade around parts of the Caribbean and beyond. But they're known for drugs, not kidnappings."

"Well, it doesn't matter. I have to tell the police. I'll need names, everything you know, so I can tell them first thing tomorrow."

He let out a loud exhale and walked over to her, sitting down a few feet away. "I have an idea that I think will be the smartest move for you now. Besides going home."

"I'm listening."

"It could be dangerous."

"That hasn't stopped me yet."

He frowned. "I know. Look, I don't know why I didn't think of it earlier today when I took you to the police station, but there are some people who can probably help you in St. Thomas."

"No, I already told you. I have to stay here. If Maddy's in St. Croix, I can't leave."

"Listen, it's a boat ride or seaplane ride away. You can always come back if you need to."

"Even if I agree to go, what's in St. Thomas that's so helpful?"

"There's an FBI office there. I remember it from years ago. My grandma talked to them about my family's murder at one point."

"But I've already contacted them, and other agencies," she said dismissively.

"But now you have more evidence. Take your sister's necklace and tell them everything that's happened. Going to them in person could really get their attention, too. I think it's worth a shot. And if you don't get more help from them, you can come here again. Meanwhile, you can stay in touch with local police, with your phone. It's not as if you'll be flying to Florida. You'll be one island over."

"I know, but I hate the thought of leaving St. Croix if Maddy is here."

"Just do this, Megan. You've got the German man and the other guys searching the island for you. If there's a chance the FBI can dive into this investigation, you need to try talking to them." He reached for her hand and took it in his. His gaze locked with hers. "Please, Megan. Even if you decide to come back tomorrow night."

His eyes begged her to hear his silent plea. His grip on her hand was secure, yet tender. A voice inside said to listen to him. Maybe it was the best move at this point. "Well, I understand. It might be worth it. So what's the dangerous part?"

Gabe sat up a little taller and released her hand. "You know that crime family I mentioned?"

"The Torrez family."

"Torrez senior is based on St. Thomas. If he *is* linked to Maddy's disappearance, you don't want to show up on his island asking questions."

"How do you think the guy with the German accent fits in? Would this family hire someone like that to do their…dirty work?"

Gabe's eyes filled with pain. She wondered if he was thinking of his family. "Yeah, from what I've heard, they would definitely hire someone like him."

Megan shook her head, putting it all together as she made her decision. It wasn't the worst idea. And she didn't have to stay in St. Thomas. "Well, I'll try it your way. For tomorrow only. I'll go, but if I don't get immediate help, I'm not staying. Mark my words, Gabe. You can't keep me away from St. Croix. Not until I find Maddy."

His brow wove together. "I believe the FBI will help you. Maybe they can discover who the men after you are and how they are linked to your twin. I want you to find her. But I don't want you to get hurt in the process. I'm only trying to help."

"It would help me if you went with me tomorrow. Will you?"

"I sure will."

34

Megan let the breath she'd been holding out. As much as she knew she should let Gabe get back to his own life, the fact the German man had been looking for her, in addition to the guy Gabe knew worked for the Torrez family, was making her fears run wild. She didn't know how she was going to sleep at all that night knowing how hot on her trail they were, but at least Gabe would go with her to St. Thomas in the morning. Maybe he could help her blend in a little better so the men chasing her wouldn't find her.

Or maybe she subconsciously wanted him to go with her because she was all of a sudden attached to the man. When he'd held her hand and peered into her eyes like that, it had nearly undone her. And when he'd said *Please*…Since when was she putty in a man's hands? What was happening to her rational, calculating style?

She had kissed him for crying out loud. She hadn't even gone on a date since her breakup four years ago, and she'd practically thrown herself at Gabe. Maddy was missing, a man had almost killed her, criminals were after her, and she was developing a thing for a man she had just met. A big thing. And now he wanted her to go to St. Thomas. To ask the FBI to figure out who these men following her were and to see if they could find answers. But what if he was wrong? If she left, would she ever find Maddy? She was so confused and overwhelmed, her head was aching.

She needed to think about something else.

She turned back to Gabe. He was observing her carefully. And his arm was still bloody. That, she could fix.

"Do you have a first aid kit? If you cut it on something in the alley, it could get infected."

"Yeah, in the bathroom."

She stood up and gestured towards it. "Come on. Let me clean it."

He followed after her and pulled the kit from behind the vanity. Standing over the sink, she washed the cut out thoroughly. She poured hydrogen peroxide on, and Gabe sucked in his breath sharply as it fizzed over his wound. "You're lucky you don't need stitches. It looks like it came pretty close to that."

Gabe studied her in the small bathroom mirror. She had thought cleaning his cut would be a distraction from her worries, but the way he observed her made her pulse speed up. She wondered what he was thinking. He was probably trying to figure out how to talk her into returning to Florida. As much as it irritated her that he wouldn't let that go, it flattered her in a strange way. It was as though he wanted to protect her. A moment ago, he'd even said he didn't want to see her get hurt. It was a reasonable thing to say, but still, it made her emotions spiral out of control. Just standing beside him made her dizzy with attraction. And tending to his wound wasn't helping. Her fingers brushed his tan, muscular arm as she worked, and she imagined tracing her hands over his entire rock-hard stomach. She'd felt his chest at the beach earlier, and it had left her wanting more. Her body temperature heated at the thought, and she withdrew her hands from his arm. Coughing, she lowered her face. This had definitely been a bad idea. Her sister was in danger, and she was drooling over a man.

"Are you OK? I can get you some water."

Megan lifted her head up, forcing herself to get it together. "Just a scratch in my throat. I'm fine now." She picked up the antibiotic cream, avoiding eye contact with him.

"You're pretty good at this," he remarked.

"Maddy was always hurting herself growing up. Climbing trees, skate boarding without kneepads. I sort of became a doctor mom at an early age," she admitted. She applied the cream and placed the gauze over the wound. She tore off pieces of medical tape and secured the bandage in place as quickly as possible. His proximity was too much for her nerves. The saltwater scent lingering on his skin wasn't bad either. She definitely needed more space between them.

"Didn't you ever get hurt? Weren't you climbing trees and having fun, too?"

"Me? No way. I was always close by, keeping an eye on her...Well, one eye on her, the other buried in a book. I'm not exactly the adventurous type."

His mouth curved upwards. "Could've fooled me. I'd say risking your life to look for your missing twin sister is pretty adventurous, Megan."

One moment he was lecturing her about safety, the next he was gazing into her eyes, and now he was complimenting her? Maybe he felt something for her, too. But if he did, he would have said something earlier about the kiss. He wouldn't have left her feeling like an idiot for making a move on him. Nothing was making sense.

"And to think, this from a guy who's been trying to get me to go home. Now I'm adventurous," she remarked casually, pointing a finger at his chest.

Gabe tensed, examining her hand where it hovered in front of him. If Megan didn't know better, she'd think he was uncomfortable with her being so close. Maybe the kiss she'd planted on him had affected him. He may not have mentioned it, but he *had* kissed her back. She dropped her hand to her side and began to clean up her mess. She shouldn't overanalyze a kiss at a time like this. But she couldn't believe she had kissed him.

Gabe cleared his voice. "Well, you are adventurous, but you're also reckless. And stubborn. Too stubborn. You might get yourself killed, in fact, if you keep being so impulsive."

Megan snapped her head up, and her face flushed. Before she could respond, Gabe went on. "But I understand why you're doing it. She's your sister. I'd do anything to save my sister if I could."

Megan gave a curt nod as they stared at each other, but neither spoke. Even if he didn't agree with her methods, he understood why she was doing it, and that made her feel a little better. She picked up the medical tape to arrange it back into the first aid kit.

Gabe straightened and reached for her shoulder. His touch sent a rush of sensations through her body, but she didn't dare move. "Thanks for cleaning the cut. I know how I can pay you back for it."

Megan's fingers fumbled the tape. She wished her brain didn't automatically return to thoughts of kissing him as soon as he'd said that. She felt her cheeks turning their usual crimson shade and refused to look at him. She stacked all of the supplies inside the kit and closed the top. When she was sure she could control her voice, she peeked at him from the corner of her eye. "How so?"

"I can feed you. I don't know how you're still standing right now."

35

As he withdrew his hand, Megan coughed. He wasn't going to mention how she'd made some ridiculous move on him at the beach earlier or bring up the kiss. Here she was replaying it over and over, and he probably hadn't even thought about it. He was going to give her something to eat. "I ate some of your plantain chips…kind of a weird taste, but it held me over."

"How about a veggie omelet? I saw you ate every bite at Captain Sully's. You have to admit, I have a gift."

She recalled his lips mingling with her own. Yes, he definitely had a gift. She grabbed the countertop and shifted away from him. Some immediate distance between them and a hot shower would clear her head. She kept her tone steady. "Sounds wonderful. Do you care if I take a quick shower? Since we were at the beach earlier…"

His jaw tensed, and he cut her off. "Go for it. Towels under the sink. I'll fix the food," he said in a rush before hurrying towards the kitchen.

Five minutes later, Megan was clean and feeling steadier. She donned a pair of pajama pants and a cotton tank top, and strolled across the studio, opting to sit down on one of the two stools beside the kitchen counter.

Gabe seemed more relaxed. He spared her a grin. "That was fast."

"I didn't know how long I could stand up. You're right, I'm tired. But the shower felt nice."

"I'd better get this order up fast. Can't have you fainting on me. You've got a big day tomorrow. You're OK with staying here tonight, right? I'm not sure it's a good idea for us to look for another hotel with a storm approaching."

"Yeah, if you don't care."

"I want you to stay," he replied at once. He paused, swallowing a lump in his throat. "I mean it's safer for you here I think. I'll sleep on the sofa. You can have the bed."

Megan hesitated. Was he flustered or was it her imagination? She shook off the thought. "Thanks."

He shrugged. "Least I can do." A teasing look crossed his face. "My grandmother wouldn't have it if I left you alone in a different hotel after the day you've had."

Megan allowed a small smile. "I'm really starting to like her."

His eyes remained on the vegetables in front of him. "She'd like you, too."

Her own grandmother popped into her mind. Grandma Lynn would like Gabe as well. Megan had taken a look around while he'd gone to her hotel. Although he didn't have much in the apartment as far as belongings, it was very organized and clean. She'd spotted his small collection of paperback fiction books and the Bible, with bookmarks marking certain chapters. The fact that he owned any books at all had surprised her, but she couldn't bring herself to tell him she felt bad about misjudging him.

She'd taken him for a beer-chugging beach bum that first morning at Captain Sully's, and though she'd searched his fridge, she hadn't seen even one bottle of beer. In fact, it had been stocked with mostly healthy food. The chin-up bar placed in the kitchen doorframe explained his muscular arms and physique. He was clearly concerned with taking care of his body, but that didn't mean he did it to impress women. Besides, if he'd been the guy she thought he was before, he'd have tried to seduce her at the beach. He would not have let her end that kiss so easily.

The only thing that bothered her about his place was that he didn't have any photographs. Was the pain of his family's murder so strong he couldn't look at their pictures? She wanted to believe he'd told her the truth about everything.

Megan stared at the cutting board and watched as Gabe diced through the vegetables for the omelet with finesse and speed. He really was good with a knife. She hoped he was telling her the truth. She'd trusted him with her life. If she'd been told a day ago she'd be staying the night in his apartment, letting him cook for her, she wouldn't have believed it. Maddy wouldn't have believed it. This was the polar opposite of her typical behavior. She never trusted men. She hadn't for a long time. But staying in Gabe's place, when there was so much about him she didn't know, was a huge leap of faith. One she prayed she wouldn't regret.

Thunder rumbled so violently, Megan flinched. Gabe placed a candle on the counter in front of her. "Gonna be a big one." He scraped the diced vegetables into a heated sauté pan and began cracking eggs into a silver bowl.

Lightning flashed outside the window as the thunder grew closer in frequency. "It sounds like it's right on top of us all of a sudden."

"Island storms move in fast this time of year. I'm surprised it held off this long actually. It was thundering in the distance on my way back."

Rain moved in fast, pounding the roof like beating drums. Megan eyed the window nervously as the lights flashed. Gabe set down the knife. "Better give you a flashlight," he remarked casually.

Megan raised a brow. "The power might go out?"

"Yep. It goes out all of the time. Welcome to the Caribbean. But don't worry. I've got a gas stove. I can finish the omelets up no problem."

Megan accepted the flashlight and wrapped her fingers snuggly around it. The smell of sautéing onions and green peppers made her mouth water. She didn't know which worried her more, the storm or her empty stomach. The thunder growled once more, answering her silent question. The storm definitely bothered her more. Gabe lit the candle on the countertop, before picking up the bowl of eggs he'd just whisked. He poured the eggs into a second hot skillet.

"I guess you don't have a generator?"

Gabe chuckled. "No, but I've got lots of candles."

The storm grew stronger and the thunder boomed right over them. The lights began to flutter and then all at once were out. Megan pressed the flashlight button, illuminating the space directly in front of her. Gabe was already lighting more candles to set around the kitchen. "How long will the power be out?"

"No telling. Could be ten minutes. Could be all night."

Megan perused the space uncomfortably. She wanted to ask if Gabe had centipedes in his apartment but didn't want to seem like a coward. He'd have plenty to say about a woman who was afraid of bugs but not the deadly men hunting her down. She *was* afraid of them, but finding Maddy was more important than her fear. Lightning struck again, illuminating his tall frame as he wiped the blade of the chef's knife clean. At once, she was reminded of how much she'd let her guard down. She had trusted a man she hardly knew with her life. And as she watched him standing a few feet away wielding a knife quite skillfully, it didn't do much to ease her doubts.

He set the plate, utensils, napkin, and a bottle of water in front of her, and took the stool a foot away. His eyes met hers in the warm glow from the candle between them, and she searched them. "I know the storm sounds bad. But we get them often. It will blow over," he said reassuringly.

She gulped, and tried to push the onslaught of negative thoughts aside. Tomorrow's plans to leave St. Croix, her unexpected feelings for Gabe, her doubts about what he was keeping from her, and thoughts of Maddy were hitting her all at once, sending anxiety through her.

When she still hadn't replied to him, Gabe covered her hand with his own. Her eyes darted to his. "Are you alright?" he asked gently.

"Just having a moment, I guess. But I'm fine. It's been a long day."

Understanding swept over his face. "You'll be safe here tonight, Megan. I'll protect you. I promise."

She searched his expression. "I know."

He squeezed her hand gently. She felt like he was good. She was sure. "Do you mind if I say grace?" he asked.

"I'd love that."

Over the noise of the storm, he blessed the food and asked that Maddy be found safe and sound, and Megan felt some peace returning to her chest. Today had been difficult. She'd found Maddy's necklace, and men had looked for her at her hotel. She had developed some sort of attachment…feelings, for Gabe, and it confused her. She still sensed Gabe was holding something back, but decided if he was, he had his reasons. Her gut told her he wouldn't hurt her. He wanted to keep her safe.

She could trust him.

36

"Glad ta have ya back, boss."

Miguel downed half of the Bloody Mary Dalbert had prepared for him and for the first time since showing up at his office thirty minutes before, he pulled off his sunglasses. His headache was beginning to clear up just enough that the morning light spilling in through the window wasn't bothering him as much.

Visiting his father hadn't eased his troubles. His father passed the time dictating orders to his crew, arranging drug runs, and partying with a multitude of women. It wasn't OK for Miguel to mess with family products, but Victor could do whatever he pleased.

His father disgusted him. Each time Miguel had tried to give him a chance to apologize for ordering the hit on Madeline, Victor had only said the same, cruel thing...He'd done Miguel *a favor*. Madeline would've caused their family trouble, and he was taking care of Miguel's best interest. Regardless of what he said, Miguel had decided his father really didn't care about anyone. With the exception of himself, of course. Victor was the most selfish, egotistical bastard in the world. And he'd never love anyone but himself, especially not his son.

Miguel had stayed up all night drinking while watching some of the crew count and prep stacks of money for transport in his father's lower level security room, and he'd returned to St. Croix on the first flight that morning. He'd only have been allowed to wallow in his self-pity for so long before his father would've snapped. Miguel needed to refocus on his duties or Victor wouldn't have any reason to keep him employed in his company.

He looked up at Dalbert standing before him. "Glad to be home, Dalbert. Did I miss anything important? I'm assuming not, since I didn't hear from you."

"Everything's good. One of the sales clerks from ISLAND GEMS asked me to have you stop by when you can. Something about a necklace one of the customers said had been stolen. She said she wanted to talk to you."

Miguel sat up taller. That was good. He needed to dive right into work so he'd stop obsessing about losing Madeline. He'd check in with all of his local cover businesses. They were mostly legit, which helped keep the illegal side of business covered up. He'd visit his employees to discuss orders for the jewelry shops, maintenance and upkeep issues with the water sports rental businesses, and look at invoices and payroll. He could go by ISLAND GEMS while he was at it. "Alright. I'll stop in there later. What about Trevor? Where is he, anyway?"

Dalbert tilted his head, contemplating his words. "Um, I haven't seen him much since you left. He told me you'd talked and he was busy taking care of some things for you."

"For me? I haven't even heard from him since I left."

Dalbert frowned. "That doesn't make sense."

Miguel scowled. "He's probably playing boss since he knew I was away. I know he's got his eye on my job. But listen, Dalbert. I am in charge of local operations here, you understand? My father has given Trevor way too much leeway."

"I understand. You want me to go by his place? See if I can find him?"

"Yes. Bring him to me. I'd like to talk to him in person."

"Yeah, boss. No problem."

With that, Dalbert left, closing the door behind him. Miguel leaned back in his office chair. He left for a couple of days, and Trevor assumed he could do his own thing. Typical. He'd straighten him out right away.

Miguel's phone vibrated once, and he pulled it from his pant pocket.

He flipped the smartphone up in his palm, and his brow wove together. It was a text message from an unknown number. He pressed the phone and a video message opened.

As a crumpled figure tied to a folding chair tossed on its side on a dirt floor came into focus, Miguel's eyes narrowed. Who was messing with him now? His stomach tightened, as he kept his eyes trained on the screen. The person holding the camera wobbled, but Miguel could see the figure better as the video zoomed in closer. The figure on the ground was definitely a woman, whose hands and legs were bound to the fallen chair, though he couldn't see a face. She wore a filthy sundress. Miguel's mouth began to dry. Something was so familiar…

A shoe rammed into the woman's side, and her head fell back as she screamed, begging for mercy. Miguel's stomach bottomed out in an instant. The hair on his neck stood on end. He'd recognize that auburn hinted red hair and face anywhere. Only the face was beaten to a bloody pulp. He felt the air leaving his chest. He couldn't breathe. But he couldn't turn away from the video.

The man bent over, and Miguel saw his face was hidden under a ski mask. He picked the chair with Madeline up, setting it upright, and yanked her face towards the camera. Miguel recognized the sundress, now torn and smeared in filth, that he'd last seen her wearing. Her beautiful hair was a mess, dirt and debris scattered throughout. Her hazel eyes glistened full of tears, and she pleaded with her attacker. "*Por favor*, stop! Please."

But the man in the mask was undeterred. He punched her in the mouth, knocking her, and the chair, backwards onto the ground. He grabbed a handful of her hair, lifting her head up, and pounded her right eye. Her head slammed to the ground, and she let out a scream. "No, *no más!*"

Miguel's stomach felt like a dagger was digging into it with each hit Madeline took. Hearing her voice, begging for her life, would kill him.

Miguel watched helplessly as Madeline became silent, lifeless on the ground, hardly flinching as the attack continued. She moaned here and there, as the disguised man hit her in the stomach, slapped her across the face, and kicked her in the ribs.

When Miguel was sure Madeline had to have died, the man knelt down and grabbed the chair, placing it on its legs once more. He wove his fingers around her neck and squeezed. Madeline's left eye shot open, the right one was already swollen shut, and she choked, her face turning bright red. Then suddenly, the man released her neck and shoved her chair, and she careened towards the ground.

The slightest movement in her chest made him believe she was somehow still breathing. The camera turned away from Madeline, focusing in on a piece of paper with large handwritten words in black ink. It was an address in San Juan with a date, SATURDAY AT NOON. Below the time, a lone sentence was scribbled. "Come alone for the girl, Miguel, or she dies this time."

Miguel stood up from the chair and began pacing. Madeline was alive, and he had to rescue her. Maybe that's where Trevor had been. He'd betrayed Miguel. If it wasn't Trevor, who was it? He thought of the warning. He'd seen what they'd already done to Madeline. It would be too risky to tell his father. And besides, his father wouldn't offer to help him anyway. He'd been the one who wanted her dead in the first place.

Anger filled him now as he thought about Madeline being tortured. His heart sped up, and a little bit of hope surged through him. The only woman who had ever trusted him was still alive. He popped a couple of Oxycodone in his mouth and swallowed them with the rest of the Bloody Mary. He'd bring her home, and this time, his father wasn't going to take her away.

37

Maddy mustered up her courage as Luis approached the cell, hiding something behind him. He had just received a phone call, spoken quickly in Spanish, then turned his attention towards her.

Her body was in agony from last night's attack. With her fingers she'd carefully grazed her swollen face, noting the ballooned jaw, cheek, and the eye still sealed shut. Blood clotted all over her face; blisters, cuts, and scratches burned her skin. With each breath she inhaled, her ribs seemed to protest, making her arrive at the conclusion Trevor must have cracked or broken a few of them. No one had given her a sip of water or anything for the pain. While she was depleted and certain she was nearing the end, if Luis was coming to kill her now, she wouldn't go down without one last fight.

Trevor had been gone for hours and though he'd been the one to beat Maddy to a pulp for the video, Luis was terrifying in his own way. He was skinny, but wiry, and Maddy sensed he could kill her without batting an eye. He opened the bars of her cell and stepped towards her.

"No," Maddy grunted, pressing her palms against the dirt floor to scoot away.

He grabbed her head and covered it quickly with a bag. But now that her legs and arms weren't tied up she could fight. She punched and kicked, squirming away from him as he attempted to pick her up. He yelled at her, words she didn't understand, and though the pain surged to all of her extremities, blindly, she fought back.

Her fingertips clasped the edge of the bag, and she ripped it off of her head. "Stay away from me!"

A determined expression came over him as he snatched a handful of her hair, pulling so hard, she cried out. She reached up reflexively and tried to pull his hand away. He gripped her aching jaw, pried it open, and something went down her throat. She grasped for her mouth, but he slammed it shut. He wrapped his arm around her throat and held her jaw firmly closed.

She felt the pill sticking to her throat and tried to gag, but he held her until she was forced to swallow it down or suffocate. The moment he released her, she dropped and rolled away, quickly shoving her finger down her throat. She started to gag, but something pounded against her temple, and she collapsed to the ground. Acceptance sank in, as her one good eye fell shut. Whatever the pill was, she'd ingested it.

She came to after awhile, but something was wrong. Everything felt numb, and though it relieved the pain she was in to an extent, a voice in her subconscious told her she needed to be alert. She told herself to wake up. To snap out of it, but her entire body was tingling, and her thoughts were foggy.

After a moment, she realized the ground was moving below her, and strange noises sounded here and there. Footsteps up a few stairs. A door swinging shut. Then suddenly, she landed hard on a solid surface, and the bag was pulled off of her head. She blinked her droopy eyelid open and strained to see in the new light spilling around her. She noted the small room and the tile surface below her fingertips but couldn't move a muscle.

A figure stepped closer and dropped down in front of her. Maddy looked at the woman, who's eyes were wide with terror. *Help me*, Maddy silently screamed. But no sooner had the woman knelt down, she sprang to her feet. She started talking rapidly in Spanish, and her voice seemed distorted and loud. Maddy's head was blaring. She wondered what sort of drug Luis had given her.

A male voice interrupted the woman, bringing Maddy back from her confused thoughts. Luis. The pair were arguing, of that much Maddy was certain, though she couldn't seem to get her head to tilt even a little so she could peer up at them.

Her head was dazed, frozen in place, propped against the wall where Luis had leaned her. After a moment, the woman's voice got louder. It strained with each word she yelled at Luis.

A popping sound blasted, and the woman's voice cut off as she staggered and fell backwards. On the floor, suddenly eye level with Maddy, the woman glanced at her briefly, then looked away as she got to her feet. Luis must have hit her.

"Bien," the woman said hostilely.

Maddy remembered that word from Spanish. It meant fine. But nothing was fine. She wanted to tell her to say anything but fine to Luis, but she couldn't seem to speak.

The next moment Luis's arms were lifting her to drag her away from the wall.

38

Gabe turned away from the seaplane ticket window and knit his brow as he noticed Megan's pale face. The baseball cap hid most of her hair, but her despairing expression was hard to miss.

He took her arm and guided her towards a bench on the dock. He led her to a seat beside him even as he scanned the area for trouble. There were a few men, dressed for work, waiting for the seaplane to St. Thomas, and one couple on vacation, who had asked a bystander to snap their photo in front of the small plane. A water taxi was a hundred yards away, making its way from the small island that housed Hotel on the Cay, over to the harbor. And other than a few fishermen hanging around boats in the harbor, there wasn't much activity.

Once he was sure no one in particular stood out as a threat, he bent closer to her. "What's wrong? You look like you've seen a ghost." He glanced at her arms, which were covered in goose bumps. "Megan, it's 80 degrees out here. Are you cold?"

She shook her head, her expression worried. "I have a terrible feeling. I get shivers all over like this when something is wrong…with either Maddy or myself. It's always happened like this to both of us," she explained, rubbing her arms lightly.

Gabe wasn't sure how to respond. Maddy was definitely in trouble, and Megan had been in trouble herself ever since she showed up on St. Croix. She could have goose bumps and a bad feeling for just about a dozen reasons he could come up with off the top of his head. But he wanted Megan to stay positive at least until he got her to his friend, Agent Hartford, at the FBI office in St. Thomas.

He was still in a little shock she hadn't changed plans to go with him this morning. She'd woken up early. He'd flinched on the couch when he heard her sit up in the bed across the room. He'd hardly slept a wink. Between listening for any intruders who might have tailed him to the apartment from the hotel and being overly aware of the breath-taking woman in his bed twenty feet away, it had been a restless night. Megan, on the other hand, had been out cold. She even mentioned how she'd slept better than she had in days and how just knowing Gabe was there had made her feel safer than usual. He decided his night of tossing and turning was worth it just to hear her say those words. Even if he had to say goodbye to her today, he knew he wouldn't forget her. He didn't think he could if he tried. Maybe it was getting a decent night's sleep, but she hadn't argued at all about his idea to go to St. Thomas. But as he studied her now, covered in goose bumps, her eyes huge with fear, it unsettled him. What if she decided not to get on the plane?

He couldn't let that happen.

"Try to keep your chin up. Just think, you'll be talking to real professionals before you know it. They can help you find Maddy."

She wrapped her arms around her waist. Her face was pale. Gabe placed his arm over her shoulders. He told himself it wasn't to feel how nice she fit in the crook of his arm, like she belonged beside him, or to treasure his last day with her, but to warm her up. She was rubbing her arms, trembling a bit. He leaned in close. "Are you OK?"

She shrugged. "The goose bumps are still there. She's in trouble, and I can't do a thing about it. What if I shouldn't go to St. Thomas?"

He ran his hand up and down her arm. He had to keep her on track with his plan. "It's worth a shot. Show them the necklace. Tell them everything. What have you got to lose? If you stay here today, do you think the police will get that much further with their investigation? The FBI has a wealth of resources. Let them help you."

She exhaled softly, glancing up at him. "I'll go. Let's face it. I need more help than I am getting here. Not that you haven't helped, of course." She bit her lip before continuing. "I guess you'll be headed to St. Croix once you drop me there?"

Gabe kept his face blank as he withdrew his arm. He leaned his elbows to his knees. She was certainly perceptive. He had felt bad enough lying to her the night before about the man in her room and for keeping everything he knew from her. He'd decided it was best to say whatever he needed to so he could get her to the FBI office. Even if that had meant leaving a few important details out of their conversation. Like how he really knew so much about the Torrez family. How there had actually been a man waiting for her in her hotel room. And how Gabe had killed him. When he'd told her he didn't want to see her get hurt, that had been true. His need to protect her was outweighing everything else.

He'd also let her assume he'd stay with her in St. Thomas while the FBI helped her out, but the truth was he needed to refocus on his undercover assignment ASAP. He was waiting to call Smith to find out if they'd identified the dead man. And if the DEA thought he could do something valuable to help find Maddy or get further involved at all, Gabe would do that. But it was up to them. Gabe's only priority was keeping Megan safe. Which meant, he had to get her to Hartford. No matter how bad her feeling about Maddy was, he'd get her on that seaplane.

"I'll make sure you get to their office. I'll stay for a few minutes or so. But then I'll probably head out."

She nodded, as she gazed at the ocean. "I bet you'll be glad to resume your usual routine, without worrying about me every second," she said, a tiny smile forming, though it didn't reach her eyes.

He brushed his knee gently to hers. She met his stare. "I'll still worry about you, trust me."

"Well, in any case, I won't call you when I return tonight. You need a break," she said with a smirk.

"Tell me you're kidding. At least give them a chance to open an official investigation. To be honest, the best thing would be for you to file your report with them and take the first flight to Florida."

"If the FBI can't help me, I'm on the first flight to *St. Croix*," she said without hesitation.

He tried not to look so disapproving, but failed. "I don't think that's a good idea. But I'm not in the mood to argue with you. Even if you are stubborn, and rash, and—"

She nudged his knee with her own, cutting him off. "I'm going to miss having you worry about my every move, Gabe." She'd said it casually, but he could sense her somber mood.

He didn't see the point in stirring her temper up right this moment by explaining to her how reckless it would be for her to return to St. Croix. He needed her to board the plane with him. He wanted to put her at ease, to see her smile. "I bet you never thought you would miss anything about this lowly breakfast cook, did you?" he asked playfully.

She tilted her head towards his and grinned. "Definitely not."

The seaplane crew called for boarding and Gabe pulled her to her feet. Megan held onto his hand. "But I *will* miss you. In case I forget to say it later…thanks for all you've done."

She dropped his hand and he gave her a huge grin. "Well, hold that thought. You aren't rid of me yet."

39

As Luis hauled Maddy's inert body into another room, she tried to form words. Her tongue was like a dead weight in her mouth. He dropped her carelessly on the floor and stocked off. The woman knelt down beside her as a door shut loudly nearby.

The sound of rushing water came from beside her. If she could get her head to turn to the left, she knew she'd see a bathtub. Maddy watched the woman as she pressed a hand to the back of her neck and lifted it gently. She held a glass of water to her lips and poured it in. Maddy couldn't quite get her mouth to cooperate, but some of the water poured down her throat. As the woman got up and turned to the counter, Maddy vowed to God she'd never take water for granted again.

The woman stepped over her and towards the tub with a small bottle in her hand. A few seconds later, a fresh aroma, reminding Maddy of lilac from her grandma's retirement home garden, filled the room.

The woman knelt down and gently pulled the sundress over Maddy's head, being careful not to touch her swollen face. She pried her undergarments off and shoved all of the clothes into the trashcan beside her. She turned the running water off and began to tug Maddy up, as best she could. But the woman was much smaller than her, maybe one hundred pounds, tops, and Maddy's limbs were useless. All she could do was lie still.

She set Maddy carefully on the hard floor and called out. "Señor."

No. Maddy tried to speak up, but nothing came out.

Luis came in and cocked an eyebrow as he hovered over Maddy.

The woman snapped at him in Spanish, and he glared at her. He hoisted Maddy's upper half while the woman helped with her legs, and they placed her in the tub of water. The woman spoke as she pointed towards the door, and Luis shuffled away, the door slamming behind him. Maddy imagined thanking her for whatever she'd said to get rid of Luis, but the thought faded away as the effects of the steamy, heavenly scented water enveloped her.

Her head and shoulders sagged heavily into the tub, and she let her eye fall shut. She could feel her open cuts and scrapes sizzle under the hot water. Though the pain was still notable even with the drug pumping through her system, she had never felt so relieved to feel clean water on her skin. She offered up a slew of prayers, begging for an end to her agony, begging for help, and once more, thanked God for water. She longed for all of the things she'd taken for granted before, like brushing her teeth, showering every day, her warm bed and room at Meg's house, and mostly for her sister.

It had taken unimaginable, horrifying circumstances for her to wake up. But now she finally understood what her sister had been trying to tell her for all those years. Living a normal, steady-job-responsible-type of life wasn't a punishment. What she would do to have a chance at that kind of life again…If she had just listened to Meg.

A wet cloth ran over her limbs, and with a touch as light as a feather, the woman cleaned each wound on Maddy's body. As the cloth lingered on her neckline, where Maddy imagined Trevor's fingertips might have left marks from strangling her, she thought of her missing emerald. She'd only noticed it was gone after they'd finally untied her arms. Her fingers had reached for the necklace at once, only to discover it missing. Knowing she and Meg had worn their matching necklaces since they were little, never taking them off, had left her feeling more devastated than ever. She longed for a second chance. To go to Meg's office and hug her twin once more.

The soap stung in so many places, but Maddy knew the woman was only helping her in the long run. She spent a lot of time on Maddy's face, being very careful as she cleaned around her eye. Next, she poured water over her hair and shampooed the web of tangled locks. The woman worked in silence, but murmured something under her breath as she tenderly cleaned Maddy's ribcage. Because of the drug, she couldn't look down to examine the bruises she expected the woman was seeing.

Once she was satisfied with her work, she picked up a towel and called for Luis. He didn't say a word this time. He helped the woman wrap the towel around Maddy and set her on the floor of the bathroom, with her shoulders to the wall. Once he left, she retrieved a fine comb from her kit and began to detangle the knots from Maddy's hair. After that, she dabbed a clear ointment from a tiny tube onto Maddy's various cuts and scrapes.

Next, she picked up a toothbrush, a cup of water, and a bowl, and placed them beside Maddy on the floor. She brushed her teeth thoroughly, rinsed her mouth out, and then repeated the process. Clothes were taken out of the bag, and Maddy watched with a sinking feeling as she wrapped a black, lacy bra over her chest. She lifted each leg and carefully pulled on a matching pair of underwear. She tugged a short, bright blue fitted dress, over her head. Just when Maddy thought nothing else could come out of the woman's kit, she took a vile of perfume out and spritzed it over her body. Finally, she applied lipstick and an array of makeup to her face, being careful to not put pressure on her cuts.

Maddy became frantic as the process wound down. They'd drugged her, cleaned her, and put sexy clothes and makeup over her wounds. She recalled the parting words of the man Trevor had called Señor Rivera. He'd said they'd have dinner together, but his intentions were quite clear now.

Maddy was being served up for dinner.

Her heart raced faster as she thought of what to do. The woman was her only way out. She focused all of her energy on moving her mouth, but nothing worked. As the woman finished up the blush, Maddy managed to move her lips. "Pl—"

The woman's gaze shot to hers.

Maddy tried again. "Pl—"

The woman looked away. But Maddy heard the words she whispered as she withdrew. "I sorry," she'd said in a hushed voice.

Maddy was sorry, too. Sorry for her past, for every decision that had led to her capture, and for the life she'd never have a chance to live. The woman gathered her supplies.

"*Señor, lista,*" she yelled.

The door swung open, and Luis waltzed in, this time with a huge smile spread across his wicked face as he ogled Maddy from head to toe.

Luis hefted her up and tossed her over his shoulder, ignoring the moan she let out as her ribs crushed across him. His footsteps sounded as he carried her quickly away from the room. She closed her eyes. Her skin covered in goose bumps.

Meg, I miss you.

40

As all eight passengers climbed into the cabin and took their seats, the engines roared, the captain spoke into the intercom, and shortly the seaplane was moving away from the dock. A few minutes later, the aircraft bounced across waves as it sped up and then suddenly, it was gliding in the air. On the twenty-minute flight, Gabe pointed out sights, including Buck Island, a nationally protected park. The island boasted pure white shores on one side and an underwater scuba trail through a beautiful coral reef on the other. He spoke mostly to calm Megan's nerves, which he could see building by the second. That bad feeling at the dock had left her shaken for sure. He figured she was ready to take the next flight to St. Croix, without even deplaning.

Once they landed in St. Thomas, he pointed out the busy traffic from pedestrians, cars, taxis, yachts, other boats, and cruise ships as the plane idled towards the dock. "Welcome to Charlotte Amalie. I think you'll prefer it to St. Croix. I get the feeling you're more of a city gal."

"I admit...the old me would've spent some time in those luxury shops I spotted on our landing."

"The old you?"

She frowned. "I'm starting to realize how meaningless all of my possessions are now. None of it matters." Her eyes started to form tears, and Gabe grabbed her hand on instinct.

"Hang in there, Meg. You'll be safe at the FBI office soon. They won't let anything happen to you."

As soon as he said it, he regretted it. Of course, she wasn't thinking of her safety. He was the one doing that, which was why he'd blurted it without thinking. Now she'd assume his only reason for bringing her there was to keep her out of harm's way. It was mostly true, but he'd known better than to use her safety as a reason to get her on the seaplane.

Her chin tilted up, and her eyes narrowed. "You think I care about the FBI office or my safety? Nothing matters to me. Not my house, my things back home, my own life. None of it. Finding Maddy is all I care about. And like I said, if they can't help me, I'm out of there. I'll be in St. Croix before sunset. Nothing can stop me from finding my sister," she snapped.

Gabe couldn't help himself. He shook his head. The woman was out of control. She'd do anything to save her sister, regardless of the consequences. And this could be his last chance to warn her to wake up. "Can't you hear yourself? Your life doesn't matter? Well, maybe it should. How are you supposed to find Maddy if they get to you first? What good will it do to get captured?" He paused, his tone low. "Or killed?"

Her cheeks flushed. "You think she's dead. Don't you? Is that why you're trying to dump me in St. Thomas? So you can get this crazy real estate agent off of your hands? Who won't stop talking about her missing sister? Her dead sister?"

"No, that's not it. And I didn't say I think she's dead. We don't know how she is. Or where she is. We don't know anything. I was—"

"You might as well have said it. And I don't care if you believe me or not. I know she is alive. I feel it in my heart, my soul, my mind, Gabe. Maddy and I have been linked to each other since we were in the womb. If she were gone, I'd know. It would kill me," she said with a shaky voice. She wiped tears away as they slid down her face. "And I sense her. She may be in a heap of trouble. But she's hanging in there. She's not dead."

Gabe's pulse shot out of control. He hadn't meant to make her cry, but to get her to think about her own life. But he had to admit, if only to himself, if he were Megan, he'd be just like her, concerned with finding his sister. But that didn't make it any easier. Keeping Megan MacKenna alive was all he could think about.

His squeezed her hand. "I believe you. I may not understand the twin connection personally, but I know you're telling me the truth. If you say she's alive, I am sure she is. For what it's worth, I think the FBI can help you find her. But I'm not going to lie to you and tell you I'm not also concerned about your safety. I told you that last night. I don't want to see you get hurt. Whether I should or not, I care about what happens to you, Megan. And maybe since you don't seem worried about yourself, it can't hurt that I am handling that part for you…for now. But after I leave you at the office…" His forehead wrinkled as he imagined her slipping out the door and catching the next flight to St. Croix. Was this a lost cause?

Megan placed her free hand on top of his. "Let's not ruin our last few minutes together arguing over my irrational behavior. Grandma Lynn always says I have a temper to match my fiery red hair."

"Fiery is one way to put it," Gabe mumbled.

Megan chuckled. "You made me forget about my chills. I guess I should thank you for distracting me." Her smiled faded. "And like I said before. Thanks for all of your help. If it weren't for you, that German man would have found me by now. Meeting you was the best thing that has happened…so far, since I flew to the island."

"Maybe you've gotten island fever. You definitely wouldn't have said that a few days ago. Come on, let me get you to the FBI."

He stood up, and tugged her along beside him. He wanted to tell her she was the best thing that had happened to him since he'd been on the island, too. Even with her hotheadedness and reckless decisions every other minute. He'd grown attached to her. And he never did that.

But his nerves got the best of him.

Maybe he'd work up the courage on the taxi ride to the FBI office. He needed to prepare himself to say goodbye. And who knew, maybe he'd be seeing her sooner than he thought. It wouldn't surprise him if she left St. Thomas like she'd threatened to. And there was no way he'd let her go parading around St. Croix alone. He'd be risking his neck, trying to keep her among the living before he knew it.

They exited the seaplane, and as Megan stopped a foot away to stare at the bustling streets, where vendors had set up shop for the day to accommodate the many tourists, Gabe flagged down a taxi. The road running along the waterfront was packed with traffic, zooming by and honking horns.

The taxi came over right away, and the driver rolled down his window. "Whe ya goin', mon?"

"We're headed to an office on the—" Gabe stopped suddenly as he noted in his peripheral vision Megan had moved. He stood up, placing his hand to his temple to shield the sun as he scanned the crowded area.

"We? It's jus da one, right?" asked the driver.

But Gabe was already on the move. He pulled his burner phone out and dialed Smith, even as he was searching for Megan. Maybe she had ducked down beside a street vendor to look at a purse...

He saw cars speeding past, boats steering away from the harbor, and people going in every direction around him.

But he didn't see Megan.

The palms of his hands grew clammy as his throat dried. "Megan!" he called out.

He walked back to the seaplane dock. "Megan!" he called out louder, ignoring the stares around him.

"Have you seen a woman with red hair? She had a baseball cap on..." he asked the attendant.

The worker shook his head, "No."

Smith's voice blared at him from the phone. "Man, what's happening?"

"I think I lost her," he said hoarsely.

"Are you sure?"

Gabe ran along the waterfront and stopped instantly when he noticed a woven, brown handbag lying on the dock near the water. It was the brown purse that Megan had been carrying around for two days. He picked it up and tore through it, discovering its contents were still there. Her wallet, with cash and credit cards, and her cell phone. He stared out into the water and made mental notes of the two large boats pulling away from the dockside.

"I'm going to read off the names and tags of some of the boats leaving the harbor. Find out who they are registered to."

Gabe rattled off the information for every boat he could see and promised to call Smith in a few minutes and hung up the phone. He took off around the area, searching more. He focused on the two boats that were gaining momentum the further they got out to sea. His stomach felt like a hole had been punched through it.

They'd found Megan.

41

A voice was calling to her. A voice she knew so well.

"Maddy!" This time it was louder.

"Maddy!"

Meg? Meg had found her?

"Maddy, wake up!"

Maddy tried to sit up, but she was a prisoner, trapped in her own unmoving body. Her limbs hung useless at her sides. No matter how she tried, she couldn't get them to budge.

Meg's voice got closer, calling to her again and again to wake up, and then all at once she was leaning over her. Her eyes were wide, and her voice was urgent. "Maddy, wake up, *now*."

As her face faded away, she called out to her twin. "Please don't leave me."

Hands clasped her shoulders and shook her. "Time to wake up," an unfriendly voice ordered.

Maddy looked up, her heart sinking as she realized Meg's voice had been in a dream. The man Trevor and Luis had called *Señor* Rivera was hovering over her with the darkest expression on his face. She must have passed out on the bed Luis had dropped her on earlier. How much time had passed? She had a fuzzy memory of the woman who'd bathed her returning and feeding her spoonfuls of soup. Chicken broth if she recalled. Had that really happened? She shuddered, remembering how they'd cleaned her up. To give her to Rivera.

He was dressed in black pants and a midnight blue button down, and his breath reeked of liquor. He assessed her face and her body, as he reached for his necktie and took it off, tossing it to the side of the bed. He unbuttoned the top of his shirt and turned away.

Maddy willed her limbs to move, but the drug was still keeping her immobile. As she strained to look in his direction, he returned to her frame, tugging a white wicker chair with him. He placed it beside the bed, then picked her up, and moved her towards the edge of the mattress. He grabbed her head, tilting it slightly, adjusting it towards the chair so she could see him. Once he released her, he retrieved a bottle of dark, single barrel rum and sat down in the chair, refilling his glass. As he downed half of the rum, he watched her.

She closed her eye and prayed. She told herself she could survive whatever happened in the room, but her fear was increasing with each second that ticked by. Who was this man? Why had he captured her? How long would he keep her alive? The not knowing was wreaking havoc on her heart and mind.

"I'm told you won't have control of your body for another hour or so. Powerful stuff Luis gave you. Very hard to come by, but Trevor is very helpful. The dose he gave you lasts anywhere from eight to ten hours. I didn't want to take any chances with your cooperation after I saw those scratches on his neck." He hesitated, as a grin curved his mouth upwards. "But I can see the men got even, ahead actually. Your face looks like it hurts."

Maddy imagined watching him on the other end of Trevor's fist and wanted to scream at him but couldn't utter a word.

He poured more rum into his glass before continuing. "I guess the drug has probably helped you with the pain, even if you can't move or talk to me. I'd advise you to choose your words carefully when you can speak again. I didn't like your tone the last time I saw you."

She wondered if he was some sort of mafia or cartel lord. Who else could take someone captive, torture them, and then talk to their victim like that? He was clearly used to being in control.

"I'm told you'll be able to speak, before you can move your limbs. In the meantime, I'll tell you a story."

Maddy hoped he'd give her answers. Maybe he'd tell her how he knew about her sister, too. She prayed Meg was far away and safe. She wouldn't wish this misery on anyone, anywhere. Maybe he'd even tell her when he planned to kill her.

"I had a wife once. Even more beautiful than you…before your face was like that, of course." He sighed. "But someone noticed her beauty, and though I tried to protect her, he found a way to get to her. She didn't return the affections of this man. When her body washed up on the seashore, she'd been beaten, raped, and strangled to death."

He regarded Maddy hatefully. She wanted to point out that she had nothing to do with his wife's murder. She wondered how Miguel fit into the situation. And then it hit her…Had Miguel murdered Rivera's wife? It was definitely a possibility. Her pulse picked up. She knew this wasn't going to end well for her.

"Our daughter was only twelve at the time. The man framed an inno-cent person for her murder, and the police bought it. Case closed. I tried to get justice the right way. The legal way, and it didn't work. Every day since, I have to look in my daughter's eyes, see my wife, and know that the man who really murdered her walks free." He emptied the contents of his glass and tilted his head, resting it on his chair.

Maddy had watched him down three glasses since she'd woken up. She wondered if he'd even be able to stand up now. He sat up, and her hopes dwindled. He definitely had a high tolerance for alcohol. She tried to move her fingers. If she could get control of her limbs, she could try to defend herself. Maybe.

He lifted the bottle and poured it, this time, spilling some of the rum over the edge. So he was feeling the effects some. That had to be in her favor she hoped.

"I've waited patiently for the opportunity to make him pay, and it has finally arrived. As unfortunate for you as it is that you were in the wrong place at the wrong time, I think it was a sign you were the one to help me. You will serve your purpose. I'm not sure what I'll do with you once justice has been dealt, but time will tell, Madeline." She loathed the way he said her name and how his eyes ran greedily over her body.

He slammed the entire glass down and set the bottle on the ground. He staggered to his feet and nearly collapsed over her on the bed. He caught himself with his hands, one on either side of her, and leaned in close. His mouth found the crook of her throat, and as he took a bite, she winced.

He withdrew an inch, his breath hot on her skin. "I told you everything I did so you can accept your situation." His tongue ran from the bottom of her throat to her ear. "Though you think you know what pain is, Madeline, just remember, you don't know the half of it. My wife knew real pain. And I live day in and day out with real pain." He heaved his leg up and fell onto her. She groaned as he smashed her ribs. She moved her tongue around in her mouth experimentally, and suddenly she had more feeling back in her jaw.

She tried to speak. "Please stop."

He jerked his head up, and grabbed her throat. "So you can talk now." He narrowed his eyes. "Remember what I said about choosing your words carefully." He squeezed her throat. "Don't tell me to stop. Accept what is happening. Or you will know real pain, Madeline."

She forced herself to agree. "OK."

He smiled, making her stomach flip. She had to act fast. There would be a price to pay, but she was willing to risk it. She'd play a role, if only for a moment. His weight pressed down on her, and she moaned from the pain, but he didn't seem to notice. He tilted the swollen side of her face towards the pillow. He ran his hand over her chest and up to her mouth. When his finger found her lips, she reacted instinctively. This was her chance.

She parted her aching mouth and at once he slipped the finger in. She bit down as hard as she could, determined to draw blood. She didn't let go. He yelled out in pain at the top of his lungs, but she clamped her teeth around his finger.

A knock sounded at the door as Luis called out to Rivera, asking him if he needed help. Rivera ignored Luis and with his free hand slugged the good side of Maddy's face. Though she tried to hold onto his finger, her jaw popped open with the second punch.

The pounding continued and the next moment Rivera's cell phone rang. He cursed her in English and smacked her once more as he stood up, gingerly holding his bloody finger as he went to the phone. He gazed at the phone, not answering, but his brow wove together. "Alejandra," he said anxiously.

He stumbled over to the door and called for Luis. The door swung open and he barked an order in Spanish. As Luis tossed her over his shoulder and started to leave, Rivera stepped in his path. He yanked a handful of Maddy's hair and growled into her ear. "I've decided I won't need you for much longer. And very soon, Madeline, I'll show you what real pain is after all."

Moments later, her head was covered with a bag, and she was rushed back to her prison. As she landed on the dirt floor, Luis tugged the cover off, and locked her in the cell.

Lying on the floor with her head to the side, she spit up fresh blood from her new injury. She may have sealed her fate with Rivera. But at least everything would be over with soon enough.

42

Ricardo stared out the window from the backseat of the Escalade as they drove along the streets of San Juan. He'd had the woman at the farm house bandage his bloody finger in a hurry. He needed to get to his daughter as soon as possible.

Evidently, Alejandra had skipped her anxiety medication that day, and the housekeeper had found her curled up in her mother's old clothes, sobbing and talking incoherently.

It had happened a few times before, and Ricardo had learned how to calm his daughter. But he was the only one who could talk her down. His brow furrowed together. Another reason to pay Victor back. He'd destroyed his daughter. Without her meds, she was hardly able to function.

They had all suffered because of Victor Torrez. Ricardo had done his best to be a good father to Alejandra, but he knew the loss of his wife Ana had changed him in many ways. He hadn't been able to cope himself, and the past three years had hardened his heart. His tender side was reserved for his daughter alone, and the little goodness he'd had in him had died with his wife. His plan for revenge was the only thing keeping him strong.

No matter how many times he tried to look within his heart for forgiveness and for peace, he couldn't do it. Ana had been a devoted Catholic, and she would hate to see the path her husband had turned down since her murder. But she wasn't here to say a thing about it. He tried to remember the sound of her voice, but like her comforting presence, it was forever gone.

Ricardo would never forget the summer she was killed or the first time he met Victor. He recalled the dress Ana had worn that night clearly. It had been a shimmery gold cocktail dress, and her long black hair had fallen loosely down the open back. As was customary, she'd lit up the fundraiser party, with her looks, gentle laugh, and charm.

She chatted politely with everyone, including her newest admirer, Victor Torrez. Victor hadn't hid his desire for her from the moment they'd been introduced. Ricardo had instantly been uncomfortable with the man and had tried to steer them away from Victor throughout the evening, but he just kept finding an excuse to talk to them, even feigning an investment interest in Ricardo's plastics company.

At one point, he'd been called aside for a private meeting and had returned to see Victor standing close to his wife, making her laugh. He had instructed Ana on the way home in the limo to avoid further conversations with the newcomer. Ana had laughed and kissed him on the cheek. "You're so cute when you're jealous, my love," she had teased him. "Never forget, you're the only man for me."

Ricardo had known Ana would never cheat on him or leave him for another man, but Victor had been a problem Ricardo had underestimated. He wished he could rewind to that summer and do it over again. This time, he would keep Ana at home, away from the public eye and parties.

A week after that first introduction to Victor, Ricardo and Ana had been invited to another gathering. Ricardo's blood had boiled when they arrived and Victor Torrez was there, smiling at them. It became a pattern. Every time they went to a party for the next six weeks, Victor was there, openly enamored with Ana. Ricardo had done some checking into Victor and learned he was a suspected crime leader, though federal agencies had yet to pin any solid evidence on him. When Ricardo had finally gotten the nerve to tell Victor to keep his distance and stop drooling over his wife, Victor had told him if he didn't want people to stare at Ana, he should keep her locked up.

Ricardo had turned down every invite after that particular party, telling Ana he wasn't feeling social anymore. Ana had of course known why they were staying home all of a sudden and had been very understanding, even relieved. "I'm glad, my love. Victor's been making me very uncomfortable lately the way he stares at me. I can't believe he's at every party we go to. Do you know, the last time he saw me, he said he had moved to his beach house here in Puerto Rico for the time being? Apparently, he has no plans to return to St. Thomas for now. It's strange, how he talks to me."

Of course, Ricardo had known that. He had found out every piece of information on Victor from the moment he had begun obsessing over Ana. He'd assured Ana he'd keep Victor away from her from that point on and not to worry about the man.

The night of Ana's death, Ricardo had been downtown for a business meeting. He'd thought that his regular security detail would keep his wife safe. And he'd been regretting that decision ever since.

His house staff informed him that Ana had received a hand written message from their priest, telling her it was very important she come to the church at once to talk with him. She had volunteered at the church regularly, never missed a Sunday service or mass, and hadn't thought twice about rushing to meet their priest. She'd left Alejandra in the care of the nanny, and she'd assured the driver and the security guard they could wait outside for her since she'd only be a few minutes and would be safe inside.

Once they realized it was taking a little longer than expected, and she hadn't responded to a text message, they'd gone in to find her. They'd found the priest, alone, in his chambers. He knew nothing about Ana, and when shown the note had sworn he hadn't written it. Immediately, they'd called the police and a search ensued.

Ricardo turned from the truck window and shook his head as he relived the nightmare. Two days later, Ana's body had washed up on a beach outside a resort in San Juan. She had a black eye, bruises all over her perfect body, and according to the ME had been raped before being strangled to death. The moment Ricardo had seen her body, cold on the ME's table, his heart had stopped beating.

He told the police it had to have been Victor, but it didn't matter. That same day, a mentally unstable man came forward, claiming to have murdered her. He had no alibi for the time of death, and he had lived near the church where Ana was last seen. It was too perfect of a story for Ricardo, and he had driven to Torrez's San Juan place and accused him of killing Ana.

Victor had gazed sincerely at Ricardo and told him how sorry he was he'd lost a woman so very perfect. Then he'd closed his eyes and described every curve of her body, as if he had felt them with his own hands. Even after what he'd done, he didn't feel remorse. And he'd taunted Ricardo about Ana's death.

Ultimately, the police had believed the young man's confession and charged him with the murder. He'd pleaded insanity and been sentenced to a mental hospital.

Ricardo pushed the memories away as the vehicle went through security gates at his home. Soon enough, Victor Torrez would have a taste of real pain and loss. He'd watch his flesh and blood die, and he'd be forced to make his confession of killing Ana. Ricardo would get the evidence to the police one way or another, without revealing his role in the confession, and Victor Torrez would spend the rest of his lonely life rotting in prison. It wouldn't bring Ana back, but it might dull some of the pain.

43

"Who dat fella been helpin' yoh?"

As the boat rocked sideways under the hot sun, Megan stared up at the man dressed in blue jeans and a black t-shirt with brown hair and piercing eyes who had been interrogating her for the last two minutes. His Crucian accent was so thick she could hardly understand him.

But she understood his fists. He had a killer right hook.

She'd been grabbed in broad daylight and shoved into the cabin of a fishing boat in less than sixty seconds. She had no idea how they'd worked so fast or pulled it off, and though she'd screamed as loud as she could, one of the men had muffled her voice with his hand.

About twenty minutes after the boat had taken off from the harbor, it had slowed down and Megan had been transported onto another vessel. Ever since, she'd been answering the questions of a man named Trevor. She'd expected to come face to face with the man who had tortured her in her room, but none of the men on either boat had spoken with a German-sounding accent.

From her knees, where she was bound on the floor, she opened her mouth slightly, stretching her throbbing jaw to the side. Trevor had been less than convinced with her last response to his question about the man someone had supposedly seen help her get from St. Croix to St. Thomas.

"I askin yoh gain' woman, who dat fella?"

"Where is my sister?"

"Answa deh question," he snapped, raising his fist.

"He's just a guy I met at a breakfast place," she replied earnestly.

"Why he helpin' yoh?"

"I don't know. He said it was out of the goodness of his heart. He was just some cook. Why do *you* think he was helping me? I figured he was interested in being more than friends with me if you know what I mean," she shrugged her shoulders, hoping to seem nonchalant.

After everything Gabe had been through to help her, she really didn't want these people to track him down, too. She prayed he had at least notified the police, or maybe even the FBI office he had planned to take her to, that she was suddenly missing, but she didn't figure he'd be able to do much beyond that.

"Tell me his name and where he work or ya neva see ya sista."

Megan closed her eyes. She'd tried her best. She'd taken a beating even, but she had no choice now.

She met Trevor's gaze. "His name is Gabe, and he works at Captain Sully's."

44

Gabe stepped away from Agent Hartford to take the call he'd been waiting on. Hartford was originally from Puerto Rico, about five' six", and had gray streaks throughout his short dark crew cut. He'd agreed to meet Gabe on neutral ground in a public place so that Gabe wouldn't have to go into the FBI office. Anyone seeing the two men would mistake them for regular guys walking through the cruise ship shopping district that was packed full of tourists.

Though they hadn't seen each other in five years, they'd helped one another out on more than one occasion when cases and leads had crossed agency paths. He'd been surprised to get the phone call from Smith about Gabe, and had assumed Gabe was still tracking down drug operations with Smith out of Miami. Gabe hadn't planned to brief him completely on his undercover op, but now that Megan had been taken, the situation had changed. Besides, he could trust Hartford, he was sure. After filling him in on everything from Maddy's disappearance to Megan's, Hartford had contacted his agency to get the ball moving for a missing persons investigation. Meanwhile, Smith had done some research.

"What have you got?" Gabe said as he answered the phone.

"We checked out all of the registrations. None of them really stood out. But one of them called *Puesta del Sol* is registered to a fisherman in St. Croix. He sells to fish markets in both St. Croix and San Juan," Smith said.

"So that might be suspicious since he was in St. Thomas today?"

"Maybe. Maybe not. Could've been a random coincidence."

"Tell me you've got more."

"I do. We got a positive ID on your dead German."

"And?"

"He's not German. He's an Austrian ex-pat, Lukas Schmidt. A professional hit man or muscle, whatever you need him for basically, with his most recent travel records flying him from Venezuela to San Juan. Four weeks ago."

"San Juan? Maybe Torrez was letting him stay at his beach house there? I've been talking to Hartford. They've had eyes on Victor's St. Thomas house for weeks, just like our guys, and they haven't seen any women meeting Maddy's description. Maybe we should check their San Juan residence. He hardly goes there, right? And he has to know the Feds are keeping an eye on his every move. Victor's smart. It might be a better place to hide someone."

"Assuming she's still alive?"

"I know it's not like him, but why did they send someone after Megan?"

"Man, you know exactly why…to clean up loose ends. I hate to say it, but neither one of them are likely alive right now."

Gabe's blood pressure flew through the roof. His voice was steely. "Don't say that." He paused, trying to calm down. "Megan was taken, not even an hour ago. I'm not letting this go. Hartford agrees, their agency will jump in for sure now that I've caught them up, and they'll help find the girls…period."

"I understand," Smith said, a hint of an apology in his tone. "Listen, we found something else, partner."

"Come on with it already."

"We decided to look into recent travel activity for anyone on the Torrez team, and we had one guy turn up. Trevor Stockton. He's been working mostly with Miguel in recent years, but it appears as though he's been working for the family for awhile."

"I'm familiar with him. I think he's the guy Raul was talking to last I saw him. I've seen him around Miguel some, too."

"Well, he's been traveling back and forth a lot recently between St. Croix and—"

"San Juan?"

"Yeah, how'd you know?"

"Just this feeling I can't shake. We haven't been paying attention to their place in San Juan. Maybe we need to check it out."

"Your instincts must be spot on. You didn't let me finish. Miguel Torrez traveled from St. Croix to San Juan this morning."

Gabe's fingers flexed around the phone. "I need to go there."

"I agree. But I have to say this, man…I still don't know why Miguel would keep the girls alive."

Gabe stared out at the ocean. He knew Megan might be dead already, but he wasn't giving up on her. She was tough. And smart. If anyone could figure out how to stay alive in the hands of the Torrez men, it was Megan. Plus, something nagged him about the case. "Maybe Miguel and Victor, neither of them, are behind the kidnappings. What if we've been looking at this the wrong way?"

"How so?"

"What if someone else is orchestrating this? I don't know. I feel like I'm missing a big piece of the puzzle. The professional hit man for example. He could've killed Megan, but he didn't. That's not a Torrez move, you're right."

"I agree. And, oh, I forgot one more thing about the guy Lukas. He received a fairly large wire transfer into an off shore account recently. We don't have the name of who sent the payment yet, but it looks like it came from an account in Grand Cayman. Our team is tracing the information as we speak. We should have a name shortly."

"As soon as you've got it, contact me. I'm headed to the Torrez Puerto Rican residence ASAP."

"We'll call you when we have something. And *be careful*, partner."

As Gabe hung up he walked over to Hartford. "I'm headed out. I need to get to San Juan."

Hartford raised an eyebrow. "Feel like company?"

Gabe nodded. "It'd probably make Smith feel better."

45

Megan clasped her hands together in prayer as her body jolted on the metal floor she lay on in the dark. Eventually, the vehicle began to slow and turned onto a gravel road.

When the engine cut, she listened to the driver door open and tried to calm herself down as she heard footsteps approaching the back. She felt a slight breeze, which was extremely welcoming after being cooped up for so long, and then the not so nice feel of hands picking her up and tossing her over a shoulder. Trevor was smart. There was no way she would know where to run if she could manage to escape since he'd kept her blindfolded since questioning her on the boat. She wasn't sure what had happened to the other men. She'd only been aware of Trevor's presence for the last hour or two. She listened as a door opened and felt the change in the air. It was stuffier at once.

"I bring *un regalo*, Luis," she heard him say with a laugh.

She had aced Spanish, and she knew for a fact that "*regalo*" meant "gift". She swallowed the new lump in her throat. She was a gift for someone? Weren't they even going to let her see Maddy? Was Maddy even here? Her heart rate picked up, and she squirmed against Trevor, trying to wiggle free.

"Don mek me hurt yoh, sista. Almost home."

She listened as metal clanged loudly and felt her palms getting sweaty. "I want to see my sister. Right now."

He set her feet on the ground and took her hands, tearing the bindings off. The blindfold was removed next, and Trevor stood grinning at her. "'Tis a family reunion." He turned to leave the cell, closing the door behind him.

Megan spun around at once, instantly spotting the small figure curled up on the dirt floor in the corner. She took in the red hair and dove to the ground beside her. Tears sprang to her eyes. "Maddy!"

Her twin's face had been beaten so badly both sides were ballooned and black, and red with cuts. Her right eye was completely swollen shut. Bruises and cuts dotted her arms and legs as well. She looked smaller than Megan had ever seen her, like she hadn't eaten for days. And worst of all, she didn't seem to be moving.

"Don't be dead. You can't be dead. I'm here. I found you. I'm here, Maddy."

Megan placed her fingertips at Maddy's throat and sighed when she found a pulse. Her sister was only passed out. Or at least she hoped. Her relief was short lived as she surveyed her condition. She wiped tears away and carefully pulled Maddy's head into her lap. She stroked her sister's hair away from her face. She'd been to hell and back. Megan wondered what horrors her twin had faced since her disappearance. She noticed the sexy dress and the makeup that had been heavily applied to her bruised face. Had the Torrez family Gabe had mentioned done this to Maddy? Who were these people?

"Maddy, please, wake up. Don't stop fighting, Sis. I'm here with you now. I won't leave you," she said with a whisper.

She started crying harder, her body shaking lightly. A soft moan came from her sister, and the next moment her eyelid fluttered open.

Maddy stared up at her and got the saddest look on her face. "It must be another dream. You look so real. Please stay this time. I'm scared, Meg."

Megan rocked her back and forth, gently murmuring to her twin. "I'm here. It's me. And I'm really here, Maddy."

Maddy closed her eye. "I hope this isn't a dream."

46

Miguel leaned over the glass coffee table at his father's San Juan residence and snorted a line of Cocaine. Since finding out Madeline was still alive, he was depending on any kind of drug, prescription, legal, illegal, and alcohol to deal with his emotional turmoil. He'd watched the video a dozen times, and each time it got worse. Waiting for the official meet to happen was tormenting him.

"It's time, Miguel. Don' wanna be late, mon," said Dalbert.

Miguel stood up from the leather sofa and fished more pills from his pocket. He grabbed the bottle of Carlsberg Elephant from the table and downed its contents along with the pills. Moments later, Dalbert climbed into a brown pick-up truck they'd borrowed from a local, and Miguel slid into his father's Mercedes, backing it out of the garage. Miguel would show up at the meet alone, as he'd been instructed, but Dalbert would be watching from nearby.

Miguel barely paid attention to traffic lights and signs as he sped to the barrio where he would meet whoever had sent the video. He was convinced Trevor was somehow involved, but couldn't be sure. He couldn't stop thinking about what had led to this moment.

After seeing the video, Miguel had waited for Dalbert to return from his search for Trevor and then confronted him in a fit of rage. He'd demanded to know in detail what had happened the day Madeline had run off in the woods. Dalbert had explained how Madeline had fallen into the ocean and hit her head on a rock, and Trevor had sent him down to retrieve her body. When he'd climbed up with her, noticing her pulse was still beating, Trevor informed him he'd phoned Victor and been instructed to kill her. Trevor had told him to start heading back and he'd take care of it. He hadn't made it too far, when Trevor caught up and said it was done. Dalbert hadn't thought anything of it at the time since the two had always worked together. He might have sensed Trevor was acting a little strange, but he'd always carried out Victor's orders.

Dalbert had gone to Trevor's house to look for him like Miguel had asked, but he hadn't found him. After showing Dalbert the video of Madeline alive, they'd tried repeatedly to contact Trevor, but there was no answer. They'd had no choice but to contact Victor and tell him their suspicions about Trevor betraying them and taking Madeline. Victor had insisted that Dalbert go with Miguel to San Juan and shadow him for the meet. But it wasn't to watch over Miguel. Victor had given Dalbert strict orders to make sure the girl died once and for all.

Miguel couldn't believe his father wouldn't change his mind about Madeline. It had been a sign, he'd argued. Madeline didn't need to die. He'd begged and pleaded, trying to reason with his stubborn father. "Let me talk to her. After everything she's been through, she'll keep quiet about what she saw. Let me do this."

"Miguel, after everything she's been through, she's probably ready to call up the Feds and turn us all in. She's a liability, and whoever took her, Trevor it seems, knows that. Maybe that's his angle. I bet the coward will tell you that at the meet. He wants money in return for her life… He knows I have money, but don't give him anything. Just get rid of the both of them. Be sure to find out where Trevor is hiding her before you finish him. She was a witness to *murder*."

"Technically, she didn't see me pull the trigger," Miguel had replied.

"Miguel, you are too weak. The girl saw enough to send you to prison and give the Feds a reason to really start interfering with our operation. I am careful and do not leave loose ends for a reason. It's a matter of survival. Are you going to do your part to stay in this family, my son?"

Miguel had sensed the question was simultaneously a delivery of a death threat. He wondered if his father would have Dalbert kill him, too, or if he'd do it himself.

"Yes, Father. I'll do my part."

As he drove down streets full of potholes and cracks, surrounded by dilapidated housing and rundown corner stores selling liquor, beer, and cigarettes, Miguel's thoughts went back to his father, who'd grown up poor in one of the worst San Juan neighborhoods. Though he mostly lived on St. Thomas now, Victor occasionally returned to his roots, although he didn't visit his old neighborhood. He stayed in his lavish, oceanfront home.

Miguel recalled the last time he'd seen his father in San Juan. A few years earlier, Victor had spent the entire summer there, working on a business deal. In a rare attempt to repair his relationship with his father, Miguel had decided to visit him. They'd grown further and further apart in the years since Miguel's mother had died. He had flown over without telling Victor because he hadn't been able to get in touch with him for days.

When he had arrived in a taxi from the airport and let himself in, Victor was standing on the balcony drinking a glass of gin. The empty bottle had been smashed into hundreds of tiny pieces that were sprinkled around the patio tiles near his feet. "*Papá*? Are you okay?"

His father had turned around quickly, startled. His eyes were bloodshot and his expression dangerous. "Go to my bedroom, Miguel. I need you to help me with something." Then, he had smiled at Miguel. "I'm glad you're here, *Hijo*."

The unusual acceptance from his father had instantly filled Miguel with a warm feeling. He had needed to hear those words from his father so desperately. Miguel had embraced his father, before walking back inside and heading towards the master bedroom suite.

He would never forget what he found there; it would be embedded into his memory forever. In the bedroom his mother and father had once shared, a woman's body was strewn across a pile of blankets on the white, tiled floor. He had seen dead bodies before. But this was different.

He studied the room, with objects smashed everywhere, from the bedside lamps to the nightstand fallen on its end and imagined the fight she had put up. Her eye was black, whelps marred her arms and legs, and a belt, one Miguel knew was his father's, was woven tightly around her petite neck. His father had only been glad to see him so he could have Miguel get rid of his latest body for him. Rejected and burning with hate, he'd gone to the balcony to confront his father.

"That's why you're glad I'm here? Who is she?"

"Just some whore, Miguel. Get rid of the body, then hurry to clean up the room."

"What was your reason this time? Was she a threat to your business somehow? What is wrong with you, Father?"

"You're not in any position to question me, Hijo. I provide for you, but that can change in an instant. I came from the gutters of La Perla and made it to where I am today. But you? You wouldn't last a minute out there. Without me, you are nothing. Now, go get rid of her." Victor had collapsed into a deck chair, then glanced towards his son, who stood frozen in place, terror and sadness rolling through him. "Don't make me repeat myself."

Miguel had dumped the woman's body into the ocean as instructed by his father, but he'd noticed every detail about her and knew his father had lied to him. She'd worn an heirloom diamond wedding ring and band. He observed the designer clothes, the soft feel of her manicured hands and feet, even the floral scent of expensive perfume lingering on her. Even in death, he couldn't miss her beauty. She had been someone's wife. Maybe even a mother. And now she was gone.

When he had gotten back to the beach house, Victor made him clean up the master suite and erase all traces of the crime. Then he'd been put to work finding an innocent guy to pin the crime on.

Miguel spotted the street he was supposed to meet Madeline's kidnapper on and turned the car down it. He had told his father he would kill Madeline or let Dalbert do it, but that had been a lie. He wasn't going to let Dalbert or anyone touch Madeline once he found her. Even if he had to kill Dalbert. Madeline would not be a victim of his father's schemes. Madeline was his.

47

Gabe peered through the FBI issued binoculars and sighed. Hartford was sipping coffee from a canister in the passenger seat of the sedan beside him. They'd pulled an all-nighter, staking out Torrez's San Juan residence. Miguel was crashing there, along with his man, Dalbert, but no one had left the house while they'd been watching.

Gabe had planned to take a closer look around the Torrez property that morning, but then Smith had phoned with the name on the wire transfer, and the higher ups had wanted them to switch gears and follow the new trail. Since Hartford's office had gotten involved, and Smith had discovered the lead, the DEA had jumped in with both feet, and a full, joint task force investigation into the missing twins, the attack by the hired hit man, and finding any connection to the Torrez family was underway.

Presently, they were parked in the high-end residential community of Ocean Park, where elegant homes and high-rise condos overlooked the palm tree-lined beach. Agency analysts had tracked down the transfer from a man named Ricardo Rivera. The DEA had dug up everything on the man, and discovered the prominent business owner, CEO of Rivera Plastics, had multiple San Juan properties. Until the recent wire transfer to Lukas, nothing had appeared out of the ordinary in his records. And if it hadn't been for the hacking skills of the analysts, the wire transfer would have remained a secret.

By all accounts, Rivera appeared to be a respected, local business-man. The only thing that rang any bells was that his wife had been murdered three years before, but the man had confessed and was serving his life sentence in a mental facility. So what was Rivera up to? Why had he really hired Lukas? The joint task force had sent in teams to snoop around Ricardo's various properties, but Gabe knew they were still missing something. He was wondering if he should drive to Torrez's once more and let the rest of the team handle the Rivera properties. Smith assured him their team in Miami was trying to connect the dots to why Rivera would've hired Lukas, but Gabe knew time was running out.

Hartford looked over at Gabe. He'd just received a text message. "My team in St. Thomas says Victor is at a bar in Red Hook having cocktails with a couple of girls. Nothing out of the ordinary on his end."

"If he is involved with the twins, or this Rivera man, he'll have his people handle any dirty work. He's good. Otherwise we would've caught him by now," Gabe remarked, agitation in his voice.

"Well, something's up with this Rivera man. We've got a team watching him at his office. He could lead us to the girls…if he's involved."

Gabe knew Hartford was trying to be positive, so he shook his head. "Yeah, he could lead us straight to them." His cell phone rang, and he was glad for the interruption. He felt more and more desperate as each minute passed. If something happened to Megan, he'd never forgive himself. He'd lost her. *On his watch*. It was Smith. "What's up?"

"Staying out of trouble?"

"I bet you wish you were here, so you could make sure of that."

"Anything new at Rivera's house?"

"Other than his daughter being taken to school? No," he said, frustrated.

"I think we've got something. We're sending in a team."

"Give me the address."

"First you're gonna want to drive to the bodega a block south of your location."

"The one on Santa Maria?"

"That's the one."

Gabe turned the key in the ignition, shifted the car into gear, and took off. "You putting someone else on the house after I leave?"

"They're already there."

"What's at the bodega?"

Smith chuckled into the phone. "I'm waiting for you to pick me up."

Gabe's mouth fell open a little, but he recovered at once. "Where are we headed?"

"We found another property, under Rivera's mother's name."

"How'd they miss it before?"

"His mother lives with them. They overlooked it. And they found out more about the wife's murder. She was beaten, raped, and strangled to death."

Gabe's mind raced. That sounded a lot like some of the past victim's they'd tried to link to Victor Torrez. "That sounds hauntingly familiar."

"It is. They tried to contact the lead detective on the case, but get this, he's gone. Up and retired, left Puerto Rico without a trace after the case closed."

"I don't like where this is going."

"We found another guy in the precinct who recalled how Rivera hadn't believed the man who confessed was guilty. Rivera told them who he suspected."

"Let me guess. Victor Torrez."

"Yep. So there's our motive. Motive to get revenge. And how do you pay someone back for murdering someone you love?"

"You murder someone they love. So Maddy was just a lure. Miguel is the real target. I should've stayed on his house so I could follow him," he snapped.

"We sent someone to his place a few minutes ago."

Adrenaline shot through Gabe's limbs. If Miguel was the target, Maddy was just a tool to get him there. And Megan had simply gotten in the way by asking too many questions. Rivera wouldn't have any use for them once he had Miguel. "I'm hanging up. I see you."

Gabe filled Hartford in as they pulled up in front of an old pay phone. Smith climbed in the vehicle, and they sped away. "Hartford, long time no see," he said, handing him the address.

"What's the matter, Miami wear you out, Smith?" Hartford returned.

"No, but worrying about Gabe did. And I can see he needs my help." He patted Gabe's shoulder and grinned. "Check out the beard and long hair. No wonder you've got women problems. Don't worry. I'm here now."

Hartford raised a brow. "You've got female troubles, Gabe?"

Gabe shook his head as he followed the directions the GPS was rattling off. "No, just partner problems. He thinks I'm gonna get shot. He's really here to keep an eye on me."

"I'm a multitasker. I'll keep you alive *and* sort out your love problems," Smith said cheerfully.

Gabe knew Smith was only trying to lighten the mood. And he couldn't say he minded the distraction, if only for a moment. "Speaking of love, how's Kate?"

Smith grunted. "She's taking some "me" time. I don't get her."

Gabe's laughed echoed throughout the sedan. "That's code for she's dumping you, man."

Smith smirked. "Yeah, I figure. I'll tell you all about it after we wrap up this little rescue mission."

Gabe's eyes met his partner's through the rear view mirror. "So you think they're still alive?"

"Maybe. Maybe not. Let's just say I feel bad for not believing you this whole time. You trusted your instincts the day you called me about Miguel's new girlfriend and when her sister showed up, too. Both times, I doubted you a little I guess. I was thinking you were too distracted with your unresolved past…the unsolved case and all. Sorry, partner."

Gabe focused on the winding road as they got further away from the city. "Forget about it. I'm glad you're here to watch my back, Smith."

He prayed Megan and Maddy were hanging in there. And that they'd get there in time to save them. He stepped on the gas.

He couldn't let them die.

48

Megan watched as Luis retrieved another bottle of a beer labeled Medalla from the cooler beside his feet. He'd dropped the empty bottles to the ground around his chair, too inebriated to even care or pick them up. He'd been chugging them down ever since Trevor had taken off awhile ago.

Maddy had managed to wake up now and then, but she was weak and her body was burning up with a fever. After her initial relief to see Megan, she'd become depressed. She said Megan never should've looked for her because neither one of them were walking away alive. Megan had told her not to give up. Miracles really did happen. She just had to believe. She'd said it as much for her own good as for her sister's. Now was not the time to give up hope. She had to think like a survivor.

Megan had gotten a few facts from her sister. The guard watching them was Luis. They both had decided they were probably on Puerto Rico because Luis didn't speak a word of English and the TV had been broadcasting Puerto Rican shows all day. Maddy had been beaten on a video that was supposed to lure the guy she'd been dating, Miguel Torrez. It was a trap. The guy Trevor had worked for Miguel but apparently was double-crossing him for his new boss. The man Rivera was orchestrating the entire thing as some sort of revenge for his wife who'd been murdered. Maddy thought Miguel might have been the one who murdered her, since she'd seen him beating a man in the woods, and that same man's body had ended up on the boat they'd transferred her in. Maddy had been drugged and nearly attacked by Rivera, but she'd bitten him and he'd punched her then tossed her to the side, promising he'd show her real pain when he returned.

As she'd listened to her sister talk, Megan couldn't believe the nightmare Maddy had already been through. Afterwards, Megan shared with her how Gabe had told her about the Torrez family being a notorious local crime family in the islands, and Maddy had shook her head, distraught. "Yeah, it's true. But I was too dumb to realize who Miguel really was. I should've listened to you, Meg, and never gone on another vacation. You were right."

Megan was terrified the fever would kill her twin. She'd never felt her that hot. She was dehydrated, and her breathing was ragged. The bruises on her ribs were awful. Maddy needed to be in a hospital. And Megan was desperate to get them out of there. Whenever Maddy had woken up, Megan had told her they had to try to escape and had been working on the best plan she could come up with. They'd have to give it a try. Because if Maddy was right, they'd kill the twins once they had Miguel.

Luis began to sag in his chair, his attention to the TV screen fading away. Now was the time to move. Megan leaned to whisper in her twin's ear. "Maddy, it's time. Remember the plan?"

Maddy shook her head. "I can feel all of my limbs finally. I'm ready to kick butt," she said dryly.

"I don't know about that. But OK. Remember, he can't know you've regained your mobility."

Maddy coughed and tilted her head towards the bars. "Luis, bathroom, *por favor*!" she yelled.

Luis glanced over his shoulder before turning to the TV.

She tried again. "Emergency, Luis. *Baño*, ahora!"

Maybe he was too drunk to care. Maybe miracles really did happen, but he stood up from the chair, swayed slightly to and fro, then shuffled over to the cell. He held up his index finger, waving it back and forth. "*Solo una.*"

Maddy pretended she couldn't get up, and Megan pulled her to her feet and draped her arm around her shoulder. She held onto her waist and hobbled towards the door as Luis opened it.

He frowned. "Una chica," he growled.

"I need to help her. *Ayuda*." Megan said, agitatedly, glaring at him defiantly.

He let out a revolting breath that swept over Megan's face. She imagined his body nearing alcohol poisoning level. He rolled his eyes. "*Vamos*."

Megan and Maddy walked out of their cell, and Luis glanced at the TV as applause sounded from the small screen. It was the only chance they would get.

Megan let go of Maddy, who managed to balance right away, and rammed her foot with all of her strength in between Luis's legs. As the one-inch heel of her sandals crushed into his groin, she thanked God she hadn't lost her shoes on the boat ride over. The prison keys fell out of Luis's hands, and he grasped onto his manhood as he fell to the ground, moaning. Megan grabbed the nearest empty bottle of beer and raised it high above her head, then smashed it with all of her might over his temple.

When she stood up, Maddy appeared shocked, but nodded approvingly. "Good idea."

Megan grabbed Maddy's hand and led her to the door. "Let's get out of here. We'll run as far as we can. We'll find a main road. I don't think it's too far."

They rushed outside, and the sun blinded them instantly. As Megan rubbed her eyes, hard metal pressed to her head. "Goin' som' where?"

Megan felt her hope, and her mode for survival drain away. Trevor stood on one side with a gun trained on her head and had another aimed at Maddy. A man she recognized from the boat ride hovered in front of them, holding a gun at a good-looking man, who's mouth was bleeding while his hands were tied behind him.

The man glanced between them, shock on his face. "Madeline?" he said, as his eyes settled on Maddy.

She leaned into Megan's side. "Go to hell, Miguel."

"We all get da chance soon enough. Inside," Trevor ordered. He picked up the phone as he led the way. "Yeah, boss. I neva heard from Lukas, but I got 'em. Got 'em all." And he hung up the phone.

49

"My sister needs a doctor, Trevor."

Trevor's laughter filled the small shed. He was pacing in front of the prison cells, glancing up at the door every so often. Apparently, he was anxious for his boss to arrive. His eyes met Megan's. "Las time I check, you weren't in position ta ask fa favas."

"She's burning up with a fever. I'm pretty sure you fractured her ribs, and her face is hardly recognizable with all of the swelling. She at least needs some water. Please, I'm begging you. I know you have water in that cooler." Megan pointed at Luis, who had his feet propped up on the table, with an ice pack over the injury she had given him. "And he certainly wasn't drinking the water," she added angrily.

Trevor shook his head, laughing. "No, no he wasn't."

Megan stroked her sister's hair. Maddy had curled up in her lap as soon as they'd been locked up. "Please, someone's going to notice I'm gone, now, too, by the way. Have you thought about that? Two missing women? Sisters? The police will have to investigate now. And the FBI," she added, thinking of Gabe. She wondered if he'd gotten to them. And what he was doing. Had he flown to St. Croix? Was he still in St. Thomas?

Trevor smirked. "Your friend the cook mighta told de police some ting, but don't matta. We looked inta him, by de wey. Bet ya didn't know he has a felony record." He watched Megan's face for a reaction, but she forced herself to stay calm. It couldn't be true. But even if it were, she knew Gabe had a good heart. Maybe he'd done something in the past. It didn't matter.

Trevor smiled. "I see ya didna know."

"Trevor, just give her some water. She's right. What do you care anyway? Do you think your new boss wants her to die before he gets here?" Miguel questioned angrily.

He was sitting behind the bars of the prison cell directly across from theirs. He'd been apologizing to Maddy, but she wouldn't respond to him at all. He had a lot to say. Lots of excuses about how he didn't order her hit. It had all been his father. Megan wondered how Miguel thought that could possibly make Maddy feel better. He was definitely drunk and high or something. But he hadn't said much that had made sense until now. Megan looked at Trevor. Would he listen to Miguel?

Trevor scowled, tilting his head towards Miguel's prison. "I ben takin ordas from yo family a long time. Eva sinc dem long ago days back in Haypenny yoh pop been havin me kill all de threats ta his business. From junkie who canna pay ta runnas who tekin what's not theirs. That's all over now. It's been twenty long years. And I'm moving on. So, no, I don think I'll give ha some wata."

Megan's mind raced. Had Trevor been the guy who'd killed Gabe's family so long ago? Gabe had been looking for twenty years. And he'd shown her the house at Haypenny, the only property there, which was his family's house. She exhaled. What did it matter now? She'd probably never have the chance to tell Gabe what she'd heard Trevor say.

"How is working for someone else moving on? And why am I here?" Miguel countered.

"Once your pop is gone, I'll be able to tek ova operations."

"You actually think you're going to kill Victor?" Miguel gave a bitter laugh.

Trevor glared at him. "Yeh, as soon as he hear we've got yoh, he'll meet our demands. He'll come. And soon, Miguel. He will."

"That's where you're wrong. My father cares about his own life way more than anyone else. He'll never come for me. Your plan is a dud. But if you let us go, I'll pay you whatever you want. You'll be rich. But all three of us have to be released. Unharmed."

"I know yo pops, Miguel. He's been havin me tek care of yoh fa eva. He'll show."

50

"What do you mean Rivera is almost to the citrus farm?"

Gabe listened with growing concern as Smith talked over the two-way radio. They were closing in on the secret property Rivera had listed under his mother's name. It was on the outskirts of the city, near the ocean. Hardly any cars had passed them at all, in either direction, for the last ten minutes of the drive.

Smith dropped the radio and frowned. "So the other agents have been tailing Rivera, and they said they couldn't get through to us. We must have lost a signal for a minute. That's why they radioed when they were within range of us. "Rivera's almost to the farm. He'll probably beat us there."

Gabe had wanted to set up surveillance before Rivera arrived. They'd planned to hide their vehicles and go by foot onto the large property so they could take positions and wait for Rivera to show up. If the girls were in his custody, they'd let him lead the way to where he was keeping them, and they would be right there to help. Now, they wouldn't have the time.

Nothing was going as planned. The agents who'd gone back to the Torrez place had come up empty. They hadn't seen Miguel, which meant he could have already met Rivera. Gabe was on edge with worry. If Rivera already had Miguel, there wouldn't be a reason to keep the twins around.

"Alright, we'll roll with it. I wonder how close he is," Gabe remarked.

"That's his Escalade I think turning down that gravel road," Hartford said, pointing half a mile ahead of them.

"He beat us here," muttered Smith. He pressed the button on the radio. "Everyone fall back. We'll wait until he's in before we move in."

As the other agents replied, Gabe sighed. "I don't like it. What if he barges in and kills the girls first thing? We shouldn't wait."

Gabe picked up the binoculars and climbed out of the car. He stood on the ledge and peered through the lenses. The Escalade was coming to a stop right past a small house on the property. It looked like a utility shed was behind it. There were so many trees and bushes surrounding the property it was difficult to be sure what he was seeing. He climbed into the vehicle.

"He's coming to a stop. We should move in."

"But we need to catch him on site if we want any charges to stick. We have to play by the book," Hartford said reluctantly. "Is he still in the Escalade or did he go inside the house?"

"I'm not sure the house is where he's even headed. There's a shed there, too," Gabe snapped.

Smith and Hartford exchanged glances.

Gabe reached over the seat and picked up the radio. "He's far enough in. Who's handling the front gate security?"

Two agents volunteered at once, and Gabe turned to Smith and Hartford. "I'm making the call."

They both nodded. "Go for it," Smith said.

"Affirmative, Carter. Move in. Make sure to take out any communication lines they have. We'll be right behind you," Gabe radioed.

"Copy that," Carter responded.

Gabe pulled the car forward and spared Hartford, then Smith, another glance. "We're bringing them out alive. Both of them."

51

Ricardo chewed a couple of antacids, then stepped into the shed, his palms damp with nerves. He was so close to getting the revenge he so desperately sought.

He wanted to see Miguel with his own eyes before he phoned Victor. Trevor was pacing the ground between the cells. At first, Ricardo hadn't been sure he could trust Trevor, but in the end, even though Lukas was MIA, Trevor had delivered and managed to get the girls and Miguel to him. Of course, he'd been paid substantially.

"Señor Rivera, good aftanoon," Trevor said enthusiastically.

Rivera noted the ice on Luis's head. "What happened to him?"

"De sista."

Ricardo walked towards the twins' cell. Megan pulled Maddy closer. "So she's as ill-mannered as her sister? Not surprising."

Megan glared at him. "We have nothing to do with this. People will be looking for us. Please just let us go."

"They'll look, but they'll find all of the wrong information. These sort of unfortunate things happen all of the time, Miss MacKenna. Don't worry. I'm sure your grandmother will be relieved to learn you were having fun at least…on the fatal scuba trip you and your twin took."

Megan's face paled. Ricardo smiled. "Sorry about your luck." He turned towards Miguel, who was watching him intently. "So you are Victor's son…I suppose I should apologize in advance for what's about to happen to you. It had to be you, and only you, Miguel. Victor doesn't have any other blood relatives."

"I can pay you," Miguel replied. "Let me and the girls go. Take my money. We'll disappear."

As Trevor laughed, Ricardo scowled. "This isn't about money."

"Then what is it about? Why did you have to pull innocent women into it? There were other ways you could've gotten to me."

"Dis was da easiest," Trevor supplied. "I saw da opportunity an I took it."

"You're going to regret this, T. Even if you manage to get out of here alive, my father will hunt you down."

"Your father won't be hunting anyone down. Not after we capture him," Rivera informed Miguel smugly. "And how can you preach to me about *innocent* women when your father has never had a problem murdering innocent women?" he screamed.

Miguel shook his head. "So that's what this is all about. Who did my father kill?"

Ricardo popped an antacid as he gazed at no point in particular on the ground. "He killed my wife, Ana. He tricked her into meeting our priest. Of course she went running to help. But it was a set up. He captured her. Then he raped her, beat her, and strangled her to death."

Miguel's shoulders slumped forward. He seemed genuinely shaken to hear the news. "I'm sorry for what he did." He lifted his chin up. "But he did it. Not me. And not Madeline or her sister."

"It doesn't matter. Someone has to pay. And I want Victor to know what the pain of losing someone really feels like. And I want to hear him confess to my face about killing Ana." Rivera paused. "How can you not act surprised or phased that I just said your father killed my wife? You must be just like him."

Miguel got to his feet and grabbed the bars. "I'm nothing like him."

Trevor cocked his head to the side. "Well, deh some definite similarities between yoh....murdera."

"Says the other murderer in the room," Miguel countered. He turned pleading eyes to Ricardo. "Do you have kids, Rivera? What would they think if they knew what you are doing? You have a choice. You don't have to go down this path. You don't have to become a monster."

"I have a daughter. But I'm hardly any good to her now. What your father did destroyed her. She can barely function without medication. She of all people would understand why I'm doing this."

"What's the plan anyway? How do you think you'll get my father here?"

Ricardo pulled his phone out and stepped away. "I'm glad you asked. I'm calling him now."

Ricardo felt the rush, the thrill of revenge running through his veins. He couldn't wait to hurt Victor. The phone number Trevor had assured him would work rang, and after three rings, Victor answered himself.

"Talk to me."

Ricardo would recognize that voice anywhere. He'd never forget the sound of it. It had been haunting his nightmares for three years. He lowered his tone as he turned towards the shed entrance and began to pace. "I have something of yours, Victor."

"I'm listening."

"If you ever want to see your son again, you'll meet my demands."

"Who is this? Did Trevor set this up?"

"It doesn't matter. This is about Miguel."

"I remember your voice now…*Ricardo*."

Ricardo came to a stop. He hadn't expected that. He swallowed the sudden anxiety that ran through him. "So, then you understand why I have your son."

"It's a crazy thing…revenge. It can cause a man to make so many reckless decisions. The thing about it is, once you start something, you better be prepared to face the consequences."

"There's only one thing I want. I want to talk to you in person. I want you to tell me why you killed Ana. If you meet me, I'll let Miguel live. I'll let him go as soon as you get here."

"We all have choices to make Ricardo. Everyday. Like are we going to put our pretty wife on display for all to admire? And act surprised when other, more powerful men notice her?"

A wave of nausea rolled through him. "Stop talking about her. Meet me in person you coward. All you've ever done is taunt me. You're too weak to say that to my face now, aren't you?"

"I'm not weak, Ricardo. I'm a survivor. And survivors make tough decisions everyday. And we learn how to live with them. Keep Miguel. Do what you want with him. He's always been weak. Just like you."

As the line went dead, Ricardo's jaw fell open, and the phone slid from his palm.

52

Megan watched as Ricardo's entire demeanor changed. Moments ago, he'd been excited about getting his revenge on Victor. But she could see the phone call hadn't gone over well. She drew Maddy's hand into hers and prayed. If there was ever a time for a miracle, it was right then.

Trevor stepped cautiously closer to Ricardo. "Every ting OK?"

Ricardo gestured towards the girls. "Bring them out. All three of them."

"Now?"

"Do it," he ordered.

Trevor shrugged, and pivoted towards the cells. "No problem boss man, no problem."

Tears poured down Megan's face. She was out of ideas. No one had come for them. And she had a sinking feeling this was it. As the prison door opened, her grip on Maddy tightened. She'd passed out, probably from the fever.

"Come on out," Trevor barked.

Megan shook Maddy lightly. "Come on, Sis. Can you stand with me?"

Maddy peered up at her. "Is it over yet, Meg? I had a dream we were home," she said in a hoarse sounding voice.

A tear spilled from Megan's eye onto her twin's face. "We're almost home, Maddy. And the best part is, we're together."

She pulled Maddy up and cradled her to her side, supporting her weight. Her skin was burning compared to her own. Maddy's head fell to Megan's shoulder. "Thanks for coming for me. I didn't think you would ever leave your job."

Megan let the tears fall, but smiled as she carried her twin from the cell. "And miss seeing you? Not a chance. You're the only thing that matters to me. I wish I would've realized that sooner. You were right, Maddy. I was too caught up in my little bubble."

"At least you were safe," Maddy replied, her words slurring slightly.

Megan held onto her. She glanced ahead towards the door. The guy who'd come in with Trevor earlier and the guy Luis were watching the scene unfold, each with a gun in their hand. They were trapped. Even if she could make it, Maddy was in no condition to run. She could barely stand up anymore. "I was safe. But I was missing out. Did I tell you what I did the other day, by the way? You never would've believed it."

"Does it top rescuing your sister from an island?" Maddy asked softly.

"Probably." She kept the slow pace, hobbling with her twin towards the man who'd seal their fate. She figured she should keep Maddy talking as long as possible. It might be their last conversation.

"I'm dying to know Meg. What did you do? Get a tattoo?"

"No, but I'll tell you what I did. I kissed a man."

"Get out of here. Now I know I'm dreaming. Either that or they've already killed us. I must be dead."

"No, it's true. I kissed him and trust me, he didn't see it coming."

"But I bet he liked it."

"I don't know. He seemed a little confused. But that's fine. I liked it. And I'm glad I did it. Even if it was a little embarrassing afterwards. It was worth it."

As they neared Ricardo, he motioned for them to get down on their knees. He had a gun trained on Maddy, and with a heavy heart Megan accepted they couldn't run. Even if she tried to escape, Maddy wouldn't make it two feet. As they got down, she turned Maddy's head towards her chest so she couldn't see the guns.

Maddy whispered. "I want to meet this guy you know. When we get home."

Megan nearly choked on a sob but forced herself to stay in control. Maddy was so delirious she really believed they were going home. "You bet. I think you'll like him. He's more your type anyways."

She tightened her grip around her sister as Trevor approached. He shoved Miguel onto his knees on the other side of Maddy. "One las reunion. Ain't it bitta sweet."

Miguel's hands had been tied behind him, but his legs were free. He started to get up, but Trevor aimed the gun straight at his forehead and motioned him down. "You don't have to do this, Ricardo. What's the point? My father won't even be sad if you kill me. He's not coming for me, right?"

Ricardo shook his head. "No, he's not."

"So what's the point then? He won't even care if you kill me! He probably told you that on the phone."

Ricardo gazed at him darkly, his fingers tightened around the gun. "I don't care what he said, losing his son will hurt him. And at this point, that has to count for something. It's time, Trevor. You do it."

Trevor lifted the gun towards Miguel. "Any last words, Miguel? For old times, yoh know?"

Miguel opened his mouth to reply, but a gunshot rang out, and blood poured from Trevor's mouth as he fell forward. Megan sat up taller, searching for their savior, but as everyone turned around, a man she didn't recognize was running from the front door with the gun in his hand aimed directly at Maddy. He had dreads down to his waist, and muscles bulging over his arms and legs. Luis and the guy beside the door raised their weapons, but the man ducked low and ran fast, aiming at Maddy.

As he squeezed the trigger, Miguel screamed and dove in front of Maddy. "No, Dalbert!"

Megan reacted, and dove as well, covering Maddy with her body. She tasted a mouthful of dirt as her face hit the ground, but she'd fallen sideways across her sister's body. Gunshots exploded all around, blaring throughout the small shed. Her ears rang as they popped, one after the other. Megan curved herself over Maddy, praying she would at least save her sister.

She waited for the pain, the burn she'd read about from gunshot wounds. But nothing came. The gunshots died down, but she couldn't move. She held on as tight as she could to Maddy. After a moment she heard voices shouting to one another. Commands. Radios echoing orders. And then hands pulled her away from her sister.

"No! Don't hurt her. Don't hurt Maddy," she screamed as she fought as hard as she could. She had to shield Maddy.

"Megan, it's over. You're OK."

She'd recognize that low voice anywhere. She quit struggling at once. He stood in front of her. "Gabe?" she asked in a meek voice.

He drew her into his strong embrace. He nearly squeezed the breath out of her, and she closed her eyes. It was Gabe.

He murmured against her ear, "Thank God, we weren't too late."

He'd found her.

But how? She retreated a step, still clinging to his arms. She scanned his body, and her jaw fell open. He had on a bulletproof vest and a hat labeled DEA. He appeared lethal. Handsome. And as usual, concerned.

Stunned, Megan tore her gaze from him and surveyed the room. An agent with a medical bag kneeled beside Maddy. There were men and women everywhere wearing the same hats and vests. Some with the DEA label, others with ones that said FBI. They were hovering over bodies. And talking into radios. One of them was calling for a life flight helicopter to come. They needed two hospital transports. Megan wondered who else besides Maddy needed a doctor. Had Miguel survived? Ricardo? Anyone? She couldn't tell in all of the confusion who was injured and who was dead. There was so much blood. She felt dizzy all of a sudden. What was happening?

Fingers pressed lightly on her arms, bringing her back. She stared up at him in a trance. Was she dreaming? "Gabe? Is it over?"

"Yes, you're safe. We took down all of the threats. We're going to get you and Maddy to the hospital."

She nodded, panic still racing through her from head to toe. She didn't have time for questions. Her sister's life was on the line. Still, she hesitated. She needed to say something to him. But clearly it was a conversation that would take some time, and she wanted to be beside Maddy. "I don't know how you did it, Gabe. But—"

He squeezed her arms reassuringly. "We'll talk later. I'll tell you everything, I promise, Megan. I know you want to go to her. It's fine. She needs you."

One of the agents called to Gabe. "Over here, Gabe, you're gonna want to hear this."

Megan looked to the agent, who was huddled over Miguel. He must have survived the gunshot wound. She glanced back at Gabe, who still hadn't responded to the other agent. "Thanks, Gabe," she said softly.

She dropped to the ground beside Maddy. One of the agents was placing an oxygen mask over her mouth. She took Maddy's hand in her own. "Hang in there, Maddy. We're getting out of here after all. Our miracle arrived."

53

Victor stood enveloped by the dark, moonless night on the edge of the marina dock, listening as the fishing boat approached in idle.

Unlike your average Boston Whaler, the center console was equipped with four 350 horse-powered outboards, which made it faster than the whalers typically seen in Caribbean waters. It had arrived on time, a little early even, on its run from Tortola to St. Thomas. There was only a tiny white light, no larger than a dot from where Victor stood, pinpointing the whaler's location. The water around the dock had an unwelcoming stagnant scent, but the gentle waves rolling in as the boat drew nearer sounded peaceful. He hadn't met one of his boats like this for years, and it reminded him of his younger days, making him smile with pride. The filthy-faced orphan running drugs for pimps and prostitutes had overcome it all. He'd built a kingdom.

He loved being here at this quiet hour. The boatyard was abandoned at three o'clock in the morning, and further shielded from the dense clouds covering the stars above. Victor's bodyguards stood on either side of him in their customary fashion, but tonight they'd help unload the shipment.

Usually, Trevor, Dalbert, and Miguel came over from St. Croix, specifically to meet this boat. It had always fallen under their responsibilities. But as far as Victor could tell, Dalbert was gone. The last phone call he'd received from him had been right after the call from Ricardo. Dalbert had caught him up on everything Victor already had learned from Ricardo, and Victor had ordered Dalbert to go inside the shed and make sure the twins were taken out. He wasn't sure if he'd made it out alive. But he'd have confirmation of that in the morning.

Miguel was dead. Of that, he was certain, because he'd refused to comply with Ricardo's demands. It had been a long time coming as far as he was concerned. Miguel hadn't been able to handle his responsibilities. Trevor was the only one he wasn't sure about, but he knew that even if Trevor had slipped away, he'd find him and deal with him eventually. Either way, he couldn't ignore his shipping schedule. He had to take care of business.

Victor's drug network reached as far as Atlanta, but also stretched to the Dominican Republic, Tortola, and down island, to places like St. Martin and Antigua. The boat arriving now contained one hundred fifty kilos of Cocaine, which would be distributed systematically, per its normal routine. Shipment times and meeting spots were ever-changing from the outside looking in but managed to follow the pattern Victor had designed himself. And Victor was confidant the Feds would never figure it out.

The boat came into full view and Victor nodded at the driver, Clive, who had been working for him for the past decade. Clive bobbed his head at Victor as the bodyguards grabbed the ropes and pulled the whaler alongside the pier.

Instantly, the team jumped into action. Victor didn't need to explain what to do. Even without the usual players, Trevor, Dalbert, and Miguel, this was a smooth ritual, polished over time. Everyone worked in silence, quietly carrying the bags full of stacks of kilos up the dock and onto the awaiting truck that would transport the product to one of Victor's hidden distribution hubs.

Victor stood inside of the truck, stacking the bags between crates of watersports supplies, such as lifejackets and paddleboards, that were sent to restock his various rental companies, one of the many cover up businesses he was involved in. He wouldn't normally be this intimately involved in the labor, but tonight was different. Miguel was dead. The more he thought about it, the higher he lifted his head. He'd done what he had to do. He did what real survivors, strong people did. What few would be able to do.

As Victor set the last bag down, he heard a voice call out from the dark parking lot. "Hands up!"

He spun around to see Clive, who'd been standing just outside the truck between the body guards, pull his gun from his waist and fire blindly at the figures in black swat gear creeping towards them.

One of the men in black fell, but not before shooting Clive in the chest. Clive landed on the gravel lot, as men yelled at them to raise their hands where they could see them. The bodyguards glanced back at Victor uneasily, but held their hands up as the agents moved in closer with Glock 40 calibers aimed in their direction.

An agent, whose bearded face wasn't concealed like the others, rushed to the injured man on the ground. "It's a shoulder wound. The rest of the shots hit your vest. Thank God."

Another agent bent over Clive, then called out, "He's dead."

"Victor Torrez, you are under arrest for trafficking and the distribution of Cocaine," said the agent with the beard as he walked closer. As the bodyguards were taken into custody, the agent continued. "You're also under arrest for the murder of Ana Montega Rivera. And a slew of other crimes. We've got so much on you, you've won a trip to federal prison for the rest of your life. Your son told us everything as he bled out on the floor of Ricardo's shed. That has to hurt just a little bit, right? A son giving up intimate details of his father's life of crime on his dying breath?"

Victor's brow wove together. "But..."

"And we recorded it all."

"Miguel wouldn't. Trevor maybe. But never Miguel. He knows better."

"You'd be surprised how a father's betrayal can get a guy to talk."

Victor began to raise his hands even as he fell to his knees in mock surrender. He grabbed the P-90 automatic weapon in front of the closest container. He couldn't go to prison. Even if he could bribe every guard and live better than the other prisoners; he wasn't built for a cage. And if Miguel had told them even the slightest thing about his operation, which he clearly had, they would put him away forever. This is what he'd been trying to get Miguel to understand. There was a reason Victor killed to protect what was his.

As the agent moved towards him, Victor jumped up with his weapon firing. He thought of the first time, at age nine, when he'd fired a gun on the streets of San Juan.

He got off one round before he went down in a blaze of bullets. As he drew his final breath he thought of his son. Even on his deathbed, he'd been a disappointment. He should've killed Miguel a long time ago.

54

Megan fussed with the hospital gown, trying to straighten it and smooth out the wrinkles, but gave up after a moment. The doctors had insisted on admitting her and treating her for mild dehydration and facial injuries.

What she would give to have her suitcase back so she could slip on some of her own clothes. Her nerves and emotions were making her restless. It had been two days since they'd arrived at the local hospital. Agents had stood guard outside the door to the room she and Maddy shared, and they'd been filing reports and talking to the twins off and on since they'd rescued them from the citrus farm.

She'd learned so much in the past two days; she was still reeling with shock and relief. She couldn't believe how close they'd come to death. And she couldn't believe how Gabe, the man she had taken for a beach bum, the man she'd kissed, had been the one to rescue them.

Megan shook her head and let it fall onto the hospital pillow as she replayed it all. After they'd arrived at the hospital and the doctors had gone to work to save Maddy, they'd tried to separate Megan from her twin. It hadn't gone over well.

Megan had sobbed while demanding they let her remain by Maddy's side until she knew she'd be OK. She'd refused the treatment they were insisting she needed and told them they couldn't touch her until they'd taken care of Maddy. As the other agents had argued alongside the doctors, Gabe had suddenly swept in, every bit the hero, looking strong and no-nonsense in his DEA uniform, and taken her side. He held the doctors at arms length, insisting they listen to Megan and allow her to stay beside her twin throughout the evaluation and procedures.

Once Megan had been assured Maddy was getting the IV fluids she needed so desperately, that her fever was starting to go down, and that she would heal from the fractured ribs and multiple facial lacerations and swelling, Gabe convinced her to let the doctors evaluate her. She'd argued at first, but he'd taken her hand and told her he wasn't going to stop worrying about her until she let them examine her. And she caved. She'd been hooked up to an IV for the first day, due to her own dehydration, and they'd patched up her mouth where Trevor's fist had left a nasty cut.

Gabe had also made sure the twins were settled into a joint room and properly guarded twenty-four seven by federal agents. After she'd been evaluated, he'd offered to answer her questions if she had them.

And she had certainly asked a lot of questions.

With a few other agents in the room, Gabe had answered them all. She wanted to know how much of his story had been the truth, how much was cover, and though she'd pieced it together pretty quickly, she had wanted to hear from him exactly why he'd helped her, why he'd tried to get her to go home, and every detail from his angle. She'd wanted to know why they hadn't taken Maddy's disappearance more seriously at first, and though he seemed sorry for the way the system and the rules behind federal cases and in their agencies operated, he'd explained every obstacle he himself had faced in getting her the help she needed.

After talking to him, she'd felt better. She'd known all along that her feeling about him was right. He'd been keeping something back from her. She just never in a million years would've thought his secret was he was a federal agent for the DEA and that he'd been on an undercover assignment trying to bring down a notorious crime ring.

His mother's maiden name was Sanchez. Technically, his name was Gabriel Walker, and he worked for the DEA in south Florida, based out of Miami. He'd taken the St. Croix assignment over three months ago, his one time home. His grandmother had moved him to Fort Lauderdale to live with her and her cousin after his family had been murdered twenty years earlier. She listened to his story of earning his degrees, including his Master's in Criminal Justice in Chicago, and then returning to Florida to work for the DEA. His partner, Paul Smith, had interjected often, filling in details he felt Gabe was keeping out, like the time he'd been shot and narrowly escaped death by the bullet that had almost hit a vital organ. She liked Paul, not only because he was funny, but because she could see he genuinely cared for his longtime DEA partner.

She imagined how conflicted Gabe must have been trying to keep his cover, keep her out of harms way, and not be able to explain how much danger her sister had gotten herself into by dating Miguel Torrez. He hadn't even been able to tell her the truth about the hired hit man he'd fought with and ultimately killed in her hotel room. She couldn't believe what he'd done to protect her. He explained everything the DEA had discovered, even how Trevor had pawned Maddy's necklace at his boss's store, ISLAND GEMS.

Megan had told him, and the other agents hovering around, in explicit details, everything that had happened in the shed, including the conversation between Trevor and Miguel, or T as Miguel had called him, about the killings twenty years ago in Haypenny. Smith had patted Gabe somberly on the back and told him it was over. It had to have been the same T who showed up at Gabe's house that long ago night. Gabe's eyes had filled with peace, and he'd agreed. It wasn't how he'd expected things to wrap up, but they finally had.

After they'd been talking for awhile, they'd received a call, approving something they wouldn't share with her, and had said they had something to take care of. Gabe had smiled at her and told her he was glad she was so stubborn and hadn't given up on looking for Maddy. On his way out, he'd promised she hadn't seen the last of "this fry cook" and that he'd return without his annoying partner to see her before she and her sister flew home.

That had been a day ago. Megan sighed as the nurse came into the room to check her vitals. Would she see Gabe Walker again? Did she really want to? Of course she did. Who was she kidding? He was constantly on her brain now that Maddy was safe. After everything she'd been through, she knew she shouldn't think about him too much. He clearly had a complicated life. And while she had definitely developed feelings for him, did he return them? It had been difficult to tell. True, he'd given her the biggest hug when he found her at the farm, but had he only been caught up in the moment? She wasn't sure. Especially, since his partner had been with him each time she had seen him since the rescue.

She told herself not to obsess about Gabe, but that was challenging. She tried to focus on her sister. After all, the important thing was that Maddy was alive and would fully recover, at least physically. They could go to Naples, and have a chance to start over. Maddy had poured her heart out to Megan earlier that morning before falling asleep. She was looking forward to a new start, even more than Megan. And Megan was going to do everything she could to help her twin. She'd stand by her no matter what, and really be there for her, wherever that led.

The DEA was sending them on an agency jet home as soon as Maddy was ready to travel. An agent had come in earlier in the morning to tell her protective custody wouldn't be necessary as far as the agency was concerned because the threat they'd been wary of, Victor Torrez himself, had died the night before. They would however, keep watch over the twins for a little while to make sure there weren't any lingering threats to them from anyone related to the Torrez family. The DEA was keeping their identity private and had made sure the press didn't know of their involvement. They said it was for the twins' safety that it stay quiet, even though the headlines would be exploding with the news of Victor Torrez's death, Ricardo Rivera's death, and the news of the charges being dropped against the innocent man who had been framed for Ana's murder.

The nurse picked up Megan's finger and placed the heart rate monitor on it. "Pulse is a little high. Are you still afraid?"

Megan frowned. "No…just thinking."

"Well after everything you and your sister have been through, I'd say it's normal to be scared. It will probably take a long time for you to feel at ease. Even then, I'd recommend some therapy. You need to talk about what happened to you. Both of you do."

"I'm sure it would help," Megan agreed with a half smile.

"It probably wouldn't hurt to talk to that good-looking agent that's been hanging around. Not the ones watching the door. The man, Walker, I think his name is…you know the one who was in here yesterday. The one who was really worried about you when you arrived. You know which one I'm talking about right?" she added with a wink.

Megan pursed her lips. She hoped her face wasn't as red as it felt. "I know which one Agent Walker is."

"Are you talking about me?"

Megan's pulse skyrocketed as his voice interrupted their conversation.

The nurse turned, to see him standing in the doorway with a huge bouquet of flowers in his hands, along with all of Megan's belongings. The bouquet was a mix of colorful Caribbean flowers, light pink Hibiscus, hot pink Bougainvillea, and bright orange Birds of Paradise.

The nurse grinned from ear to ear, blushing herself. "Why speak of the devil. And he brought flowers. I like him." She turned back to Megan, raising a brow at the heart rate monitor before taking it off. "Yep, pretty fast," she mumbled, casting a sly look at Megan. "I'll check on you later, Miss MacKenna. And we can talk about my recommendations."

"Thanks," Megan replied dryly as she left the room.

55

Megan's heart rate kept climbing as she watched Gabe approach. He set the bouquet down on the table beside the bed and rolled her suitcase beside it. He placed the purse on the table as well, briefly holding it open to show Megan the cell phone, wallet, and even Maddy's necklace within. As promised, he'd gotten everything sent over from St. Thomas as soon as he could.

Her palms were clammy, and she became more nervous by the second. If he had come to say goodbye, she wasn't ready. "Thanks for getting my things. I can't wait to give Maddy her necklace when she wakes up. And the flowers are beautiful." She tried to keep her voice even.

He shrugged. "I thought it might make you feel better. Besides, you can't get fresh Caribbean bouquets quite like this in Florida."

He set a chair right beside her bed and sat down as close as he could. It reminded Megan of the first time they'd met, when he'd sat down beside her at Captain Sully's, only this time instead of a grease spotted ripped and faded t-shirt, he wore jeans and a polo-style short sleeved shirt. Without holes. And this time, even though she wasn't sure how he felt, she wasn't interested in putting any space between them. If only this weren't goodbye.

"How are you feeling today?" he asked.

She imagined telling him the truth. She was a bundle of nerves. In emotional turmoil. She didn't want this to be the last time she saw him. But she couldn't. "I'm fine. They finally took the IV off after I insisted. And Maddy's moving along well. No fever today, but they gave her meds for the pain, and they are making her sleep a lot. But they said she'll have a full recovery. Though she might have a scar or two, we'll see."

"So what was that all about with the nurse? She has recommendations for you? Are you OK? Did they miss something on their initial evaluation the other day?" he asked anxiously.

"And here I figured you wouldn't have to worry about me anymore," she teased.

He raised a brow. "I can't help myself. I'm developing an addiction to it I guess," he paused. "So, is everything OK?"

"She was just being funny. Trying to cheer me up. She says I've been through a lot that might be hard to cope with in the months ahead."

"That's true. It will take some time," he said, his fingers trailing over the scar on his chest. Megan recalled pressing her own fingers on that perfectly sculpted chest, right before she kissed him at the beach, and her face flushed. But fortunately, he was dazing off and didn't notice.

She'd put it together the day before after Smith had told her about the near death experience. Gabe had a habit of rubbing the scar when he was thinking. She wondered what had him thinking so hard right now. She wanted to ask. But figured after bombarding him with a million questions the day before, she should give him some space. And the one question she wanted an answer to, now that he was alone with her... *Did he have any feelings for her*, seemed so absurd, she couldn't bring herself to ask. Besides, now that the case was over, they'd be going their separate ways. She told herself that it shouldn't make her feel sad. But it did. She'd found her sister. Life would be fine. Time would heal the emotional wounds. Naples, her job, her home, her structured life was waiting for her.

But what about Gabe Walker?

As crazy as it sounded, she'd miss him. But she couldn't tell him without sounding ridiculous. And she'd already made a fool of herself one too many times with him...that day at the beach when she'd kissed him.

Why couldn't she forget that kiss?

She fumbled with the edge of the blanket below her fingers. "So, I can't tell you enough how thankful I am you brought my suitcase. I can't wait to get out of this hospital gown."

Gabe glanced over her and smiled. "I'm sure you're ready to pull out your designer dress and shoes, but you'd look good in a potato sack, Megan."

Megan cleared her throat and imagined pulling the hospital blanket over her head and hiding until he left. Was he flirting with her? Why did he have to mess with her head?

She ignored the remark and went on. "And thanks for the phone. I called Grandma Lynn last night from the room phone. I told her we are coming home tomorrow and I'd visit her as soon as possible. I decided to wait to tell her the truth until I get there. I hate to worry her. Besides, she sounded so excited. She wants to hear all about our vacation. You should have heard her. Talking about how I'd finally taken time off work to do something relaxing."

"Well, there was that one day at the beach," he said, holding her gaze, an amused expression coming over him.

Megan wanted to look away, but couldn't. Was he intentionally taunting her? Was he talking about the kiss she'd planted on him? "Yeah, the day at the beach was…nice." Until I looked like an idiot and kissed you, she added to herself.

Gabe leaned in closer and swallowed. Why did he suddenly look uncomfortable himself? "There's something I want to say, Megan."

Megan waited. Was this goodbye? "Yesterday I told you everything you wanted to hear, but when I left I realized I hadn't even thanked you or Maddy."

"For what? Driving you crazy? It had to have been difficult having me interfere with your investigation and cover assignment…even though I had no clue what was going on with you for real."

"No, I mean yeah, you were…fiery," he said with a chuckle. "But

I'm glad you came. And Maddy. I've spent twenty years chasing down Victor Torrez and the guy who killed my family, and then you two show up, and in the blink of an eye, it's over. Not only do I get to return to Florida and my regular job, I have closure. I'll always carry some of the pain from the past around…I'm sure you can relate to that. But now I'll have to get used to not looking around every corner for something linking the case I'm working to my past. I know who killed my family, and I can finally let it go."

"I never expected to hear you thank me for anything. Especially after all of that time you tried to get me to go home. But I'm glad you told me that. I feel a little better about everything, knowing you are better."

"Yeah, and I need to pay my grandma a visit myself. She has no idea what I've been doing on this assignment. She's going to find the cooking part quite funny. She spent years trying to teach me to cook."

"Well, it worked. I've never tasted an omelet so amazing."

"You should have my Lechon. She made me master it. It's even better."

Megan laughed. "Yeah, maybe one of these days when you're not chasing down drug dealers."

As soon as she'd said it, her face blushed. She just kept digging a hole. Though he'd flirted with her for sure, off and on since they'd met, if he'd really been interested in her, he would've said so, and that day at Haypenny he wouldn't have blamed the kiss on her getting too much sun.

"There's something else I wanted to say. You know how I told you the other day how I had no choice but to keep my cover from you?"

"Yeah. I understand."

"I know, but I also had to keep something else from you for your safety and also because I didn't expect things to end like they did. What I'm trying, not very eloquently to say is…"

"Checking in with you, time to get lunch orders." Megan glanced up as a different nurse barged into the room.

Gabe leaned back in the chair as the nurse handed Megan a menu card. Megan wanted to yell at her to leave. Gabe had been about to share something with her, and she needed to hear whatever it was. She checked the boxes for menu item number one, not even noticing what it was and tossed the card to the nurse.

Once they were alone, Gabe grinned. "Hopefully, there won't be anymore interruptions." He took Megan's hand in his. "I'm not very good at this. It's been awhile. But my grandma always told me when you know you know. And…"

"And?" Megan enquired, her pulse picking up.

"And I wanted to keep kissing you that day at the beach. In fact, if you hadn't ended the kiss, I'm not sure I would've been able to."

Megan's mouth fell open an inch, but she closed it at once. She swallowed. "But you said I got too much sun."

He ran his thumb over the top of her hand, then met her gaze. "I couldn't tell you how I felt. I wanted to keep you at a distance so I could concentrate on your safety. I was trying to get you to go home so I could stop worrying about you. But the truth is, Megan Mackenna, even after the bust, after last night, after everything, you're all I can think about… since the moment I saw you in Captain Sully's." He paused, leaning in closer. "I know I'm not your type. But what would you say about me taking you out on a real date, like you deserve…as soon as I can. Once we're both in Florida. I'll even shave the beard and get a hair cut first."

She chuckled. "I'd love that…I mean the date part. I can't imagine how you'd look without the beard and long hair. I don't know. I kind of like it. "

"So that's a yes?"

"I wouldn't say yes to anyone but you."

He sunk his head, letting out a sigh. "I'm glad you'll go. Miami is only two hours from Naples. I'll plan it all."

"You didn't think I'd go?" Megan couldn't believe that. Was he blind?

"I was a little nervous. I know you can be difficult to persuade sometimes. Speaking from experience."

"Well, I'm glad to know Mr. DEA has nerves on occasion. You seemed so intense there for a second, I thought maybe you were going to try to kiss me or something."

His smile widened, and his grip on her hand tightened. "I thought about it, believe me."

"Well, it's probably a good thing you didn't. You know how I am about being rational and making carefully thought out decisions."

"Honestly, I don't know that Megan. I know the reckless one who goes running into dangerous situations trying to save her sister and not even thinking about herself."

"Well, I assure you, those were special circumstances."

"I don't know...I think a lot has changed since the day I met you at Captain Sully's. Maybe this new you could let go of some of the old rules," he said, edging closer, his voice husky.

His face was inches away. Electricity was shooting through her from the touch of his hand. She could hardly think straight. "I'd have to agree. I could change a few things."

"That's good. Because the old you wouldn't have approved of me kissing you right now, for example. Before even taking you out on a first date."

"Yeah, the old me definitely would not have approved," she replied, eyeing his mouth. "She wouldn't have approved of me kissing you at the beach either."

"OK then, it's settled. The old you doesn't need to know about that kiss at the beach...or this."

"Or wha—"

Before she could complete the sentence, his mouth met hers. She wove her fingers into his hair and pulled him closer. He took his time, kissing her slowly. Her heart beat wildly in her chest as warmth spread from her head to her toes, and Megan lost track of her thoughts and every worry in her mind.

After a moment, he grinned, his voice low. "Remind me to thank your sister again for going on vacation."

"I'll thank her for the both of us," she said breathlessly.

Moments later, Gabe was gone and a smile rested across Megan's face as she laid on the pillows.

"If you don't marry that man and have his babies, I swear I'll never forgive you."

Megan sat up. "Maddy? You're awake?"

"Did you hear what I said? *Never forgive you*...That man is head over heels for you, Sis, and oh my, what a catch."

Megan couldn't help but laugh. "How long have you been awake?"

"Long enough to know Mr. DEA is definitely a keeper, Meg. He rescues us, he brings flowers, he cooks? And he's drop dead gorgeous?"

"I told you, you'd like him. He's more your type."

"No, not for me....too dangerous of an occupation. I'm a changed woman myself. I'm looking for non action. No adventure. A man who takes minimal risks. Maybe an accountant or something," she said with a giggle.

Megan shook her head. "Good. Because I was kind of hoping you'd let me keep Gabe."

"Don't worry about that. I heard him, and I saw the way he looks at you. That man isn't letting you go anywhere. And you like him. I can tell. A lot, Meg. I can't believe you're finally relaxing a little. My *older*, calculated, rational sister."

"I'm only older by one minute."

"It counts, believe me. And Grandma Lynn is going to fall out of her chair when I tell her about you falling in love."

"Oh let's not get ahead of ourselves, Sis. I think the pain medication has got you talking crazy."

"I admit, I'm feeling much better already. But it isn't the meds. I want you to be happy. I'm just speaking the truth, Meg. You'd best catch up. I have a feeling my future brother-in-law just walked out that door."

Megan sighed. "Anyway…no matter what happens, I think I should make it official."

"What's that?"

"My thank you."

"What are you thanking me for?"

"For buying that ticket to St. Croix."

"That's what kid sisters are for old lady."

"One minute older, remember?"

"Yeah, yeah…," Her expression sobered. "Thanks for coming for me. I prayed someone would find me. I hate what you had to go through… but I'm glad it was you. You never gave up on me. Most people would've thought I was dead."

"I could feel you. You must have been sending vibes my way. I knew you were alive."

"Every time I got goose bumps, I wondered if you were in trouble, too. I'm so glad you trusted your instincts. I love you, Meg."

"I love you, too, Maddy."

A mischievous look crossed Maddy's face. "Now tell me everything about that kiss at the beach. I want to hear all of the juicy details about you meeting Gabe Walker. Start with chapter one…*They meet at Captain's Sully's*. Maybe we can have a Captain Sully's themed engagement party for you two."

"Oh Maddy, you're hopeless."

As her twin, safe and sound in the hospital bed beside her, egged her on, she started at the beginning. She opened up her heart to her best friend and dreamt of the days to come. Life was giving her a second chance, and Megan was going to take it.

A Note from the Author

Thank you for reading my book. If you enjoyed *Last Vacation*, I'd love for you to tell a friend or post a review. I read every review and appreciate them all. I would also like to invite you to stay up-to-date with me on social media for upcoming book releases. Thank you for your support!

Acknowledgements

Thanks to Natasha Brown for the amazing book cover art for *Last Vacation*. Thanks to my editor, Sherry Foley, for finding time in your busy schedule to take on a new client. I am so grateful for your editing talents. You took my manuscript to another level. Thanks to Odyssey Books for formatting and typesetting. Thanks to Brand Photo Design for making me look pretty.

I'd like to thank my mother, Jacquelyn, for inspiring me to write. Thank you for always being the first set of eyes on my first drafts and for your feedback. Mostly, thank you for being my therapist. I don't know what I'd do without you, and I love you. You are the best mom in the entire universe. And I am not just saying that to kiss up. I already know I am your favorite. Thanks for passing down the family writing genes, thanks for your continued pep talks and prayers, and thanks for not telling Sam and Coleen that I am actually your favorite child. I'd hate to hurt their feelings.

To my dad, Mark, I am so grateful you are my father, and I can't begin to express how much I love you. Thanks for teaching me a thing or two about thinking like a survivor, and thanks for making me watch every action movie under the sun. You are always there for me, and I can't thank you enough.

Thank you to my siblings, Sam and Coleen, for your encouragement, support, and for always having my back. As the middle child, I watched you fight over who had to share the hotel room bed with me and who would get the trundle, who would get shotgun and who would be stuck in the back of the car with me for my entire life. Still, I know that both of you would track me down if I ever disappeared on vacation. I am blessed beyond words to be your sister.

Thanks to my husband, Charles, for always believing in my abilities and for encouraging me to go after my dreams.

Thank you to my children, my nieces, and my nephews for always making me smile. I love you so much. And God loves you even more.

Miss Copenhagen, my pal Sonja, I am still waiting on that move to America. But in case that isn't on the table, I'll start planning my next trip to Denmark. I'll always love you, Señorita Dinamarca.

To Grandpa Doc, you keep inspiring me. I miss you and love you so much.

To all of my family, friends, and readers, thank you for your support, reviews, and for sharing my work with your friends. I couldn't do this without you. May God bless you.

~Sarah Elle Emm

About the Author

Sarah Elle Emm is the author of the HARMONY RUN SERIES and MARRYING MISSY. She has lived in Germany, England, Mexico, the U.S. Virgin Islands, including St. Croix and St. Thomas, and traveled extensively beyond. Sarah currently resides in Florida with her family. When she's not walking the plank of her daughters' imaginary pirate ship, she is writing. Visit her website at SarahElleEmm.com. Follow her Facebook page, Sarah Elle Emm.